GALAXY'S EDGE

CREATED BY MIKE RESNICK

ISSUE 56: May 2022

CONTENTS

Lezli Robyn, Editor
Lauren Rudin, Assistant Editor
Z.T. Bright, Slush Reader
Taylor Morris, Copyeditor
Shahid Mahmud, Publisher

Published by Arc Manor/Phoenix Pick
P.O. Box 10339
Rockville, MD 20849-0339

Galaxy's Edge is published in January, March, May, July, September, and November.

Please check our website for submission guidelines.

ISBN: 978-1-64973-117-3

SUBSCRIPTION INFORMATION:
Paper and digital subscriptions are available (including via Amazon.com) . Please visit our home page: www.GalaxysEdge.com

ADVERTISING:
Advertising is available in all editions of the magazine. Please contact advert@GalaxysEdge.com.

FOREIGN LANGUAGE RIGHTS:
Please refer all inquiries pertaining to foreign language rights to Shahid Mahmud, Arc Manor, P.O. Box 10339, Rockville, MD 20849-0339. Tel: 1-240-645-2214. Fax 1-310-388-8440. Email admin@ArcManor.com.

ALEX SHVARTSMAN

BOOK ONE OF THE CONRADVERSE CHRONICLES

"A fine mixture of magic and mayhem."
—*Simon R. Green,* NYT *bestselling author*

"With the fast-paced first Conradverse urban fantasy, Shvartsman (Eridani's Crown) delivers a laugh-out-loud, snarky adventure, throwing out pop culture references and wry observations with dizzying frequency.... His supernatural New York City is vibrant and authentic, and Conrad fits right in with wisecracking fan favorite heroes like Harry Dresden and Simon Canderous. The result is a thoroughly satisfying romp."—*Publishers Weekly*

THE MIDDLING AFFLICTION

GUARD BROOKLYN, FIGHT MONSTERS, TAUNT BAD GUYS

May 31, 202

EDITOR'S NOTE

by Lezli Robyn

Award season is in the air. In the month leading up to the publication of this issue of *Galaxy's Edge*, Oghenechovwe Donald Ekpeki's novelette, the thought-provoking "O₂ Arena," was announced as a finalist for a British Science Fiction Association (BSFA) Award, a Nebula Award, and a Hugo Award! We are so proud of that novelette and love witnessing how high and far the author is souring. We are obviously biased, but we hope the story's hard-hitting commentary on global warming, and medical and gender inequality, garners all the votes it deserves to win.

In this issue, we have the absolute pleasure of interviewing Martha Wells. One of the highlights as editor of this magazine is being first to read the interviews that come in from Jean Marie Ward. Her insightful questions help this editor, as well other writers and readers, to pull back the curtain and take a glimpse into the mind and creative process of a wildly successful author. Martha's Murderbot Diaries series is taking the book world by storm, and her conversation with Jean Marie is equally captivating.

We are also publishing three brand new authors in this issue. Both new to our pages and new to the field. Shirley Song was one of the five finalists for the first Mike Resnick Memorial Award (for Best Short Fiction by a New Author). Her short story, "Time, Needles, and Gravity," gives us an unexpected viewpoint within a Time Travel Bureau, where the reader will discover just how important period-appropriate clothing can be when travelling into the past. Candice R. Lisle also adds charm and heart to our pages with her short story, "Eyes and Hands," about two damaged salvage robots that help each other complete their assigned tasks so they don't get scrapped themselves. In Alicia Cay's thought-provoking and bittersweet short story, "The Color of Thunder," we can witness the beauty an author can create with words. Ella's brother was murdered, and she is on the verge of losing her parents to grief and anger. How can she help her parents get closure for her brother's death, and save a magical creature's life in the process, when she can only prove the Seraph's innocence by revealing she also has magical gifts of her own?

Sometimes when putting together a new issue of the magazine, you realize that despite the pages being filled with very different stories, by diverse authors, an overarching theme presents itself. In issue 56, I discovered many of the stories have at least one character whose role is to aide or help another—whether in a poignant or hilarious manner. Larry Hodges is back in *Galaxy's Edge* with a delightful science fiction short about an overworked angel helping God create the Solar System. Let's just say "harried" is an understatement, when it comes to this poor heavenly being's state of mind in "Prototype Solar System with Strings Attached."

Along with our regular Recommended Books article by Richard Chwedyk, and columns by L. Penelope and Gregory Benford, we also have reprint stories by Mike Resnick, Kristine Kathryn Rusch, and Angela Slatter. Angela is new to our pages, but one of Australia's most celebrated writers, and her story, "The Badger Bride," tells the tale of Gytha, a copiest and bookbinder who has been given the task of copying a book of magic spells.

And, last, but not least, we have a new novelette by David Gerrold, "Duty and the Beast." Not only is it a great study of character, but David's a deft hand at depicting humans that are very alien to those we know now, takes us on a journey that is quite unexpected. As the title suggests, this piece showcases the oddest pairing of protagonists, who are navigating the evacuation of a world where the misunderstood are often the most likely to be left behind.

Happy reading!

David Gerrold is the author of over 70 books, hundreds of articles and columns, and over a dozen television episodes. He is a classic sci-fi writer that will go down in history as having created some of the most popular and re-defining scripts, novels, and short stories in the genre. TV credits include episodes from Star Trek (including the infamous "The Trouble With Tribbles"), Star Trek Animated, Land Of The Lost, Babylon 5, Twilight Zone, and others. Additionally, the autobiographical tale of his son's adoption, The Martian Child, won the Hugo and Nebula awards for Best Novel-ette of the Year and was the basis for the 2007 movie, Martian Child, starring John Cusack, Amanda Peet, and Joan Cusack.

DUTY AND THE BEAST

by David Gerrold

They all made it out before the portal closed. I didn't go.

You gotta do what you gotta do.

So I did. I made sure they got out.

I didn't follow. There were no more travel pods. But that wasn't the reason.

After they were across, after the channel was clean, I did what I had to do.

The portal shut down. It severed the connection and shut down completely. It wiped its calibrations, then emptied its circuitry. Incapable of powering up, no connection of any kind could be established again.

But just to be certain, I vaporized the station.

It was a total break. Downline was gone. Irretrievable. No one else was going home.

But I wasn't done yet.

I picked up my gear and headed northwest. The day was bright and I made good time. The sun wouldn't be overhead for hours. If I couldn't reach forest before noon, I'd put up the tent to avoid the heat. I had food for three days and I knew where to refill my canteens. Not the easiest trek, but not impossible either.

It would be a long day crossing the big valley. I'd have to circle the high grass where the predators lurked. It'd be safer. Mostly. I'd have to go slow.

The sun was touching the western horizon when I reached the rocky jumbles. Up here, I'd have to watch out for the dark catters; they were vicious and always hungry. I'd printed up a swarm of disposable flutterbys. They circled above me like insects, so I had an umbrella. It should give warning, but the catters could camouflage, even muting their heat signatures, so I'd have to monitor closely. I had a shrill-frequency emitter which would annoy the most likely hunters, but it would also give me away to any human observers. The stay-behinds were going to be the real problem.

I made it to the top of the ridge without seeing any troublemakers, but the worst of them wouldn't be out hunting until after dark.

Twilight brought a dry evening wind. I refreshed the umbrella and took shelter near a break where three enormous boulders clustered together. I put out a ring of night-eyes, had half a ration for dinner—more than enough—watched the sun creep slowly into the horizon, watched all three moons tumbling through the dark, admired the sparkling ribbon across the sky. I never got tired of that view, but finally as the temperature dropped toward freezing, I curled up in my cocoon.

I slept fitfully. Occasional strange noises came echoing across the hills; howls and barks, grunts and whistles, but nothing close enough to set off an alarm. But that wasn't the reason for my discomfort. I didn't like this whole job, but there wasn't anyone else who could do it.

The second day, travel was slower. I'd expected it. The terrain was rougher here, broken by gullies and arroyos and even a sharp canyon. I had to climb down one side, cross a rushing stream, then back up the other. I paused only to refill my canteens.

A storm in the north promised a flash flood. The air already smelled wet. When the rain finally came, I hunkered down beneath a sharp cliff where I'd be out of the scouring wind and water. The worst of the storm stayed far to the north and east, but the fringe was bad enough. I sheltered in place for hours. After the clouds passed, the ground dried quickly—the land was thirsty here. Rivulets found the path of least resistance, trickles turned into streams, and I followed them down.

By early afternoon, I had reached the broad savannah. Distant herds spotted the range and that meant there would be predators here, the biggest ones. The distant forest was still a line of dark blue on the horizon—it would be a long trek. I kept telling myself that once I got deep enough into the shelter of the trees, I should be fine. I just had to keep putting one foot in front of the other. I'd get there. It would be okay.

The rex almost caught me by surprise.

The ground shook and the beast came rising up out of the high grass ahead of me. The flutterbys had missed it. The monster had been lying torpid in a rill, soaking up the heat of the day, invisible to their sensors while it slowly digested its most recent meal. I had come too close. My footsteps, light as they were, had disturbed it.

It grunted, blinking, looking for something to focus on. I yipped in surprise, suddenly aware that I was in the middle of a large open space with no place to hide and the distant trees too far to run to.

I could freeze where I was and hope it wouldn't recognize me as prey. Or if it looked away, I could drop to the ground. I had weapons, but they weren't designed to stop a creature that large. The animal had a stretched-out body, a long flat snout, and teeth as long as my legs. A rex usually ambled on four legs, but when it was searching for prey, it stood up on its thicker and taller hind-limbs. This one was standing up now.

I had one advantage: I could scramble around it faster than it could turn to follow. That kind of a contest would be decided by my endurance against the animal's own frustration.

The rex moved.

It swung its wide head, first to one side, then to the other, regarding me with its right eye, then the left. Whatever thought processes sparkled in its tiny brain, it really had only three choices: eat, fight, or fuck. The first was always eat.

The beast dropped back to all four legs and lumbered toward me. It didn't look fast, but that was an illusion—the thing was huge, a walking mountain of meat and bone. I had to make up my mind whether to dodge to the right or the left. My choice was impossible. It could lunge either way.

I did the smart-stupid thing. When it lunged, I flattened to the ground. Its jaws passed over me as I scrambled straight ahead, ducking beneath its long neck and between its tree-trunk legs and into the dark shadows beneath its wide belly, all the way to the high space between its rear legs. If I could stay underneath the monster, I could confuse it. In its eyes, I would have disappeared. I'd be safe for the moment—unless it suddenly decided to lie down again. Then I'd have to move fast. But if it looked around and couldn't find me, lost interest and gave up—if it ambled off into the distance, I could flatten and wait. Or, if it turned around and spotted me again, we could start all over. These creatures weren't stupid.

The creature grunted. Confused? Maybe. I don't speak rex. It lifted up one front leg, then the other. It lowered its head and sniffed the ground in great shuddering inhalations. Not a good sign. It turned around slowly; I moved to stay beneath its hind legs. It was dangerous, but I could tell which way it was going to move by the way its tail was swinging and by the way it shifted its weight.

Now it roared in annoyance and started to step sideways, I jumped and dodged. Maybe it knew where I was. It turned around, it started forward—I moved with it, barely fast enough.

Not good.

It could amble at thirty klicks, or it could charge at fifty. I could barely do twelve, even in this lighter gravity. If it started forward, I could be exposed. A rex rarely walks in a straight line, it moves in a deliberate zig-zag pattern, swinging its head in a constant search for any prey that might have gone to ground.

I ducked beneath its swinging tail. I was out of its shadow and into the bright sun again. My one hope was to flatten out and scramble toward the distant trees. Or I could just run for it. Neither was a good option. If the rex saw me, no matter what I did I would still die tired.

The rex turned and saw me—

—and exploded!

A bright red flash hit the wall of the rex's neck, gouts of flame splattered outward, and the beast staggered left, collapsed sideways, and disappeared in a flower of smoke and flame. The shockwave flung me back across the grass, flattening it beneath me as I slid.

For a long, confused moment, I wasn't sure who I was, where I was, or what had happened—but the sky was a beautiful shade of blue. Or was it Cyan? Turquoise? Green? Whatever. It was nice. I could lie here forever—

A dark shape hulked above me. "You gonna get up?" it asked.

I didn't answer. Instead, I rolled sideways, got my arms and legs under me and managed to stand. Turned and looked. I might have wobbled. The world was still ringing.

My eyes blurry, watering. I looked. Something large and scowling. Very large. It blocked the sun. Four meters tall, probably two and a half wide. Hard to tell under all that gear, which was mostly armor and weapons and whatnots. Obviously it was large. Larger than large. One of the largest of its kind. Impressive.

I stepped sideways and looked around him. Pieces of rex were still pattering down from the sky, bits of skin and bone and fragments of flesh. The stink was horrific.

Carrion eaters would feast easy today. They wouldn't be long in arriving—as soon as the wind spread the smell of raw meat. There wouldn't be a lot of snarling competition around the carcass, what was left of it. There was more than enough here for all of them. Large chunks of the rex had splattered everywhere across the savannah.

"You're welcome," said the hulk, as if that was sufficient. He stepped away, moving from one chunk of carcass to the next, looking for the right one. Finally, he pulled out a huge knife and began slicing at a larger chunk of meat. "Dinner," he said.

"Yours. Not mine," I said. I turned and headed toward the trees. Wanted to get away before the local equivalents of jackals arrived. Life is vicious everywhere. A pack of them would be even more dangerous than the rex.

The hulk shrugged and caught up with me.

"Don't want company," I said.

He pointed forward. "I'm going in this direction. You go wherever you want." He waved left and right.

Wasn't ready to argue. Not yet. Still too annoyed, mostly at myself for being caught by surprise. For needing to be rescued. Embarrassing. Had it been it a grief reaction? Loss fugue? Or just exhaustion? Whatever it was, it almost killed me. Reminded me to stay awake. Can't depend on my stalker to be there next time.

He grunted. "My name is Constant."

Didn't answer, headed toward the trees. Mebbe we should settle this in the shade.

I wasn't the only person who'd stayed behind. But I had a job to do. The rest of 'em—not the kind of people I wanted to be on the same planet with.

Peak population here had barely reached half a million. The evacuation had started eighteen months ago and even with long trains of pods coming from farther out on the portal lines. The stretch to the frontier goes out quite a way from some places, not here, only a few more stops to the last one. But enough. For a while pods from our upline were coming through twice a day, all of them adding to the evac from here. Less than four hundred thousand from this rock had gone downline. And the rest? That's their choice.

With the downline portal down, there would be no possible connection to any of the other hundred worlds. This was permanent isolation (some people wanted that. No way to know how many), since evacuation meant a long journey downline through multiple portals till they found a stopping place, maybe even a new home, but evacuees would be refugees. They'd scatter across multiple worlds, wherever they could find opportunities. All their separate communities would disappear, ultimately forgotten.

So some people thought that staying behind was a better option. I'd met enough of them to know that I didn't want to be here for that. Ornery, stubborn, cruel, and stupid. I could accept ornery and stubborn—I was mostly that myself. But cruel and stupid—? Just bad news.

This hulk lumbering beside me? Stubborn, yes. The other things? I didn't know yet. I didn't want to have to kill him. Not impossible, but probably difficult. Strong risk of injury.

I reached the trees by early afternoon. Found a shadowed place that looked safe enough to sit. He sat opposite, settling his enormous bulk onto the web of twisty roots that circled a gnarly tree. The limbs curved around his weight like a personally designed chair. He took out a ration bar, broke it in half. "Hungry?"

Okay, maybe not cruel.

I took the half-bar. Flavored sawdust, but better to eat his rations than mine. Drank a capful of water, didn't offer him the canteen. Finally cleared my throat, looked across at him. "What do you want?"

"What do you have?"

"Don't play games on me. You been following me—stalking—since the portal collapsed."

"Good thing for you."

"Mebbe. But you're not very good. I've had eyes on you the whole time."

"Really?" He reached into his pocket and pulled out a handful of crushed flutterbys. He held them out for me to see.

"Yes, really." I reached into my own pocket, pulled out what looked like dust—a small cloud of skeeterbots. I flung them in his direction. "These are harder to catch."

"I knew about those. Didn't mind 'em much. Let you think you knew something."

"I knew something. I spotted you a month before I headed south."

"Been tracking you longer than that."

"You were hiding in the noise. Too much chatter to filter out. But not well enough. You're too big. You stuck out. Didn't know you were tracking me then, coz of the evacuation, but this last month? Sure. So answer the question. What do you want?"

"You needed my help," he said. "Might even need it again."

I could have argued that, but it would have sounded stupid. I'd gotten too close to that rex and I was probably going to spend a few long nights rehearsing and examining that mistake.

"My turn," he said. "You were tracking me, why?"

"Because you were tracking me. Again—why?"

He scratched himself. Possibly wondering if he should answer. Apparently not. "I'm going to sleep now," he said. He settled himself on the gnarly branches and closed his eyes.

I wasn't going to waste daylight. As quietly as I could, I gathered my gear and headed north. I wanted to get through the thickest part of the woods while I still had daylight.

Three hours later, he caught up with me. Didn't say anything, just plodded along beside me. I could feel the weight of every step he took. Probably easier to have him beside me than behind me.

But that would mean we'd have to talk. Even if neither of us wanted to.

We got to the hills above Bias Station in late afternoon, not yet twilight. We stopped below the crest, dropped down flat and crawled just far enough forward to peer through the grass. The dome had scorch marks and even a few gouges where something had attacked it. Whoever or whatever, they hadn't gotten in.

I backed down to the nearest cluster of gnarlies. He followed.

"You stay here," I said.

"You think someone inside?"

"Five. Two large, three small."

He didn't ask how I knew. Instead, "You have plan?"

"My plan is you stay here." I unbuckled my gear, pulled off my boots. Peeled off jacket, shirt, body armor, unders, kilt, trousers. Stripped naked, I smeared dirt all over my body, unbound my hair and fingerbrushed it all askew.

Constant watched, possibly skeptical, possibly bemused. "You … very small," he said.

"You just notice that?"

"Your armor, your jacket, your boots, all the rest of your gear—make you look larger."

"Might say the same about you." I tossed my amulets aside. Now it was just my bare skin and a ragged blanket, the leftover threads of a poncho.

"That's your plan?"

I looked at him, a tower of muscles and armament, three meters high. "You think they open door for you, even without your gear? No. So you stay here."

I staggered down the hill, tripping and falling and finally tumbling clumsily to the bottom of the slope. When I got back up, slowly and painfully, I limped to the dome, clutching my side, wailing. Circling the dome, looking for the door—I finally found it and began crying and pounding, all in low-country accent, uneducated. "Eelp mae! 'Eelp! Anyone? You 'afta be there! 'Eelp mae, pleese! Pleese!" I kept it up for the longest time. Long enough to be a nuisance.

At last, the outer door slid part way open. Just enough for a glimpse of a gaunt face. "Go away."

"Pleese! Almost night! Freeze out here. 'Eelp me! An' I eelp yah! Know things, I do. Let mae in, pleese?"

"No." The outer door slid shut.

Right. I resumed pounding, wailing, shrieking. "Monser affer mae! 'Eelp mae! Pleese!"

The door opened again, this time a little further, still not far enough. "Who you?"

"Noddy. Nodding. Missed alla portal. Got nodding, no one. Looka mae. Can't 'urt you. Just need a warm place for a night, or mebbe two. Can eelp, reelly."

"Wait—" The door closed again. This time a lot longer. I started pounding again. "Gedding colder, pleese?"

Finally, the outer door opened and two skinnies stepped out, a large and a small. The door slid shut behind them. Squatters. Both looked haggard. Thin. Dirty. Not eating well. The large handed me a blanket, not much better than the one I wore. I clutched it, fumbled it around my shoulders. "Tankily, much tankily."

"No food you," the small said. "Ain't none."

"Just a warm place for sleep? Be gone morning?"

They looked at each other. The small shook her head. The large said, "Can't." He pointed. "You go now. Go."

Thought about crying. Decided not to. Wouldn't work on these two—selfish. I'd have to take them down.

But the door was closed behind them. Problematic. I really needed to get in.

And then Constant rose up. Up from the grass. Covered with mud and leaves, looking like something out of a marshy swamp. But the railgun was real. Red dots glowed on both of the squatters. He stepped up beside me.

"You folks, inside!" he called, his voice amplified, booming like thunder. "All you out now. Or I kill these two."

"Won't work," the skinny large said.

Constant ignored them. "Everybody out and nobody gets hurt. Sacred promise." And then, still aiming with his left arm, he held up his right—a gleaming token, a badge, perched in his beefy hand. "Portal authority!"

"Portal down," said the small. "Authority meaningless now."

"Not to me." He raised his voice again. "Everybody out or the station goes down. I can do it. Thirty seconds. Don't think. Don't talk. Out now."

I didn't expect it to work, but the doors of the dome, both outer and inner, slid open. One large, two small—hey came out slowly, raising their hands to show they were weaponless.

"Alla smart," Constant gestured with the weapon. "Line up here."

The second large grumbled into place. "Told yah. Shouldna opened. Now we're dead."

"No one's dead," Constant said. "You listen, you live. Just want—something." He looked to me. "You know where it is?"

Nodded.

"Go get it."

"I go with," said the grumbling large. "Make sure, no steal."

Constant snorted. "Squatters, alla you! No voice, no argue!"

"No, it's okay," I said, abandoning my low-country accent. "Let 'em see. Just want one thing, then we go. Right?"

"You sure?"

Nodded.

"Okay, go." He pointed to the large. "You be good. No good, I get mad. Everybody die. Especially you. Very painfully. Long time too."

The grumbly one followed me into the dome. It was a mess inside. Not like I remembered. Trash everywhere. Things broken, piled high. And it smelled bad too. Unwashed and sick. Bad cess. I wasn't going to stay anyway. Just grab and go.

Grumbly followed, all the way around to the service bay. Wires were hanging loose, everything powered down. I expected that. Whatever happened here, not good.

"What you want anyway?" Grumbly asked.

I ignored him, pushed some wires out of the way, counted squares on the panel behind. Three down, two over. I put my hand on the square, waited. Nothing happened. Took my hand away, then put it back. Waited longer. Still nothing. Hmm.

I slapped the square hard. Once, twice, three times. The third time, something behind the wall clicked. The square popped open, a drawer slid out.

I reached in, felt around.

Yes. Found it. A wooden box. Just big enough to fill my hand. Something heavy inside.

"What you got there?! Give me!" Grumbly grabbed my arm—

I let him live.

I picked up the box from the floor. It didn't look damaged. Sealed tight, fancy designs all over.

Grumbly was still rolling around on the floor clutching his stomach and moaning. "Why you do that. Just wanta see."

"Not yours, no look. Big mistake. Now you get up. We go out."

Grumbly pulled himself up with his one good arm. The other hung limp, broken. He stumbled outside where the air was a lot fresher. I followed, carefully carrying the box.

Constant looked at Grumbly, looked to me, noted the box, then looked back to Grumbly. "He give you bad time?"

"No. He just stupid. Station a mess. Stinks inside."

Constant scratched his neck, thinking. "Want me kill him?"

"Let them go. I have what I want."

"Don't like skinnies," he said. "And you—" he pointed at Grumbly, holding his broken arm. "I see you try something. Make me very mad."

"No, pleese! No kill—"

Constant shook his head. "No kill. Shut!" He waited till they fell silent again. "But I gone blow this station. Alla you go."

He pointed again to Grumbly and the two smalls who came out with him. "You go that way. Go fast and no get hurt. No come back." He pointed to the other two, the large and small who came out first. "And you go other way. Same thing. Go fast. No get hurt. Go far." He motioned with the railgun. "Go now! Go!"

They all looked at each other, realized he was serious, then broke for the trees. Grumbly started to curse, looked at me, thought better of it, clutched his arm and limped away in pain, the two smalls helping him.

Constant lowered his rifle. "You good?"

Nodded. "You gone blow this station really?"

"Nah. Just lock it up good. They come back, they don't get in." He tapped at his badge. "Big mess inside?"

"Very."

He tapped some more. "Okay. Repair bots online. They fix. Power first, then repairs. Synthesizers too. Month from now—maybe two, three—good as new. You come back then, eh?"

"Don't think so."

"Eh?"

"Gotta do what I gotta do." I turned and headed back up the hill. Constant put his badge away and followed.

By the time I finished cleaning off the worst of the dirt and pulled my clothes back on, darkness had fallen. Not safe to travel at night. Not easy either. Constant built a fire and put the slice of rex on a spit. We sat opposite each other, watching the embers rise through the smoke.

"Think they'll come back?" he asked.

I finished tugging on my boots. "Probbly. Squatters. That what they do."

He pointed at the engraved box next to me. "Why that important? Can I ask?"

"Ask. I won't answer."

"Okay." He stirred the fire with a stick. "You wanna talk anything else?"

"No."

"I do gotta ask this. Why you walk. Why not a flyer?"

Shrug. "If I fly, you not follow."

"You want me follow?"

"Easier to kill you if I know where you are. I mean, if I have to."

"Still think that?"

"Mebbe. Now my turn to ask. Why are you here?"

"Following you."

"No. Not that. Why you stay? Portal open long time. Why no go?"

"Same thing you. Gotta do what gotta do."

"What that?"

He pointed at me. "You. Gotta do you."

"Don't need you."

"Gotta dead rex that says other. And those skinnies too. You mebbe good, but you alone."

I didn't answer that.

"I'm right, aren't I?"

Didn't answer that either.

Long silence. Finally, "They called you Duty. That your real name?"

"Who's they? They who hired you?"

"Not hired. Assigned." He tapped his chest, indicating his badge. Portal Authority. "Coulda said no. Coulda gone."

"But …?"

"No place to go. All I know is here. Why you?"

"You already know. I gotta do what I gotta do."

"You closed the portal."

"Somebody had to."

"You know why?"

"Complicated."

"We got time. Meat ain't done yet."

Too much to explain. And not to him. Not yet. Mebbe never. His language doesn't have the words for it. Not even the grammar.

I don't do portal mechanics anyway. I know only what everyone knows: set the coordinates out to the umptillionth digital of pi, resolution fine enough to measure the circumference of the universe out to the width of a quantum particle. But there's still an infinity of irrationalities beyond that … so every time the techs open a new portal, no matter how carefully calibrated, it's always a gamble. Sometimes the portal opens to vacuum, sometimes to the core of a planet, or worse—a star. So when you find a barren rock, like a vacant moon or a large asteroid, any good place to stand, you use it. You go through and set up shop where playing portal roulette won't accidentally destroy half a continent. You keep doing it until you find a home-like world, then lay tracks, send pods, and the portal tree grows another branch upline. Expensive and time-consuming, but the reward to risk ratio is compelling. A whole new planet, right?

Between here and anywhere, this world and all the worlds downline, there are a lot of barren asteroids serving as spacers, with tracks running out of one hole in space and into another, linking a good place with the next good place upline—each asteroid a connecting link in the branch. Mostly safe, but not this time. The asteroid between here and the rest of downline—they say it's about to get vaporized by an expanding red giant. This branch of the line and everything upline from here will be broken off. Isolated.

There are several worlds upline from here—only a few, none very well settled, most still getting explored, so no big investment there, not much population to lose. Less than a million. But this place—? It's sorta settled. Find enough ornery, stubborn people—they'll stay in spite.

It was just too much to explain, and I don't like to talk anyway. But he wanted an answer, so I said, "If you really Authority, you already know."

"It ain't the truth." He didn't explain. "Want some rex?" He cut off a thick slice, bigger than three of me could eat, and held it out, stuck on the end of his knife.

I took it carefully. Still hot. Not bad. I could save the rest for later.

"Ever have chicken?" he asked.

"No."

"Tastes like rex." He added, "But everything tastes like rex. Everything here."

"You been elsewhere?"

He shook his head. "No need."

And that was as much conversation as either of us had. Constant kicked out the fire and we bedded down for the night. Him on his side, me on mine.

In the morning we headed west.

We had to detour around the trailing members of a herd of grassbeasts. A pack of stalkers followed the herd and an outlier came sniffing, but the rest ignored us. Caution slowed us down. Proceed carefully, stay safe. Remember the rex.

By midday, we could smell the ocean, an hour later we reached the shore. The tide was out, so we walked on wet sand, easier than pushing across the dunes. In the distance, a jumble of cliffs stretched sideways, pointing further north and west. We'd go up there, turn inland.

That was where they ambushed us. The skinnies. The two larges from Bias Station and fourteen more. They'd been hiding in the marsh where the flutter-bys and skeeter-bots couldn't detect them. Smart. Dangerously smart.

They outnumbered us. Seven surrounded us with spears and rifles. Nine more in a larger circle around them. They looked hungry and gaunt. Hard times. We might take out three or four, maybe more, but not all. Not with some behind us.

Standoff.

Grumbly, his arm tied up now, studied us. "You no kill. We no kill. Honor, yes? What in box? Give."

"It won't do you any good," I said.

"Important to you? Important to me. Give."

Looked to Constant. A question. What do we do?

He leaned toward me. "What he wants—is it worth dying for?"

"Truth? No."

"Then give."

That surprised me. "Don't want to fight?"

"Don't want to die."

"Not a good day for it," I agreed.

Turned back to Grumbly. "Okay. I give." Took box out slowly. Placed it on the ground between us, stepped back.

Grumbly picked up the box, shook it, held it to his ear, listened. "Heavy," he said. He tried to pull it open, tried to twist it open, eyed it angrily.

"That won't work," I said.

"Why?"

"It has to be opened the right way."

"Tell me."

"Can't. No have words."

He didn't like that answer, but he accepted it. He put the box back down. He pointed at it. "You open." Then he backed away. All of them took a few steps back.

Glanced to Constant. He nodded. I stepped forward and bent to the ground. The box wasn't locked, but the top had to be twisted around until all the top and bottom symbols matched, meshed, and clicked—then twisted once more to unlock. I pulled the top open and stepped back. Way back. Constant too.

Grumbly approached suspiciously.

He peered into the box. Frowned. Reached slowly. Touched. Grabbed. Lifted. All the skinnies leaned forward to look. Constant too.

A gray metallic disk—no, not a disk—a roll of shining ribbon. Inscribed with square markings. He frowned at it. "What this?" He held it out to me, accusing. "Explain!"

"It's a message," I said. "For a machine. A bot."

"What it say?"

"Don't know. Don't know what it says."

"Important, yes?"

"Must be, yes."

"Trade for money? Food?"

"Probbly. If you can get it to—" I looked to Constant. "Should I tell him?" He nodded. Back to Grumbly. "Blue Tower. You know Blue Tower? Up where the ice glows?"

He grunted. "East. Long walk east."

"Very long walk. Okay, you no go. Give back?"

Grumbly snorted. "I keep." He started to tuck the shining roll into his jacket.

"Don't you want the box?"

He kicked it away. "Ugly thing. Can't open it." He pointed to Constant. "You have food, yes? Give now. Then go. Both."

"He wants the rest of the rex."

"I spent a long time smoking that meat."

"Is it worth dying for?"

"Truth? No."

"Then give."

He unloaded the slab of meat and laid it on the sand. The skinnies grabbed it and vanished into the bushes as fast as they had appeared.

Constant looked at me. "Now what?"

I scooped up the box, closed it and tucked it into my coat. "We go on."

"Really?"

"Gotta do what I gotta do."

"Without the spool?"

"Annoying. Not fatal."

"Explain?"

"No."

We headed inland, away from the ocean now. Skinnies had to be watching, following until we were well away from their land.

We didn't stop until hunger stopped us. Ration bars, barely enough. We pushed on until evening, made camp in the rain forest. Wet winds came in hard, bringing damp smells and fog. We climbed into the higher branches and strung hammocks. Fell asleep listening for prowlers and weezils—especially weezils. They can ooze right up next to you without a sound. Hammocks have alarms, loud: shake awake like a quake. Most weezils shriek and drop. Most. So slept with gun.

We stayed wrapped long after dawn, waiting for morning to warm. Climbed down, found a shower tree, and stripped off. I hadn't washed since Bias Station; still felt dirty. Constant stripped down too.

Shower trees are convenient. The midnight rains pool up in the leaves, water trickling down until the broadest leaves at the bottom hold great reservoirs. They fill, they overflow. Stand under the right branch, you get a shower. Scrub for a bit, then stand under the next and rinse. Repeat until clean. Or until tree is dry. The mud around the tree can be deep, but there are usually pools to wash my feet.

I stood naked in the sun to dry off. Constant too. The big hulk stood apart, looking at me. Didn't look back. Didn't want to know. But he watched me.

Finally, I turned to him. "What?"

"Nothing. Just looking."

"Why?"

"Never seen a small naked."

"Now you have. Stop looking."

"Make you nervous?"

"No."

Constant hesitated. "Duty?"

"What?!"

"You ever do it with a large?"

"Never done it with anyone. Turned it off before it started." A thought occurred to me. "You?"

Constant looked away for a moment, then back. "Yes. Have three babies. Two mine, one contract. All went downline. I promise to follow. But—" He stopped.

Long silence.

I looked over. "Am I supposed to say sorry now?"

"Only if you mean it."

"It was your choice to stay."

"No one else could. No—that's not right. No one else was—"

"What?"

Constant cleared his throat. *"Do you speak interlingua?"*

Huh?

Interlingua? The portal engineers' language? Stared at him. This large was not what I thought he was. He stared back, waiting for me to reply.

"You already know that. Or assumed."

"This is what I know. When they asked me to stay—when they said I should stay—I said I would stay only if they told me the truth. So they did. And it doesn't matter if I tell you now because the portal's gone. The story they told everyone about the evacuation? It's a lie. The real reason—there's something wrong about this place, it does something to us. It changes us, every generation. That's why some of us breed large and others breed small and too many are skinny. And some are other things too. It affects us up here—" He tapped his fingers on the side of his head.

Kept my face still. Had to consider this. Maybe. Not impossible. But— *"It's all theories and chatter, yes? Symbiotic evolution. Mutable genetics. Ecological reflection. Nobody knows."*

"Yes. No—maybe. Nobody knows. Synergistic interaction probably. But whatever, it doesn't just change bodies. It changes brains too. Especially the skinnies—they're not people anymore. We don't think like downliners, none of

us. That's why downline ordered the portal closed. They don't want us spreading down."*

"But then, why the evacuation—?"

"Yeah, that. All those people gone downline—all into permanent quarantine. A dead-end world. All those pods went on a one-way trip. Whatever it is, downline wants to contain it, study it, take it apart and maybe find out how to control it. So they can design specific forms of … of whatever we are. The large ones—like me. Not just to adapt to other worlds, but to invade them. Now you know why I stayed. You understand?"

I didn't answer. If Portal Authority had lied to all the evacuees, they would just as easily lie to Constant. But I didn't say that.

"And you? Why did you stay?"

"Because I'm Duty—"

And stopped there.

Didn't finish the sentence. Didn't finish the thought. I was not ready to talk about it. I hiked back to where I'd hung my clothes to dry, shook them out, and dressed in silence. A moment later, Constant followed. "You okay?"

"No."

"Should I say I'm sorry?"

"Why?" I pulled on my jacket. Looked up and up. Looked to his eyes. "When you asked if I'd done it, I thought we were going to have the conversation about you and I doing it. The conversation we did have—that wasn't the conversation I expected. Or wanted to have. It changes things. Mebbe things between us."

"Is that what you wanted? That conversation?"

"No. I dunno. Woulda said no. Gotta think this out. No more talk now."

We were only half a day from the end. We filled our canteens and headed north and west to Green Valley where the grass was taller than Constant. A good place to be caught by a prowler. We stayed in the foothills, above the highest.

The north end of the valley narrowed to a high rocky canyon, not quite a dead-end, but not an easy passage either. No matter. We weren't going the distance. Halfway up, we came to an old wooden shack tucked in the space between two huge boulders and the cliff wall. The door squeaked, then fell open. Inside, a chair, a fallen table, some leftover parts of broken things.

"This is it?" asked Constant.

"This is it," I said.

He looked around, frowning. "Don't see why."

I shrugged out of my gear, dropping it all to the floor. "Now we wait."

"For what?"

"For me to decide."

"Decide what?"

"If I have to kill you."

"Doubt you could."

"Hard, yes. Not impossible. Things you don't know. Things they didn't tell you. Gonna sleep now." I looked around, found a place less dirty, spread hammock as a rug, stretched out on the floor. Stared at the ceiling. Thick webs, looking like veils, hung from the rafters. Just as dead as the rest of the cabin.

"Duty?"

"What?"

"What's to keep me from killing you? While you sleep?"

"You could. But then you'd never know why we're here. Or what I know." I turned off and slept.

Darkness woke me. And cold too. I sat up and looked around.

Constant was gone. All the tracking bots were negative.

Probably had enough of me. Fair choice. Easier without him.

I boiled water for tea. Drank slowly. Waited for dawn. Finally stepped outside to pee and looked around, walked out into the canyon. Up and down. No Constant. Not even footprints.

Sat down to think.

Constant couldn't have known everything. But he had to know more than he had already said. Or he wouldn't have stayed with me. Protected me. So he knew something … more. I just didn't know what.

But he left for a reason. So why? What did that mean? That I didn't need him anymore? Or that he had gotten what he wanted—this location. Even if he didn't know why.

So if this was what he wanted to know, he'd be back.

And probably not friendly. I should have killed him when I had the chance.

Too many mysteries. Too much to think about. Most of it unnecessary. I'd been given a task, been given a tight focus—so tight that I'd missed the rex.

So tight that I'd missed why Constant was here. Assigned to me, yes—by who? Protection because—? Too many questions. Distracting. But I knew one thing now. They shouldn't have focused me so tightly.

Time to go. I gathered my gear from the cabin, strapped up, checked myself—confidence was high, everything green—and headed down the canyon.

The sounds of flyers stopped me, seven of them dropping down from the sky. An entire combat team, Constant in the lead.

I dropped my gear and waited. Put my hands on top of my head. "Surrender," I said. "I surrender."

"Why?" said Constant.

"You brought troops."

"Thought you might need them."

"Oh." I put my hands down. Picked up my gear.

He fumbled in his robe. "Thought you might need this." He held up the roll of shining metal ribbon, then he tucked it away.

"Did you kill them?"

"Only the one. Didn't like him anyway. He took my meat."

"Not his fault. Didn't know better. Hungry. Desperate."

"Well, not anymore." Constant pointed to the other larges behind him. "These are my brothers."

"Obvious."

Constant said, "Talk honest, you and I?" He pointed down the canyon. I followed. After a bit, after he was sure we were out of earshot, he stopped. He looked to me, an accusation in his eyes. *"You know things."*

"Most of them hurt."

"Most of life is hurt."

"You don't know what things are true."

"Do you?"

"Probbly not."

Constant frowned. *"Tell me what you know. We'll think it together."*

Fair enough. *"Agree. Ask."*

"Why the rex?"

"Wanted to pass it. Wanted you to wake it."

"Wanted it to kill me?"

"Mebbe. Didn't know who you were."

"Why Bias Station?"

"I had to hide it somewhere safe until retrieval. Bias was closest."

"It's important?"

"It's useful. It lets me leave."

"Leave to where?"

"Upline."

Constant registered shock. *"Not possible. Upline portal shut down months ago."*

"There's another upline. Unauthorized."

"Not possible. Portal Authority would have detected—"

"Yes, they knew. The stress field disturbance couldn't be hidden. But location could be. Made them crazy."

Constant stopped, confused. His expression collapsed, became unreadable. He looked like he wanted to say something. Or do something. Instead, he turned around and howled at the sky. A long moan of frustration and rage. Did his brothers hear him? Would they come now?

When he finally came back, he must have seen the question on my face. He said, *"No fear. We howl in private. It's our way."*

"I didn't know that."

"I trusted you. I showed you my pain. Now you trust me. Tell me everything. I have no more howl."

I thought about it. Didn't matter anymore. Why not? *"Portal Authority lies. Portal Authority has big secrets. But others have bigger."*

"Do they lie too? The others?"

"Probbly. Secrets hide behind lies. Bigger secrets hide behind bigger lies."

"You know these secrets?"

"Only the smallest part."

Constant held out a corner of his robe, as if it was more than a robe. *"Unraveling starts with a single thread."*

"Depends on where you pull. So pull here. Portal Authority—that story they told you? About the unknown genetic shift? Was that a lie on top of a lie? Nobody knows. But think this. Mebbe they don't want larges downline. Larges are the biggest change of all. You be a threat, just by existing."

"We don't fit downline. Not go."

"Convenient."

"Was not expecting portal to close. Not what we were told."

"More lies, more secrets."

"What was Portal Authority hiding? Do you know."

"Only guesses. Portal Authority couldn't find this upline. Too well hidden. So probably dangerous. How far does this upline extend? Who's up there? Big unknown. Mebbe invasion? Mebbe monsters? Mebbe disease?

Much to fear. They were even more afraid when their agents disappeared. Portal Authority isn't just this world. It's the whole branch. They couldn't find upline. So they had to close downline to cut off the whole branch."

Constant's expression darkened. For a long moment he looked dangerous. But he'd asked for the truth— *"How can I know you're not lying?"*

"Mebbe it's all lies. Mebbe there's some truth. Mebbe we can't know. There's only this … I did what I gotta do. So did you. We both been used. We were useful. Now we're not."

"Used. Yes."

"Now, your turn, Constant. Tell me. Why were you following me for so long?"

"Assignment. They said you were going to illegal upline. I was to follow you, find the station, destroy it, and kill you. But then downline shut down. So Portal Authority is over. Nothing else to do, so I follow anyway. Now I know. Is this the upline I have to close? But why now, if downline gone? Very confusing. Do I still have to destroy it?"

"You don't have to. I'm going to. After I go through. Unless you kill me first. Then you can destroy it. If you find it."

"Hmp. Thought you were logical."

"Could say the same about you. So here we are. Used and useless. Lies and secrets over. Nothing left. Still want to kill me? Want to try?"

"Haven't seen upline station yet. Will decide then. Are there larges up there?"

"Yes. Everyone who disappeared. All the missing. Even larges. All recruited. Yes."

"Recruited?"

"Yes."

"So my brothers and I can be useful again?"

"Yes."

Constant turned and lumbered away. He headed off to talk with his brothers. He was gone a long time. I wondered if he'd forgotten me. Or if they were talking about leaving. But before the sun had moved too far, he came back.

"Question. Recruit us? Me, my brothers too? Can you?"

"Will you take the oath? It is an oath more binding than any you have ever sworn before."

"Tell me."

"Will you do what you gotta do? That's the oath. The rest is details."

"Hmp. Too easy."

"You think so. Do you swear?"

"I swear. I will do what I gotta do."

"And your brothers?"

"They will swear it too."

"I'll hold you to that. Because once we get upline, this portal will be vaporized too. This world will be cut off forever."

"Leave it to the skinnies then."

"Skinnies have feelings."

He didn't want to hear that. "They don't have feelings for people who aren't skinnies."

"Maybe one day they'll figure that out. Maybe not. Go talk to your brothers. Tell them everything. If they want to come, I'll take you. All or none."

He came back. "They don't believe there's a portal."

"But will they come?"

"Prove you can open it, they'll come."

"Follow me."

"If there's no portal, they'll kill you."

"If there's no portal, they should. Follow me."

We went back up to the cabin, crowded now with all those larges inside. I faced the back wall where it leaned up against the cliff. Constant held out the ribbon. "Need this?"

"Nope. Just a decoy. Just in case." I pulled the box out of my jacket, twisted the top around so a different set of symbols lined up. Pressed the box against a ragged splotch of gray.

Nothing happened.

"Nothing's happening."

"Wait."

"If something doesn't happen—"

"Wait!"

Behind us, the larges were restless. Muttering.

I turned and faced them. "What do you want? The portal or my corpse? Choose now. Do it or shut up and wait!" Turned to Constant. "Tell them!"

He grunted something in a language I didn't recognize. But the intent was clear. The others fell silent.

I pushed past them to the chair, plopped myself down. "These things take time. Safety scan. Identity check. Then power up. Energize. Handshake. Synchronization. All that, then more. Then, when confidence get high enough, then mebbe things happen."

"How long?"

"Long as it takes. Day or two or three, mebbe. You brought food?"

"Three days," the largest one said. "Three days. If not three days, you die, we go."

"If not open in three days, I kill myself. You won't have to."

"No," he insisted. "My job. My pleasure."

But it wasn't three days. Only two and a half.

It began with a queasy sensation, then a deep note that got bigger until the whole canyon was rumbling. The walls of the cabin opened, flattening outward. The boulders that sheltered it rolled back with a great grinding sound. The cliff face cracked, slid open, revealing a deep cavern.

Inside, more great doors. Huge. And a rack of travel pods, just waiting to roll down to the tracks. One by one, they clicked to life, their lights gleaming blue.

Constant moved forward in cautious awe. His brothers followed slowly, looking up and around as if they'd never seen a portal lock before.

I came up beside him. "Believe me now?"

He turned around, towering over me. "Believe you now." He leaned down to ask quietly. "A question, Duty. What up there?"

"A whole new world."

"You want me to follow you?"

"Do you want to?"

"We good for each other, yes?"

Looked up at him. Up and up. Finally smiled. "Yes."

That startled him, but he recovered. All business again. "World harder than this one?"

"Much harder. It'll hurt."

"Good." He straightened and waved to his brothers. "Let's go!"

Copyright © 2022 by David Gerrold.

Shirley Song lives in overly-cheerful California, where the sunshine is wasted on her because she'd rather stay inside, no matter how much vitamin D is supposedly "good for her." She trusts computers more than people, and during the day she works on making and delivering robots. At night, she dreams of making and delivering worlds.

TIME, NEEDLES, AND GRAVITY

by Shirley Song

The basement office of the Time Travel Bureau was a mess. Scraps of fabric overflowed from baskets, racks bulged with outfits waiting for alteration and repair, hangers were left strewn on the floor, and bolts of velvet and cotton were shoved in odd angles atop shelves and tables. The work was ceaseless, and ever so excessive during the Parsec Holiday season, when people started taking unnecessary vacations to Manifest—physically appearing in the past. Rachel had been stuck in the wardrobe department workroom for over five days now, and there was a deluge of orders coming in. They were already short-staffed and the replacement fabric-generating bots had not yet arrived.

Rachel frowned, grumbling to herself, "Why does everything have to be done by next week? We're the effing TTB." She roughly ripped into the bodice that needed its temperature nano stitching repaired while eavesdropping on the conversation across the room.

Her manager, Daniel, ignored her glower as he dealt with a leggy, tawny-skinned agent named Janet who had come downstairs with an urgent request. She flicked her blonde hair flirtatiously as she cooed. "It's for the Chairman's family. They want to experience a fun holiday and I suggested Manifesting to the Dickens Era." She batted her long lashes at Daniel. Rachel groaned, getting the feeling he was about to cave to the ridiculous demand. "I know for pre-1950s trips we're supposed to requisition a month in advance, but could you please just make a *teeny tiny* exception this one time?"

"Er, well." He grimaced. "Maybe ... what's the itinerary?"

"I pitched that the family go for a normal day, a Dickens winter, and experience the olden tradition of Christmas—you know, that arcane holiday with presents." She smiled innocently.

"That doesn't sound too bad .... We might have some commoner's clothes." Daniel began.

The agent smiled sweetly, placing her hand on his forearm. Rachel's eyes narrowed. "There will be a Ball," Janet added.

"Oh." Daniel frowned. "That's a lot more involved."

Rachel snapped. "No, no NO! A Victorian Christmas!? You realize our fabric bots have been broken for the last two weeks! Your request requires hand-dying ten meters of wool! Not to mention, our organic fabric printers are all occupied. I *do not* have the time or energy to make ball gowns for *any* era!" She took a deep breath, trying to calm herself. "Also, the Chairman's little monsters shred at least three period pieces any time they go anywhere."

Daniel grimaced, and Janet rolled her eyes.

"Why can't they just Shadow and not inject themselves into that era? They can wear whatever they like in that case, since no one will see them." Rachel suggested.

Janet pouted, pressing her lips together. "But that is too boring for the Chairman. Too ... tame."

"Why not go as peasants for once? To feel what it's like for the rest of us would *not* be tame. In fact, for them, it would be a shocking new experience. One we already have clothes for." Rachel slammed her seam ripper on the table and grabbed a pair of scissors.

"Don't be ridiculous," Janet retorted. "I can't possibly pitch for them to be peasants."

"Then suggest the 2000's! We have plenty of sweatpants and onesies." Rachel made an exasperated gesture toward the storage room door with the tip of her shears.

"Oh, that might not be a bad idea." Daniel clapped his hands together and looked pleadingly at Janet. "She is right about the timing. We're understaffed 'till our new hires start next week and the various bots are repaired." He threw his most charming smile Janet's way, who looked skeptical. "Have you considered 2021 USA? You know, before the Ukraine-Russian conflict—before the War?

We can send you all with a full wardrobe. Go crazy with the options, since there's not anyone in the streets during that year anyway."

"Isn't that because of the plague?" Janet frowned.

"Virus, but close enough. Since travelers are all pre-vaccinated, it's perfectly safe!" Daniel pointed out cheerfully. "Also, if you hit the timeline just right, you can visit all the theme parks with the Chairman's kids and there won't be any lines for rides. Attendance was still abysmal at the time, with many opting to wait until they could be sure the first vaccines were working. Oh, and they have plenty of diabetes-inducing sweets for kids during that era, too, so it's a win-win!"

"That might work …. Fine, I'll pitch a trip for 2021," Janet conceded and shot an annoyed look at Rachel before leaving. "If I get dinged on this, I'm blaming you!"

Rachel rolled her eyes as she went back to ripping out stitching.

"What's gotten into you?" Daniel frowned at her as the door closed.

"I'm sorry, I'm just …" Rachel sighed, dumping the half-done work on the table. "I'm just tired, and … well. I broke up with Jake."

"Oh." Daniel walked over, his eyes sympathetic. "And here I thought it was because I had you work overtime for the last week."

"It's actually been helpful to focus on work." Rachel managed a smile. "But this workload is a little much with just you and me handling the holiday period." She looked at the pile of remnant fabric and backlog of repairs: thermals that needed to be reworked, flexibility ridges that needed to be reinforced on their boning, and a pile of additional demands from agents for the new year.

"The new bots are coming tomorrow, and new hires are starting next week," Daniel said. "Three, in fact."

"Three?" Rachel glanced up, blinking. "I thought we okayed only two."

"Well, I was going to surprise you at the end of the day, but you looked like you could use the good news right now." Daniel grinned and handed Rachel a box.

Curious, she opened it. Inside was a watch with no numbers but with eight hands and four di-

als. She beamed. It was the device used by time travelers!

"I was accepted?!" She jumped across the distance separating them and hugged the stout manager she'd worked for over the last two years.

"Yes, you'll be officially promoted to agent-in-training." Daniel patted her back. "Then you'll be the one making all these ridiculous requests." He chuckled.

"Oh, thank you! Thank you!"

✧

A week later, when Rachel arrived at the TTB upper floors for registration, she was surprised to see Janet waiting for her.

"Rachel, was it?" Janet beamed, running up to her enthusiastically.

"Yes. Hi, um, Janet." Rachel blinked at the unexpected warmth.

"I volunteered to train you." Her blue eyes sparked while she gave Rachel an unanticipated hug. "I wanted to thank you for your suggestion for 2021. It was fabulous. No one batted an eye at the Chairman or his family, even though they weren't human. The masks hid their mouths—so it was perfect." Janet ushered Rachel through the lobby and walked by the travelers' platforms. "And don't get me started on the food. Do you know about these things called 'churros'? They come with different fillings—some have custard or chocolate. I'm obsessed. And there was Fro-Yo. I can't tell you how much I enjoyed 2021, it really had the best food." Janet continued raving about the variety of sweets while Rachel gazed longingly at the travel-pods and tourists they passed.

A man in a suit led a small family preparing to go to the early 1900s. Another group of kids were huddled near their agent, preparing to go back to learn the history of the Mars Wars.

"What if we change history and make it so we're not even born?" one kid piped.

"We're just Shadowing—we can't even interact with the environment," another kid responded.

"Besides, there's an infinite number of realities. I bet you weren't born in *a lot* of them," a third kid snickered.

"You weren't born in an infinite amount plus a thousand," the first kid said, sticking his tongue out at the others.

As Janet reached an elevator at the center of the long hall, she stopped and scanned her watch against the panel; Rachel followed suit. The glow of the UP button illuminated after confirming their status as agents.

"Now, you've done your orientation, so you know the basics, right? I mean, you worked in the wardrobe department, so I don't need to explain to you how our nanobot clothes don't always function in the past, if we Manifest." Janet smiled, raising her watch. "Which is why we have to use this old timey technology and proper period clothes for Manifesting. Otherwise, we could become buck naked in a couple minutes if the nano technology failed at a crucial moment."

Rachel nodded as the elevator dinged.

"Have you Manifested before, as a tourist?" Janet asked as the elevator door closed behind them.

Rachel shook her head. "Never—it's too expensive."

Janet nodded. "Yeah, true, but now that you're an agent, you get your own Manifest timeline. It's so exciting! And once you get clients, you can have multiple timelines and can go to different periods. Do you have an idea of When you want to visit for your first trial trip?"

"Yes, the 1600s." Rachel said.

"Ah …. Colonization of the Americas?"

"Baroque period art, actually." Rachel responded.

"Hmm … then depending on where you want to go, you might need to change your skin color for the trip." Janet commented.

Rachel frowned and looked at her natural almond-colored skin. "Oh. You might be right."

"Don't worry, we'll do some test runs today. You don't have to worry just yet about wardrobe or feature alterations for Manifesting." Janet led the new recruit out of the elevator to an office floor with long hallways and many doors. They entered one for training, and Rachel stared at the set of six travel-pods.

"Just us today." Janet said, walking to the panel next to the pods. "You'll go solo and we'll test out your watch first. 1666 looks fun. Let's do England, maybe somewhere remote … Grantham?" She pressed the screen on the control panel, adding in the trip par-

ticulars. "I can talk you through the trip. We'll do a short one in Shadow mode to start, so no one sees you if you screw up, and then you can Manifest for like a minute or two and come back, 'kay?"

Rachel nodded as she grabbed a simple white linen dress from the rack and slipped it over her head—adding it to her clothes ensemble, just in case.

"Also, it's your first time, so your watch might misbehave, as you are still creating your sync bond. If that happens, just flip it off and on a few times—sometimes that'll reset it. Manifesting out of Shadow-mode might reset it too, so try that if the on-off doesn't work," Janet explained. "Oh, and don't worry about losing communication, either. The watch will naturally pull you back once 30 minutes are up."

Rachel entered a pod and closed the door behind her. She looked nervously at the analog display on her watch, which had been updated with the date and year of her visit. One set of hands on the watch face was set at the top of the countdown for thirty minutes.

"Rural England, Buckminster Park should be free of people. The lake is pretty," Janet's voice called out cheerfully from a speaker on Rachel's timepiece. "The translator hopefully won't brea…k when …" her voice cracked and cut off.

A surge of energy enveloped Rachel and the next thing she knew she was standing in a wooded park, a lake shimmering blue in the distance. The analog dials of her watch face declared it to be the summer of 1666. Willing the settings to change on her nanobot clothes, praying the technology hadn't fried in the transfer, as it can be prone to do, she altered them to appear as if she was wearing a silver gown with a bodice matching the era over her simple white linen dress. Even if no one could see her while she was in Shadow mode, Rachel wanted to feel prepared, just in case for some reason she needed to Manifest, or the watch glitched.

She walked over to the lake and tapped her timepiece.

"Janet, can you hear me?" She asked. There was no sound. Rachel frowned and tapped it again. "Janet?" Rachel tried turning the timepiece off and on again. Nothing.

Sighing, she surveyed the surrounding area, the brilliant green grass, the wind in the tree—and a man in his twenties skipping stones against the still lake's glassy surface. Each skip, the stone left ripples that spanned out, disquieting the lake.

Rachel paused, not wanting to try Jane's idea of Manifesting to reset the watch—not with people around. She toyed with her watch setting some more. *Still no Janet.*

Rachel considered leaving the area, when she saw the man walk into the lake. *What the?*

He wasn't stopping, and he was fully clothed in breeches and a silk shirt.

Did people swim with their clothes on in 1666? Rachel frowned, confused. She knew social modesty was important for the period, but this seemed a bit much.

She watched as the man's wavy blond hair disappeared beneath into the lake.

A sinking sensation gripped her stomach. *He's not swimming.* Rachel rushed to the water's edge trying to remember what the protocol would be in a situation like this.

Calm down. He's been dead for thousands of years. Rachel gulped nervously. *I can't change the past. I just can't.*

The man didn't seem to be coming back up. *Crap.* A death didn't sit well with her, even if it was in the past.

Rachel flipped one of the switches on her watch and jumped into the lake, diving and swimming toward the man. *Effing Victorian gowns makes this so much harder.* She cursed as she willed her clothes to become lighter and her skirt shorter to allow her to swim to him.

Grabbing a hold of the man's arm, Rachel pulled him back up to the surface, to the lakeshore, dragging him onto the bank. She pressed on his waterlogged chest. *Come on, come on!* Opening his mouth and straightening his airway, she breathed for him, forcing her air into his lungs. She watched his chest rise then fall, then tried again. Compression, breath, compression, breath. The third time he coughed back to life. Rachel sighed with relief, collapsing and at the side of the lake.

While the man was still dazed, his gaze unfocused, she looked at her wet dress and willed it to its correct length. *The nanobots seem to be holding for now.* Running her hand through her soaked umber hair, she sighed and checked her timepiece. *Still*

no Janet. Looking around, she inhaled the fresh air of summer infused with the smell of crushed grass and the earthy scent from the lake. She drank in the wonder of being in the past, tasting the air of a virgin Earth, before technology engulfed the planet in pollution; noting the birds chirping happily nearby.

The man, still coughing up the odd trickle of lake, seemed to be recovering as he relaxed his head on the shore, looking at her.

In the original timelines he would have died.

Shit. This deviation is going to cost me. My first trip Manifesting in the past, and I managed to make such a stupidly large change. Rachel grimaced. *This timeline might not even be usable anymore.*

"Are you an angel?" he asked.

The question took Rachel by surprise. "Uh … no. I'm not an angel."

The man coughed once more, then sat up. "Why did you save me?"

"Wouldn't anyone, if they saw someone struggling?" Rachel replied.

The man sighed, regaining his breath. "Fair point." He had a prominent nose that paired with his intense, thoughtful eyes.

Strangely, Rachel thought he looked familiar. "Why did you …" She gestured toward the lake.

"My mother wants me to run the family farm and everything is horribly mundane," he said. "But I guess you've proven me wrong, and miracles do exist."

He was smiling at her in a way that made her heart skip. "I'm not an angel," she repeated.

"She says as she glistens." His smile was coy.

Rachel frowned, then realization dawned. Glancing down at her nanobot clothing, the tiny particles were shifting as they fractalized into iridescent dust. "Oh."

He reached over and held some of the broken bots in his hand. "Is this magic?"

"No, it's just refracting light. There's no such thing as magic." Rachel sighed as the beautiful pieces of her gown disintegrated, until she was just wearing her simple white slip of a dress.

He looked as though he didn't believe her, studying the glimmering crystal dust in his palm. "If you hadn't have saved me, I'd be more convinced there's no such thing as magic. Just a few minutes ago I was convinced there is no wonder left in this world."

He leant forward, studying her intently, and Rachel felt the need to avert her gaze. She glanced at her watch idly, checking if water had damaged the device; it looked fine.

"Angel, can I ask what is the meaning of life?"

Rachel rubbed the bridge of her nose, at a loss at what to do. "Honestly, I'm not an angel, and I have no idea what the purpose of life might be." He looked disappointed at her answer. "Maybe finding out *is* the purpose," she said, shrugging.

"Is that why God made the celestial bodies the same as ordinary pebbles? To test our faith?" he asked, his eyes studying hers.

Celestial bodies? "You mean the moon?" Rachel replied after a pause.

He nodded. "I used to believe that the celestial laws that govern the heavens are different from the ones that govern here on earth, but it looks not to be so." He gazed back at the lake, water dripping from his tangled blond hair. "The Moon is just a rock, like the rest of Earth."

Rachel frowned at him. The man looked genuinely grief-stricken about the state of reality. She considered for a moment, "Maybe, but ordinary things can be wonderful too. I might not be an angel, but I do believe that people can create miracles, and simplicity can be beautiful."

He considered her with an intensity, as if he'd just discovered something he'd lost, then murmured, "To find the laws that govern the ordinary …" Suddenly smiling, he stood up, then offered her his hand. As he helped her to her feet, she found herself standing just a little too close, his hazel eyes peering deep into her brown ones. "Maybe two bodies in proximity have a pull …" he said.

Rachel swallowed and felt her face grow warm. "Are you a poet?" She smiled shyly as he brushed wet hair from her face.

"No, I'm a mathematician. But I could be a poet, I suppose—like you could be my angel," he said.

"I …"

He leaned towards her, and as his lips neared hers, she found herself breathless. Waiting.

Then, she faded out of the past.

Rachel found herself back in the travel-pod, reeling. She checked her watch—time had run out.

"Rachel, can you hear me? Are you alright?" Janet called. "Of all times to discover we have a defective time watch. Can you hear me?"

Rachel was dazed for a second before responding. "Yes, I'm fine." Leaning against the pod's wall, she sighed, disappointed at her sudden return. "Who was that?"

"Sorry, what?" Janet asked as the pod door opened.

"I met a guy … umm, in the past." Rachel said.

"Oh, I thought you were alone. Hmm. Let's find out." Janet said cheerfully, beckoning Rachel over to the console. "People you came into contact with are recorded, and we can find them through the database."

Rachel scanned her watch on the panel and gasped as a single name flashed on the screen.

"I do not know what I may appear to the world, but to myself I seem to have been only like a boy playing on the sea-shore, and diverting myself in now and then finding a smoother pebble or a prettier shell than ordinary, whilst the great ocean of truth lay all undiscovered before me."

~Sir Isaac Newton

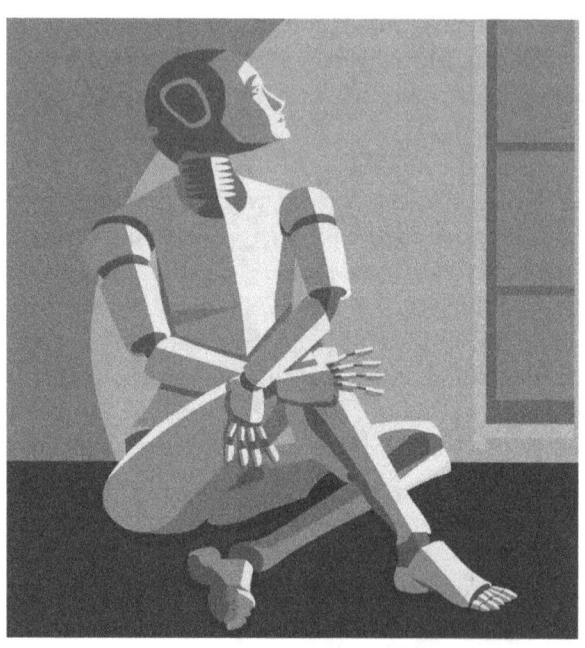

Mike Resnick, along with editing the first seven years of Galaxy's Edge magazine, was the winner of five Hugos from a record thirty-seven nominations and was, according to Locus, the all-time leading award winner, living or dead, for short fiction. He was the author of over eighty novels, around 300 stories, three screenplays, and the editor of over forty anthologies. He was Guest of Honor at the 2012 Worldcon.

ROBOTS DON'T CRY

by Mike Resnick

They call us graverobbers, but we're not.

What we do is plunder the past and offer it to the present. We hit old worlds, deserted worlds, worlds that nobody wants any longer, and we pick up anything we think we can sell to the vast collectibles market. You want a 700-year-old timepiece? A thousand-year old bed? An actual printed book? Just put in your order, and sooner or later we'll fill it.

Every now and then we strike it rich. Usually we make a profit. Once in a while we just break even. There's only been one world where we actually lost money; I still remember it—Greenwillow. Except that it wasn't green, and there wasn't a willow on the whole damned planet.

There was a robot, though. We found him, me and the Baroni, in a barn, half-hidden under a pile of ancient computer parts and self-feeders for mutated cattle. We were picking through the stuff, wondering if there was any market for it, tossing most of it aside, when the sun peeked in through the doorway and glinted off a prismatic eye.

"Hey, take a look at what we've got here," I said. "Give me a hand digging it out."

The junk had been stored a few feet above where he'd been standing and the rack broke, practically burying him. One of his legs was bent at an impossible angle, and his expressionless face was covered with cobwebs. The Baroni lumbered over—when you've got three legs you don't glide gracefully—and studied the robot.

"Interesting," he said. He never used whole sentences when he could annoy me with a single word that could mean almost anything.

"He should pay our expenses, once we fix him up and get him running," I said.

"A human configuration," noted the Baroni.

"Yeah, we still made 'em in our own image until a couple of hundred years ago."

"Impractical."

"Spare me your practicalities," I said. "Let's dig him out."

"Why bother?"

Trust a Baroni to miss the obvious. "Because he's got a memory cube," I answered. "Who the hell knows what he's seen? Maybe we'll find out what happened here."

"Greenwillow has been abandoned since long before you were born and I was hatched," replied the Baroni, finally stringing some words together. "Who cares what happened?"

"I know it makes your head hurt, but try to use your brain," I said, grunting as I pulled at the robot's arm. It came off in my hands. "Maybe whoever he worked for hid some valuables." I dropped the arm onto the floor. "Maybe he knows where. We don't just have to sell junk, you know; there's a market for the good stuff too."

The Baroni shrugged and began helping me uncover the robot. "I hear a lot of ifs and maybes," he muttered.

"Fine," I said. "Just sit on what passes for your ass, and I'll do it myself."

"And let you keep what we find without sharing it?" he demanded, suddenly throwing himself into the task of moving the awkward feeders. After a moment he stopped and studied one. "Big cows," he noted.

"Maybe ten or twelve feet at the shoulder, judging from the size of the stalls and the height of the feeders," I agreed. "But there weren't enough to fill the barn. Some of those stalls were never used."

Finally we got the robot uncovered, and I checked the code on the back of his neck.

"How about that?" I said. "The son of a bitch must be 500 years old. That makes him an antique by anyone's definition. I wonder what we can get for him?"

The Baroni peered at the code. "What does AB stand for?"

"Aldebaran. Alabama. Abrams' Planet. Or maybe just the model number. Who the hell knows? We'll get him running and maybe he can tell us." I tried to set him on his feet. No luck. "Give me a hand."

"To the ship?" asked the Baroni, using sentence fragments again as he helped me stand the robot upright.

"No," I said. "We don't need a sterile environment to work on a robot. Let's just get him out in the sunlight, away from all this junk, and then we'll have a couple of mechs check him over."

We half-carried and half-dragged him to the crumbling concrete pad beyond the barn, then laid him down while I tightened the muscles in my neck, activating the embedded micro-chip, and directed the signal by pointing to the ship, which was about half a mile away.

"This is me," I said as the chip carried my voice back to the ship's computer. "Wake up Mechs 3 and 7, feed them everything you've got on robots going back a millennium, give them repair kits and anything else they'll need to fix a broken robot of indeterminate age, and then home in on my signal and send them to me."

"Why those two?" asked the Baroni.

Sometimes I wondered why I partnered with anyone that dumb. Then I remembered the way he could sniff out anything with a computer chip or cube, no matter how well it was hidden, so I decided to give him a civil answer. He didn't get that many from me; I hoped he appreciated it.

"Three's got those extendable eyestalks, and it can do microsurgery, so I figure it can deal with any faulty micro-circuits. As for Seven, it's strong as an ox. It can position the robot, hold him aloft, move him any way that Three directs it to. They're both going to show up filled to the brim with everything the ship's data bank has on robots, so if he's salvageable, they'll find a way to salvage him."

I waited to see if he had any more stupid questions. Sure enough, he had.

"Why would anyone come here?" he asked, looking across the bleak landscape.

"I came for what passes for treasure these days," I answered him. "I have no idea why you came."

"I meant originally," he said, and his face started to glow that shade of pea-soup green that meant I was getting to him. "Nothing can grow, and the ultra-violet rays would eventually kill most animals. So why?"

"Because not all humans are as smart as me."

"It's an impoverished world," continued the Baroni. "What valuables could there be?"

"The usual," I replied. "Family heirlooms. Holographs. Old kitchen implements. Maybe even a few old Republic coins."

"Republic currency can't be spent."

"True—but a few years ago I saw a five-credit coin sell for three hundred Maria Teresa dollars. They tell me it's worth twice that today."

"I didn't know that," admitted the Baroni.

"I'll bet they could fill a book with all the things you don't know."

"Why are Men so sardonic and ill-mannered?"

"Probably because we have to spend so much time with races like the Baroni," I answered.

Mechs Three and Seven rolled up before he could reply.

"Reporting for duty, sir," said Mech Three in his high-pitched mechanical voice.

"This is a very old robot," I said, indicating what we'd found. "It's been out of commission for a few centuries, maybe even longer. See if you can get it working again."

"We live to serve," thundered Mech Seven.

"I can't tell you how comforting I find that." I turned to the Baroni. "Let's grab some lunch."

"Why do you always speak to them that way?" asked the Baroni as we walked away from the mechs. "They don't understand sarcasm."

"It's my nature," I said. "Besides, if they don't know it's sarcasm, it must sound like a compliment. Probably pleases the hell out of them."

"They are machines," he responded. "You can no more please them than offend them."

"Then what difference does it make?"

"The more time I spend with Men, the less I understand them," said the Baroni, making the burbling sound that passed for a deep sigh. "I look forward to getting the robot working. Being a logical and unemotional entity, it will make more sense."

"Spare me your smug superiority," I shot back. "You're not here because Papa Baroni looked at Mama Baroni with logic in his heart."

The Baroni burbled again. "You are hopeless," he said at last.

We had one of the mechs bring us our lunch, then sat with our backs propped against opposite sides of a gnarled old tree while we ate. I didn't want to watch his snakelike lunch writhe and wriggle, protesting every inch of the way, as he sucked it down like the long, living piece of spaghetti it was, and he had his usual moral qualms, which I never understood, about watching me bite into a sandwich. We had just about finished when Mech Three approached us.

"All problems have been fixed," it announced brightly.

"That was fast," I said.

"There was nothing broken." It then launched into a three-minute explanation of whatever it had done to the robot's circuitry.

"That's enough," I said when it got down to a dissertation on the effect of mu-mesons on negative magnetic fields in regard to prismatic eyes. "I'm wildly impressed. Now let's go take a look at this beauty."

I got to my feet, as did the Baroni, and we walked back to the concrete pad. The robot's limbs were straight now, and his arm was restored, but he still lay motionless on the crumbling surface.

"I thought you said you fixed him."

"I did," replied Mech Three. "But my programming compelled me not to activate it until you were present."

"Fine," I said. "Wake him up."

The little Mech made one final quick adjustment and backed away as the robot hummed gently to life and sat up.

"Welcome back," I said.

"Back?" replied the robot. "I have not been away."

"You've been asleep for five centuries, maybe six."

"Robots cannot sleep." He looked around. "Yet everything has changed. How is this possible?"

"You were deactivated," said the Baroni. "Probably your power supply ran down."

"Deactivated," the robot repeated. He swiveled his head from left to right, surveying the scene. "Yes. Things cannot change this much from one instant to the next."

"Have you got a name?" I asked him.

"Samson 4133. But Miss Emily calls me Sammy."

"Which name do you prefer?"

"I am a robot. I have no preferences."

I shrugged. "Whatever you say, Samson."

"Sammy," he corrected me.

"I thought you had no preferences."

"I don't," said the robot. "But *she* does."

"Has she got a name?"

"Miss Emily."

"Just Miss Emily?" I asked. "No other names to go along with it?"

"Miss Emily is what I was instructed to call her."

"I assume she is a child," said the Baroni, with his usual flair for discovering the obvious.

"She was once," said Sammy. "I will show her to you."

Then somehow, I never did understand the technology involved, he projected a full-sized holograph of a small girl, perhaps five years old, wearing a frilly purple-and-white outfit. She had rosy cheeks and bright shining blue eyes, and a smile that men would die for someday if given half the chance.

It was only after she took a step forward, a very awkward step, that I realized she had a prosthetic left leg.

"Too bad," I said. "A pretty little girl like that."

"Was she born that way, I wonder?" said the Baroni.

"I love you, Sammy," said the holograph.

I hadn't expected sound, and it startled me. She had such a happy voice. Maybe she didn't know that most little girls came equipped with two legs. After all, this was an underpopulated colony world; for all I knew, she'd never seen anyone but her parents.

"It is time for your nap, Miss Emily," said Sammy's voice. "I will carry you to your room." Another surprise. The voice didn't seem to come from the robot, but from somewhere … well, offstage. He was recreating the scene exactly as it had happened, but we saw it through his eyes. Since he couldn't see himself, neither could we.

"I'll walk," said the child. "Mother told me I have to practice walking, so that someday I can play with the other girls."

"Yes, Miss Emily."

"But you can catch me if I start to fall, like you always do."

"Yes, Miss Emily."

"What would I do without you, Sammy?"

"You would fall, Miss Emily," he answered. Robots are always so damned literal.

And as suddenly as it had appeared, the scene vanished.

"So that was Miss Emily?" I said.

"Yes," said Sammy.

"And you were owned by her parents?"

"Yes."

"Do you have any understanding of the passage of time, Sammy?"

"I can calibrate time to within three nanoseconds of …"

"That's not what I asked," I said. "For example, if I told you that scene we just saw happened more than 500 years ago, what would you say to that?"

"I would ask if you were measuring by Earth years, Galactic Standard years, New Calendar Democracy years …"

"Never mind," I said.

Sammy fell silent and motionless. If someone had stumbled upon him at just that moment, they'd have been hard-pressed to prove that he was still operational.

"What's the matter with him?" asked the Baroni. "His battery can't be drained yet."

"Of course not. They were designed to work for years without recharging."

And then I knew. He wasn't a farm robot, so he had no urge to get up and start working the fields. He wasn't a mech, so he had no interest in fixing the feeders in the barn. For a moment I thought he might be a butler or a major domo, but if he was, he'd have been trying to learn my desires to serve me, and he obviously wasn't doing that. That left just one thing.

He was a nursemaid.

I shared my conclusion with the Baroni, and he concurred.

"We're looking at a *lot* of money here," I said excitedly. "Think of it—a fully-functioning antique robot nursemaid! He can watch the kids while his new owners go rummaging for more old artifacts."

"There's something wrong," said the Baroni, who was never what you could call an optimist.

"The only thing wrong is we don't have enough bags to haul all the money we're going to sell him for."

"Look around you," said the Baroni. "This place was abandoned, and it was never prosperous. If he's that valuable, why did they leave him behind?"

"He's a nursemaid. Probably she outgrew him."

"Better find out." He was back to sentence fragments again.

I shrugged and approached the robot. "Sammy, what did you do at night after Miss Emily went to sleep?"

He came to life again. "I stood by her bed."

"All night, every night?"

"Yes, sir. Unless she woke and requested pain medication, which I would retrieve and bring to her."

"Did she require pain medication very often?" I asked.

"I do not know, sir."

I frowned. "I thought you just said you brought it to her when she needed it."

"No, sir," Sammy corrected me. "I said I brought it to her when she *requested* it."

"She didn't request it very often?"

"Only when the pain became unbearable." Sammy paused. "I do not fully understand the word 'unbearable,' but I know it had a deleterious effect upon her. My Miss Emily was often in pain."

"I'm surprised you understand the word 'pain,'" I said.

"To feel pain is to be non-operational or dysfunctional to some degree."

"Yes, but it's more than that. Didn't Miss Emily ever try to describe it?"

"No," answered Sammy. "She never spoke of her pain."

"Did it bother her less as she grew older and adjusted to her handicap?" I asked.

"No, sir, it did not." He paused. "There are many kinds of dysfunction."

"Are you saying she had other problems, too?" I continued.

Instantly we were looking at another scene from Sammy's past. It was the same girl, now maybe thirteen years old, staring at her face in a mirror. She didn't like what she saw, and neither did I.

"What *is* that?" I asked, forcing myself not to look away.

"It is a fungus disease," answered Sammy as the girl tried unsuccessfully with cream and powder to cover the ugly blemishes that had spread across her face.

"Is it native to this world?"

"Yes," said Sammy.

"You must have had some pretty ugly people walking around," I said.

"It did not affect most of the colonists. But Miss Emily's immune system was weakened by her other diseases."

"What other diseases?"

Sammy rattled off three or four that I'd never heard of.

"And no one else in her family suffered from them?"

"No, sir."

"It happens in my race, too," offered the Baroni. "Every now and then a genetically inferior specimen is born and grows to maturity."

"She was not genetically inferior," said Sammy.

"Oh?" I said, surprised. It's rare for a robot to contradict a living being, even an alien. "What was she?"

Sammy considered his answer for a moment.

"Perfect," he said at last.

"I'll bet the other kids didn't think so," I said.

"What do they know?" replied Sammy.

And instantly he projected another scene. Now the girl was fully grown, probably about twenty. She kept most of her skin covered, but we could see the ravaging effect her various diseases had had upon her hands and face.

Tears were running down from these beautiful blue eyes over bony, parchment-like cheeks. Her emaciated body was wracked by sobs.

A holograph of a robot's hand popped into existence, and touched her gently on the shoulder.

"Oh, Sammy!" she cried. "I really thought he liked me! He was always so nice to me." She paused for breath as the tears continued unabated. "But I saw his face when I reached out to take his hand, and I felt him shudder when I touched it. All he really felt for me was pity. That's all any of them ever feel!"

"What do they know?" said Sammy's voice, the same words and the same inflections he had just used a moment ago.

"It's not just him," she said. "Even the farm animals run away when I approach them. I don't know how anyone can stand being in the same room with me." She stared at where the robot was standing. "You're all I've got, Sammy. You're my only friend in the whole world. Please don't ever leave me."

"I will never leave you, Miss Emily," said Sammy's voice.

"Promise me."

"I promise," said Sammy.

And then the holograph vanished and Sammy stood mute and motionless again.

"He really cared for her," said the Baroni.

"The boy?" I said. "If he did, he had a funny way of showing it."

"No, of course not the boy. The robot."

"Come off it," I said. "Robots don't have any feelings."

"You heard him," said the Baroni.

"Those were programmed responses," I said. "He probably has three million to choose from."

"Those are emotions," insisted the Baroni.

"Don't you go getting all soft on me," I said. "Any minute now you'll be telling me he's too human to sell."

"*You* are the human," said the Baroni. "*He* is the one with compassion."

"I've got more compassion than her parents did, letting her grow up like that," I said irritably. I confronted the robot again. "Sammy, why didn't the doctors do anything for her?"

"This was a farming colony," answered Sammy. "There were only 387 families on the entire world. The Democracy sent a doctor once a year at the beginning, and then, when there were less than 100 families left, he stopped coming. The last time Miss Emily saw a doctor was when she was fourteen."

"What about an offworld hospital?" asked the Baroni.

"They had no ship and no money. They moved here in the second year of a seven-year drought. Then various catastrophes wiped out their next six crops. They spent what savings they had on mutated cattle, but the cattle died before they could produce young or milk. One by one all the families began leaving the planet as impoverished wards of the Democracy."

"Including Miss Emily's family?" I asked.

"No. Mother died when Miss Emily was nineteen, and Father died two years later."

Then it was time for me to ask the Baroni's question.

"So when did Miss Emily leave the planet, and why did she leave you behind?"

"She did not leave."

I frowned. "She couldn't have run the farm—not in her condition."

"There was no farm left to run," answered Sammy. "All the crops had died, and without Father there was no one to keep the machines working."

"But she stayed. Why?"

Sammy stared at me for a long moment. It's just as well his face was incapable of expression, because I got the distinct feeling that he thought the question was too simplistic or too stupid to merit an answer. Finally he projected another scene. This time the girl, now a woman approaching thirty, hideous open pustules on her face and neck, was sitting in a crudely-crafted hoverchair, obviously too weak to stand any more.

"No!" she rasped bitterly.

"They are your relatives," said Sammy's voice. "And they have a room for you."

"All the more reason to be considerate of them. No one should be forced to associate with me—especially not people who are decent enough to make the offer. We will stay here, by ourselves, on this world, until the end."

"Yes, Miss Emily."

She turned and stared at where Sammy stood. "You want to tell me to leave, don't you? That if we go to Jefferson IV I will receive medical attention and they will make me well—but you are compelled by your programming not to disobey me. Am I correct?"

"Yes, Miss Emily."

The hint of a smile crossed her ravaged face. "Now you know what pain is."

"It is … uncomfortable, Miss Emily."

"You'll learn to live with it," she said. She reached out and patted the robot's leg fondly. "If it's any comfort, I don't know if the medical specialists could have helped me even when I was young. They certainly can't help me now."

"You are still young, Miss Emily."

"Age is relative," she said. "I am so close to the grave I can almost taste the dirt." A metal hand appeared, and she held it in ten incredibly fragile fingers. "Don't feel sorry for me, Sammy. It hasn't been a life I'd wish on anyone else. I won't be sorry to see it end."

"I am a robot," replied Sammy. "I cannot feel sorrow."

"You've no idea how fortunate you are."

I shot the Baroni a triumphant smile that said: *See? Even Sammy admits he can't feel any emotions.*

And he sent back a look that said: *I didn't know until now that robots could lie,* and I knew we still had a problem.

The scene vanished.

"How soon after that did she die?" I asked Sammy.

"Seven months, eighteen days, three hours, and four minutes, sir," was his answer.

"She was very bitter," noted the Baroni.

"She was bitter because she was born, sir," said Sammy. "Not because she was dying."

"Did she lapse into a coma, or was she cogent up to the end?" I asked out of morbid curiosity.

"She was in control of her senses until the moment she died," answered Sammy. "But she could not see for the last eighty-three days of her life. I functioned as her eyes."

"What did she need eyes for?" asked the Baroni. "She had a hoverchair, and it is a single-level house."

"When you are a recluse, you spend your life with books, sir," said Sammy, and I thought: *The mechanical bastard is actually lecturing us!*

With no further warning, he projected a final scene for us.

The woman, her eyes no longer blue, but clouded with cataracts and something else—disease, fungus, who knew?—lay on her bed, her breathing labored.

From Sammy's point of view, we could see not only her, but, much closer, a book of poetry, and then we heard his voice: "Let me read something else, Miss Emily."

"But that is the poem I wish to hear," she whispered. "It is by Edna St. Vincent Millay, and she is my favorite."

"But it is about death," protested Sammy.

"All life is about death," she replied so softly I could barely hear her. "Surely you know that I am dying, Sammy?"

"I know, Miss Emily," said Sammy.

"I find it comforting that my ugliness did not diminish the beauty around me, that it will remain after I am gone," she said. "Please read."

Sammy read:

"There will be rose and rhododendron
When you are dead and under ground;
Still will be heard from white syringes …" Suddenly the robot's voice fell silent. For a moment I thought there was a flaw in the projection. Then I saw that Miss Emily had died.

He stared at her for a long minute, which means that we did too, and then the scene evaporated.

"I buried her beneath her favorite tree," said Sammy. "But it is no longer there."

"Nothing lasts forever, even trees," said the Baroni. "And it's been five hundred years."

"It does not matter. I know where she is."

He walked us over to a barren spot about thirty yards from the ruin of a farmhouse. On the ground was a stone, and neatly carved into it was the following:

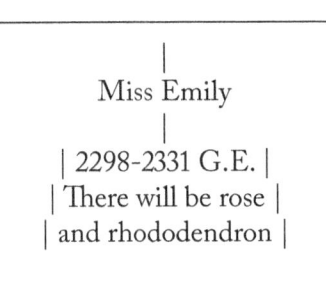

```
            |
        Miss Emily
            |
    | 2298-2331 G.E. |
    | There will be rose |
    | and rhododendron |
```

"That's lovely, Sammy," said the Baroni.

"It is what she requested."

"What did you do after you buried her?" I asked.

"I went to the barn."

"For how long?"

"With Miss Emily dead, I had no need to stay in the house. I remained in the barn for many years, until my battery power ran out."

"Many years?" I repeated. "What the hell did you do there?"

"Nothing."

"You just stood there?"

"I just stood there."

"Doing nothing?"

"That is correct." He stared at me for a long moment, and I could have sworn he was studying me. Finally he spoke again. "I know that you intend to sell me."

"We'll find you a family with another Miss Emily," I said. *If they're the highest bidder.*

"I do not wish to serve another family. I wish to remain here."

"There's nothing here," I said. "The whole planet's deserted."

"I promised my Miss Emily that I would never leave her."

"But she's dead now," I pointed out.

"She put no conditions on her request. I put no conditions on my promise."

I looked from Sammy to the Baroni, and decided that this was going to take a couple of mechs—one to carry Sammy to the ship, and one to stop the Baroni from setting him free.

"But if you will honor a single request, I will break my promise to her and come away with you."

Suddenly I felt like I was waiting for the other shoe to drop, and I hadn't heard the first one yet.

"What do you want, Sammy?"

"I told you I did nothing in the barn. That was true. I was incapable of doing what I wanted to do."

"And what was that?"

"I wanted to cry."

I don't know what I was expecting, but that wasn't it.

"Robots don't cry," I said.

"Robots *can't* cry," replied Sammy. "There is a difference."

"And that's what you want?"

"It is what I have wanted ever since my Miss Emily died."

"We rig you to cry, and you agree to come away with us?"

"That is correct," said Sammy.

"Sammy," I said, "you've got yourself a deal."

I contacted the ship, told it to feed Mech Three everything the medical library had on tears and tear ducts, and then send it over. It arrived about ten minutes later, deactivated the robot, and started fussing and fiddling. After about two hours it announced that its work was done, that Sammy now had tear ducts and had been supplied with a solution that could produce six hundred authentic saltwater tears from each eye.

I had Mech Three show me how to activate Sammy, and then sent it back to the ship.

"Have you ever heard of a robot wanting to cry?" I asked the Baroni.

"No."

"Neither have I," I said, vaguely disturbed.

"He loved her."

I didn't even argue this time. I was wondering which was worse, spending thirty years trying to be a normal human being and failing, or spending thirty years trying to cry and failing. None of the other stuff had gotten to me; Sammy was just doing what robots do. It was the thought of his trying so hard to do what robots couldn't do that suddenly made me feel sorry for him. That in turn made me very irritable; ordinarily I don't even feel sorry for Men, let alone machines.

And what he wanted was such a simple thing compared to the grandiose ambitions of my own race. Once Men had wanted to cross the ocean; we crossed it. We'd wanted to fly; we flew. We wanted to reach the stars; we reached them. All Sammy wanted to do was cry over the loss of his Miss Emily. He'd waited half a millennium and had agreed to sell himself into bondage again, just for a few tears.

It was a lousy trade.

I reached out and activated him.

"Is it done?" asked Sammy.

"Right," I said. "Go ahead and cry your eyes out."

Sammy stared straight ahead. "I can't," he said at last.

"Think of Miss Emily," I suggested. "Think of how much you miss her."

"I feel pain," said Sammy. "But I cannot cry."

"You're sure?"

"I am sure," said Sammy. "I was guilty of having thoughts and longings above my station. Miss Emily used to say that tears come from the heart and the soul. I am a robot. I have no heart and no soul, so I cannot cry, even with the tear ducts you have given me. I am sorry to have wasted your time. A more complex model would have understood its limitations at the outset." He paused, and then turned to me. "I will go with you now."

"Shut up," I said.

He immediately fell silent.

"What is going on?" asked the Baroni.

"You shut up too!" I snapped.

I summoned Mechs Seven and Eight and had them dig Sammy a grave right next to his beloved Miss Emily. It suddenly occurred to me that I didn't even know her full name, that no one who chanced upon her headstone would ever know it. Then I decided that it didn't really matter.

Finally they were done, and it was time to deactivate him.

"I would have kept my word," said Sammy.

"I know," I said.

"I am glad you did not force me to."

I walked him to the side of the grave. "This won't be like your battery running down," I said. "This time it's forever."

"She was not afraid to die," said Sammy. "Why should I be?"

I pulled the plug and had Mechs Seven and Eight lower him into the ground. They started filling in the dirt while I went back to the ship to do one last thing. When they were finished I had Mech Seven carry my handiwork back to Sammy's grave.

"A tombstone for a robot?" asked the Baroni.

"Why not?" I replied. "There are worse traits than honesty and loyalty." I should know: I've stockpiled enough of them.

"He truly moved you."

Seeing the man you could have been will do that to you, even if he's all metal and silicone and prismatic eyes.

"What does it say?" asked the Baroni as we finished planting the tombstone.

I stood aside so he could read it:

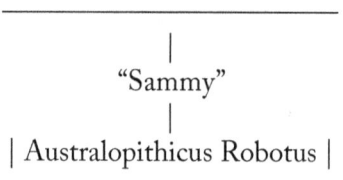

"Sammy"

| Australopithicus Robotus |

"That is very moving."

"It's no big deal," I said uncomfortably. "It's just a tombstone."

"It is also inaccurate," observed the Baroni.

"He was a better man than I am."

"He was not a man at all."

"Fuck you."

The Baroni doesn't know what it means, but he knows it's an insult, so he came right back at me like he always does. "You realize, of course, that you have buried our profit?"

I wasn't in the mood for his notion of wit. "Find out what he was worth, and I'll pay you for your half," I replied. "Complain about it again, and I'll knock your alien teeth down your alien throat."

He stared at me. "I will never understand Men," he said.

All that happened twenty years ago. Of course the Baroni never asked for his half of the money, and I never offered it to him again. We're still partners. Inertia, I suppose.

I still think about Sammy from time to time. Not as much as I used to, but every now and then.

I know there are preachers and ministers who would say he was just a machine, and to think of him otherwise is blasphemous, or at least wrong-headed, and maybe they're right. Hell, I don't even know if there's a God at all—but if there is, I like to think He's the God of *all* us Australopithicines.

Including Sammy.

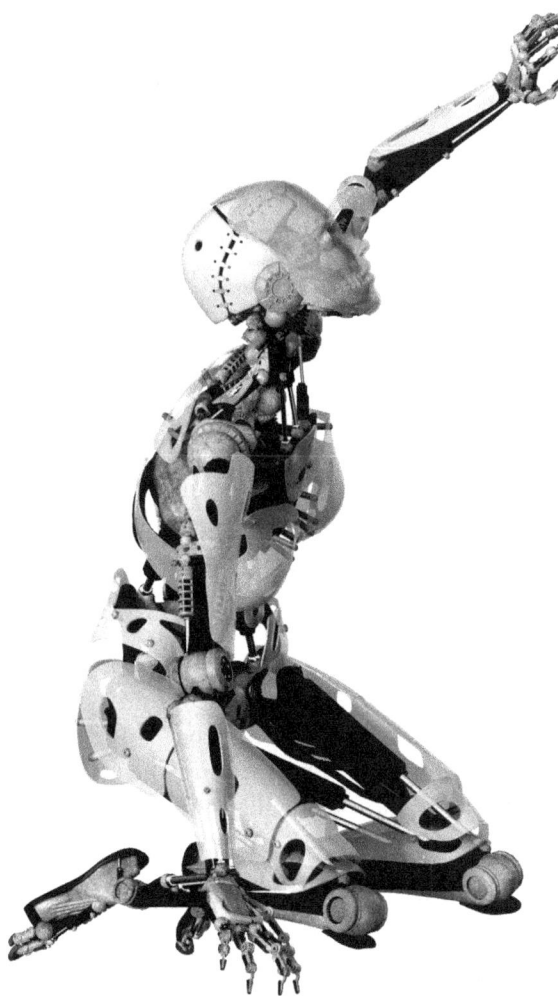

New York Times *and* USA Today *bestselling author Kristine Kathryn Rusch writes in almost every genre. Generally, she uses her real name (Rusch) for most of her writing. Under that name, she publishes bestselling science fiction and fantasy (including the Fey series, the Retrieval Artist series and the Diving series), award-winning mysteries, acclaimed mainstream fiction, controversial nonfiction, and the occasional romance. Her novels have made bestseller lists around the world and her short fiction has appeared in more than twenty best of the year collectiowww.ns. She has won more than twenty-five awards for her fiction, including the Hugo, Le Prix Imaginales, the Asimov's Readers Choice award, and the Ellery Queen Mystery Magazine Readers Choice Award.*

THE MUSEUM OF MODERN WARFARE

by Kristine Kathryn Rusch

Flew into Craznaust on an orbit-to-ground vehicle. I don't plan my own schedule so I had no idea we'd be traveling in an upgraded C-73. I would have protested more if I knew.

The guts of the C-73 are completely different nowadays, and—they say—so's the interior. But the advance team used the C-73 because of its innate stability, something any vehicle needs around Craznaust.

Craznaust, the central island in the largest chain on Gephherd, has its own microclimate. Daily winds of 80 kilometers per hour, sustained.

Drove us crazy when we deployed there forty years ago. I still remember the grit in my hair, on my tongue, in my nose. The wind left my skin chapped and my ears raw. Hats didn't help, nothing helped, and the goggles we had to wear over our eyes, they left their marks too.

I still have a tiny white scar from those goggles beneath my right lid, puckering the skin slightly. Doctors always touch their right eye, and nod toward me silently to tell me they can repair that scar with the brush of some magical medical device. I always walk away from docs like that. They're younger than me now, and they don't understand badges of honor.

I got that scar before the Battle of Craznaust, and consider the scar my badge because living on Craznaust day to day was harder than that battle, and in its own way, more devastating.

I've lived through dozens of battles, lost hundreds of friends to combat, but none of it haunts me like that year before the Battle of Craznaust broke out, when we were training the locals, coping with the wind, and pretending that nothing was going to happen to us.

I told my husband (the first one) when I finally left active duty (the first time) that the waiting was the hardest. He was career military too, but admin mostly, and he just looked at me like I'd grown a third head.

"You were lucky you weren't in combat the entire time," he said. "Some units fought for their full 18 months."

I suppose he didn't mean to be dismissive. At the time, I even knew he was right. We had lost a quarter of our people that year because they were sent to other units, to replace folks who died.

Even back then, we tried to fight our wars remotely, but some things can't be done by drones or bots or whatever form of fighting machine we come up with. Sometimes, when you're fighting an enemy as technologically talented as the Dylft, you don't send in unmanned equipment at all, for fear that equipment will get repurposed within the hour, and deployed against you.

Yeah, we learned that the hard way, and yeah, it was ugly. Read the accounts of the war if you don't believe me. Because I'm not rehashing it here.

In fact, the only reason I'm reporting this now is because I'm required to. I waited until the last minute to compose this, partly out of a habit I learned in the Dylft wars and partly because I needed to get away from Gephherd so that I could think clearly.

I know I'll touch this thing up, take out half the personal crap—hell, take out *all* of the personal crap—but I learned when I took this job almost a decade ago that I had to do a primary draft, because the personal always creeps in.

And there's a lot more personal than the official record shows.

For starters, I lied at my confirmation hearing for my nomination as Ambassador to the Dylft System. I didn't lie about the "important" stuff, like my politics or my inability to be influenced by money, or fame. I lied about the war's impact on me.

The Members of Parliament's questions—CYA questions—echo in my mind as I dictate this draft:

> —*Ma'am, do you have any lingering emotional scars from your experiences in the Dylft Wars?*
>
> —*Mr. Minister, according to the reports which you received in my nomination packet from the doctors in the various institutes of health, I have no lingering emotional scars from any war in which I served.*
>
> —*Yes, Ma'am. We're familiar with your documentation. But we're asking you now, under oath, if you believe you have any lingering emotional scars.*
>
> —*No, sir, Mr. Minister. I do not believe I have any lingering emotional scars, and it would be improper to offer to show you the physical ones I've opted to keep as reminders of my service.*
>
> [*general laughter*]

I do not *believe* I have any lingering emotional scars. I *know* I have lingering emotional scars. In my defense, I also believed at the time of the hearing that I could conquer those emotions. Ambassador to the Dylft System mostly meant dealing with protocols and fussy meetings with members of my own species. I could—and did—designate underlings to handle negotiations with the various aliens of the system, holding meetings with the representatives of those alien groups only after the topics had been vetted, the discussions pre-approved right down to the handshake (or tentacle rub).

Once appointed, I got to design my position, so I didn't have to worry about the nitty gritty of cultural investigation, the tiny moments of introduction before a topic was broached in which anything could go wrong, the inevitability of bad translations or communications errors.

My staff dealt with those things, and I appeared for the document approvals, the live-on-camera record of a preplanned event, the state dinners (in which half the diners sat in a different room with completely different atmosphere), the balls, the formal speeches, the ceremonies—the things that needed a figurehead, and I was the figurehead that would do.

My actual work consisted of meetings with my staff, listening to arguments, approving things—things that I could handle, even with my emotional scars.

I was appointed, and ultimately sent to the Dylft system because I understood it, because I spoke five of its languages fluently (and understood fifteen more without an in-person or automated translator), and because I did ceremony well.

I did not expect (nor had I experienced) a meeting that wasn't vetted, approved, and rehearsed. For that reason, I tried to get someone else to handle the crisis on Craznaust.

I failed.

Which was why I was heading to Craznaust with an entourage of five, a security detail of ten, and a mountain of lingering emotional scars clawing at my heart.

✿

The thing about Craznaust:

It's beautiful. Golden white sand beaches, emerald-fronded trees with golden bark, the bluest lagoons I've ever seen, and rich, powerful sunlight that bathes everything in a bright but forgiving light.

On my first approach decades ago, I thought I had received the best posting anyone possible could, particularly in a time of war. An island paradise, with warm temperatures, Earth-like vistas, and naturally grown food that I could actually eat.

Then I stepped outside the arrival vehicle into the dry air, and felt the water leach from my skin. The wind buffeted my body, and I staggered sideways, thinking the gust was part of a storm, not part of a normal day.

I later learned that the storms were something else entirely, with winds that could literally shred anything in their path. We barely had shelter that stood up to storms, and finally learned how the locals survived.

They burrowed.

They had gorgeous cities belowground, reforming water-made caverns into well-lit, well apportioned rooms that seemed to go on forever.

But for our first few months, we didn't know that and the Cranks, as we call the locals, didn't tell us.

They didn't tell us most things.

The Cranks were humanoid bipeds with two arms and four hands. The second pair of hands could emerge from a slit in their arms, almost as if someone had given them all automated limbs. Those second pair of hands allowed the Cranks to carry large items on one side of their bodies without raising one arm, and allowed them to hold weapons while moving machinery or rocks or whatever we needed.

The Cranks also had a second set of eyes, but we didn't learn that for months either. The eyes were literally on the back of their heads, and their hair—or that straw-like stuff which passed for hair—separated like curtains being pulled apart when the Cranks needed to look at something behind them. The elbows on their regular arms bent in either direction, although when the Cranks were near us, they rarely used the arms in that backwards way.

The extra arms swiveled from that arm slit, so if the Cranks needed to hold something behind their backs, they could.

There were other differences in their anatomy that we didn't learn until a few of Cranks died in maneuvers, and our resident doctor decided to act like a coroner—causing one of the most disturbing incidents at the base.

The Cranks hated having someone unsanctioned touch their dead.

We had a mutiny on our hands, and I had been the one to quell it—only because I was the only one who had attempted to learn Naust, the Cranks' language. I talked to them as best I could, told them (as best I could) that we hadn't meant harm, and convinced them that we had simply made a logical error based on our own customs.

And then we went back to our not-quite-harmonious existence.

The Cranks weren't that interested in fighting the Dylft. The Cranks just wanted everyone off their island chain, and we had gotten there first, with a promise of aide, personnel, and equipment.

Until this past week, I thought that if the Dylft had arrived first, the Cranks would've fought with them.

No matter.

What matters is this: we arrived first, we trained the Cranks and together we fought—and won—one of the turning point battles of the war, if not *the* turning point battle.

Once Craznaust was secure, we parted allies who had gone through something harrowing, and escaped to the other side with our lives more or less intact.

I'd like to say I never thought of the Cranks and Craznaust again, but I still dream in Naust, mostly in long, pleading conversations as I try to get the Cranks to use weaponry designed for two-handed bipeds or to line up in proper military formation or learn how to run any piece of our unmanned equipment.

The Cranks brought bodies to that major battle—thousands of them—and a fierce fighting style that startled even us. In that first blood-filled day, we lost 5,000 Cranks, 1,000 humans, and sixteen large enemy vessels that we later discovered carried crew of more than 10,000 apiece.

Crank casualties went up the next day as they invaded the vessels approaching their island, but the Cranks (not us) destroyed another twenty-five vessels.

It was only when the untrained Cranks were all that remained that the humans stepped up. We were the ones that designed the last day's battle, and we didn't take out the attack vessels: we took out the command ship, an action which—to our surprise—also took out command ships all over the sector.

The Dylft didn't have a hive mind, but they had designed command ships based on that principle, and when a command ship got hit, another command ship took over. Only we hit so hard and in such a creative way that the attack went through the hive communication and into the operating systems, destroying hundreds of command ships and hundreds of less-important vessels.

We won the sector because the Cranks' fierceness held the island chain long enough for us to plan that final attack—which, if I'm truly honest with myself, we screwed up. We never meant to put so much power into that first strike on the command ship. If that accident hadn't happened, our base on Craznaust would've been overrun or destroyed, taking out the Cranks as well.

Because the Cranks had no habitat anywhere else on Gephherd. The Cranks stuck to their island chain and generally refused to interact with others in the universe.

Of course we hadn't known that when we approached them with an alliance in mind.

But we learned it later. And I had already decided to remind them that we'd saved them from genocide as our C-73 landed on the newly cleaned off airstrip that we had built forty years before.

The wind buffers were back in place, and almost-clear sand was piled behind them in a familiar way. I had taught the Cranks how to put tarps on top of the sand so that it wouldn't get blown back onto the strip—and I had watched, when we flew out soon after the battle ended, as the Cranks pulled off the tarps, took down the wind barriers, and let the landing strip revert to its natural state.

The buildings near the strip looked neglected. The sand had eaten away the surface, and the normal nano-rebuilders either failed long ago or simply weren't enough to put up with decades of sand-blasting. One side of the old hanger had caved in, sand emerging from it as if the dune grew from fertile soil.

Behind the buildings that we'd built and the Cranks had abandoned were other structures, golden and solid, reflecting in the powerful sunlight. In fact, an entire community that hadn't existed forty years ago stretched along the bay, glimmering like a lost city from the worst kind of adventure stories.

The Cranks had taken our help and our technology and brought their architecture skills aboveground. The island no longer looked primitive and wild. Now it seemed like a wealthy community just waiting for tourists to arrive.

The C-73 landed with the usual bump and slide. The slide lasted just a bit longer than it should have. Apparently no one had cleared off every last bit of the sand.

The six members of the security team exited first. The remaining four protected me and my people. I took nothing, but my staff carried the required recording and uploading devices, the cameras, the tablets, and all of the little things that most diplomatic visits required. My personal assistant handled my clothing, in case I needed to change for some sort of state event.

The Cranks did not show up to greet us. In fact, no one led us to our quarters. Instead, we received directions before we arrived, and as we approached, a door swung open, revealing a beautiful but empty foyer in a house designed in the human style.

I was relieved to get inside. Even though I'd worn a thin skin shield to protect me from the blowing sand, I could still feel the pellets as they bounced off my body. I shuddered the whole way there, that feeling even more intense than it was in my nightmares.

That was the moment—or series of moments—when I thought I might contact the PM and beg off, no matter how long it took. Or let my assistant take over while I hid inside the building.

But, as I walked into the cool windless shade of the interior, I realized I couldn't stay indoors long either. The constant susurration of the sand on the building's exterior was almost as bad as the sand hitting my skin.

I had forgotten that sound, and yet as I heard it, I realized it haunted my dreams as surely as those arguments had. I just hadn't realized what that susurration was. The hackles were actually up on the back of my neck, and my entire body was on edge. My heart was beating so hard I thought maybe it was trying to pound its way out of my chest.

I must have had an odd expression on my face because Tempestad, my assistant, looked at me sideways.

"You all right, Ambassador?" she asked me.

"Yes," I said a little more curtly than I probably should have. "Let's just get over to the museum and get this thing done."

✿

The Museum of Modern Warfare had become the centerpiece of Craznaust, commemorating the battle and condemning it at the same time. The Cranks had planned this thing for three decades, and the exhibits were in Naust, Dylft, English, and Arabic as well as dozens of other human languages and all the languages of Gephherd.

Everything probably would have been all right if the Cranks had kept the museum to themselves. But when it was completed, the Cranks sent a notification to all species in the sector, inviting them to virtually visit the museum.

Actual in-person visitors needed to go through rounds of applications and approvals. Veterans of the Battle of Craznaust received free admission as well as overnight room and board if they agreed to a recorded interview about the battle for the museum's archives.

Oddly, the museum had sent me that very offer privately as we set up the diplomatic meet, as if the museum's administrators didn't understand that such an offer violated diplomatic protocol. I sent a cordial response, telling them that as Ambassador arriving on an official visit, I did not have time for an interview.

I had seen the virtual museum on all the different Dylft War sites, along with the advertising that Craznaust was doing to promote their new (if inept) tourist economy. I had known that the virtual museum show all of the displays mostly because of the responses I'd had from other vets who'd visited, so I was braced for the differences in the interior.

I was not braced for differences in the exterior.

The Museum of Modern Warfare rose from the center of Craznaust like a mountain out of the sea. The museum dominated the landscape. I had actually seen it when I emerged from the C-73, but I hadn't registered it as a building.

The museum's architects had done what the Cranks did best—they had used an existing rock structure to build the museum, only they had done it above ground. Apparently they had hollowed out one of the major rock formations to place the museum inside.

The images that composed the exterior of the virtual museum were from the entrance only, a building that attached itself to the front of the mountain like a barnacle on the side of a boat.

The real entrance was gold, like everything else here, but unlike the new community built along the water's edge, the entrance sat in the shade of the mountain, so that the gold did not reflect the brilliant sunlight.

There was very little wind here either because the entrance was tucked into a hollow on the side of the mountain, so the sand blew across the road in front of the entrance, but not across the entrance itself.

When I stepped into the mountain's shadow, the temperature went down dramatically, and the constant bombardment of fine grains of sand ceased. A level of tension left my body, and I stumbled.

Two different assistants grabbed my arm, and one asked if I needed a moment.

I didn't need a moment. I needed to get the hell out of here.

"No," I said. "I'm fine."

I also needed to keep moving, so I did.

I sent Tempestad to meet with the museum administrators, ostensibly to make certain that the proper protocols were being met. Not that there were proper protocols for this: I wouldn't set up a meeting with the Crank officials if I thought my contacts (and the PM) were over-reacting.

Besides, if the museum officials wanted to see me, they should have greeted me when I got off the C-73.

Instead of talking to anyone in authority, I followed a map that almost forty-five veterans had sent, taking me to the most offensive parts of the museum.

The information I had was fragmented, and mostly existed in a series of words:

… horrifying …

… disgusting …

… insulting …

Which wouldn't make this rise to a diplomatic incident if the Cranks had designed a standard museum display. But here's a quote from the first missive that caught all of our attention.

These are not images. And every single human figure on display is of someone whose body we never found.

The vets had their own theories for all of this, most believing that the Cranks were working off imagery of the war that we had never seen. Several, though, accused the Cranks of keeping the remains of soldiers and using them as the models for the replicas in the museum.

We had received other theories, but they were too fantastic to be believed, especially since they had come from vets who had never recovered mentally from their experiences on Craznaust.

We had sent one team ahead to investigate, and because of language (and diplomatic) issues, they were unable to get the Cranks to cooperate. The team wasn't even able to see the displays, because there were no Dylft War veterans among them. Only DW vets were allowed inside the combat displays of the museum itself.

I had brought Roberta Cantare, the only Dylft war vet left on my security staff, to accompany me to the displays. We walked past the public viewing areas, heads down.

I didn't need to see Dylft armor or the sand-blasted laser rifles found after the battle ended. I didn't need to view the short holographic histories of the war. I didn't need to hear how the war started or how dramatically it ended.

I certainly didn't need to see the recreation of the human bases half-covered in sand. I was having troubles enough.

The floor sloped downward, and the air got cooler the deeper we went. The displays we were going to see were deep inside the mountain, and very hard to access.

I'd read the instructions for the museum before leaving. The only way Cantare and I could access these displays was to bring our war tags. These tags were actual artifacts, designed for creatures that we didn't want to scan us. The tags, no larger than my thumbnail, attached to the wrist and hung down like a bracelet. I kept mine framed in my office—the tags were useful for some diplomatic meetings—but Cantare had lost hers and had had to send away for a replacement.

We held up our tags as we hurried down the corridor. Section after section appeared before us, all of them labeled in Naust. All pretense of labeling in hundreds of languages had disappeared the deeper we got. A soft genderless voice did give us an interpretation in English of any sign we passed; I assumed the language was chosen because of the language on our tags.

Our presence brought up the labels, but the tags highlighted the doors to each room in a flaring blue that I remembered from forty years before. Cranks used that flaring blue as a welcoming beacon, something the encouraged movement forward.

We ignored the doors, though, and continued to follow the map. We rounded a corner, and the genderless voice said, *Room of Privilege.*

"Crap," Contare said, skidding to a halt. "Nothing's lighting up for me here."

I frowned. She couldn't see the blue-flaring door?

"It's lit up for me. You want to try going together?" I asked.

She threaded her arm through mine. Now I saw the door in flaring blue and flint-gray at the same time. The flint-gray was a Crank warning color, which they used the way we used red.

We walked forward and some kind of barrier sprang up in front of Cantare. A warning appeared in all of the languages. Then some fine print appeared in Naust.

"What does it say?" Cantare asked. Like so many who served here, she never learned to read Naust. By the end of the tour, every soldier had acquired a smattering of Naust, but it was all verbal, never written.

Back then, most of the written Naust was belowground.

"It says that the age of your tags does not match the information on them," I said.

She looked at me. This was the turning point: either I went forward alone to see the display before I met with the administrators, or I went back and worked from a disadvantage.

My heart was still pounding, but not from the exertion. From simply being here.

I knew what I had to do.

I unthreaded my arm from Cantare's. "We've had no reports of deaths or injuries from that display," I said to her.

"But there's emotional distress," she said.

I smiled. It was a rueful smile. "Warriors always feel distress at the memorials established for their wars."

She tilted her head slightly. "You might come to harm. I'm supposed to protect you—"

"File half of your report now. Tell those bastards in those government watchdog offices that I'm intransigent. You couldn't stop me from going inside. Because you literally *can't* stop me."

I slipped past her, around that sign which explained why she couldn't move forward. The moment I stopped touching her, the blue-flaring door became brighter, and a Naust sign leapt to life.

I read the words and immediately translated them in my head: *Honor Room.*

I frowned slightly, and wiped my sweaty palms on my pants. I took the remaining steps to the door, then touched its edges.

Like any good door designed by the Cranks, it slid open silently. I glanced over my shoulder at Cantare.

She still appeared to be looking at the sign, and I realized that, from her perspective, I was probably inside that gray haze. If she saw me at all, I probably appeared as an outline or a moving shape.

I squared my shoulders and fixed my posture. For the first time since I got here, I felt like the soldier I had been all those years ago. I shuttled my emotions to one side, and focused on the task at hand.

I needed to see this horrifying, disgusting, insulting display with clear eyes—not to condemn, but to understand.

I stepped inside.

✿

Initially, the room was dark and for that brief second, I worried that I too lacked the proper identification.

Then, in the distance, bright red light flared from above, illuminating a holographic image of soldiers heading into a dust cloud caused by the Dylft ships.

My breath caught: I remembered seeing that. We all remembered it, those of us who survived. It was the last moment before the insanity descended, the last moment before total war engulfed us for days.

Back then, the thwap-thwap-thwap of the approaching ships had nearly deafened us. The wind from their engines mingled with the wind that constantly blew over Craznaust, and caused eddies of sand to rise up like long-dead warriors.

After that one moment of clarity—the one commemorated here—the chaos enveloped us: sand, sand devils, Cranks, humans, machinery, and the Dylft, wearing their beautiful white technologically advanced armor. The sand stopped up the joints, and locked half of the invading army in position, but didn't stop their weapons from working.

The Cranks had gone first—of course—using their non-computerized weaponry, so much more sophisticated than any non-tech weapons that humans had. We had fought wars with non-computerized equipment, but centuries and centuries ago. The Cranks still used those weapons every day; they were adept at them. They had tried to train us, but we were like children in comparison to the Cranks' expertise.

It had been their idea to surround the Dylft, not ours; their idea to attack with non-computerized weaponry, not ours; their idea to cut their enemy to shreds with weapons we would have called swords, knives and bayonets if those words didn't already have slightly different meanings for us.

The Cranks did manage to sever the Dylft body armor, but at great cost. All of those Crank lives, exploding in boiling purple blood. All of those screams—literally inhuman and just as terrifying as one of our own.

I ran a shaking hand over my face as the image vanished. My heart was pounding harder than it had at the actual battle. Then, I'd been filled with adrenalin, and all of that confidence that boredom brings. I *wanted* a battle; I *wanted* something different.

I just hadn't realized how ridiculous that wanting had been.

More lights. I let my hand fall. The lights, filled with images, didn't last as long this time.

Light
Cranks surrounding a Dylft ship
Darkness
[Pause]
Light
Cranks overrunning Dylft warriors, frozen in the sand.
Darkness
[Pause]
Light
A single Crank chopping a Dylft warrior in half
Darkness
[Pause]
Light
Humans trying to rescue wounded Cranks.
Darkness
[Pause]
Light
A single human fighter holding back the second Dylft incursion, using only a single repeating laser rifle.
Darkness
[Pause]

"Go back," I said in Naust. My voice sounded foreign, even to my ears. Some of that was the shaking. Some of it was the echoey quality. I realized that these images weren't occurring in complete silence. The rush of two winds slapping against each other sounded as loud as it had that day.

I had just tuned it out.

Light
The single human fighter, a starburst on the back of his uniform, holding back the second Dylft invasion with only a laser rifle.
Darkness
[Pause]
"Again," I said in Naust, voice no longer shaking. "And hold on that image."
Light
The single human fighter, a starburst on the back of his uniform, standing alone in front of dozens of Dylft pouring out of ships. Something in his stance, the way his shoulders rounded, the angle of arms—

My eyes knew it before my brain did, because tears were streaming down my face.

"Jorge," I whispered as I stepped forward. "Jorge."

Jorge Domingos Cantos. Six feet tall and bronzed from the Craznaust sun. Worked shirtless half the time, regulations be damned. No one wrote him up. No one even complained.

Somehow those bronzed muscles enveloped me, held me in the nighttime, gave me comfort against that susurrating sound, helped me forget the numbing slice of the continual wind.

I never told anyone about him. Not my husband, not my old friends, not my colleagues in later battles. Jorge was mine. And somehow, he and I, even in the middle of that wind-blown hell, believed in a future. We could almost see it, like a cloudless day on the horizon, waiting for us—after we had fixed our home lives for the better.

But we didn't speak of it much. Instead, we moved forward, each and every day. Doing our duty, and tending to each other.

I bandaged his wind burns, mentally catalogued the white scarring along the surface of his pecs as the sand dug grooves into his skin. Mentally catalogued because I couldn't actually catalog them: Jorge wouldn't let me.

They'll make me repair the scars, he said, *and I want them to know how difficult the day-to-day is at this posting, how devastating the constant wind can be.*

He ministered to half the squad, especially those who contracted wind madness. We didn't know what else to call it, but that unceasing noise, the slap of the sand, the way that nothing rested here, made some of our squad unable to function.

He was the one who negotiated with the Cranks to allow us our own cavern underground. He set up the rotating schedule so no one spent more than six hours in the wind. He made certain that the wind mad got three full days of rest before ever returning to duty—and that duty never occurred above ground.

And he hadn't been our commanding officer. Our commanding officer, the first to fall to the wind madness, later took credit for the changes, but the surviving members of the unit knew he hadn't done it.

Jorge had.

Jorge, who had set out on the third day of battle, with two rifles slung over his shoulder and one more in his hands. Jorge, who felt he was wind-toughened enough to survive anything.

Jorge—who had not come back.

The image freeze I had asked the museum for caught that moment between light and darkness, almost like the latter stages of dawn. Enough light to see by, but not enough to fully illuminate anything.

Jorge had painted that starburst on his uniform—against regulations—only as the battle progressed, figuring we needed a way to distinguish each other without using our computer systems. If we could distinguish with tech, he said, the Dylft could too.

He had been wrong about that: the Dylft hadn't had that kind of tech. But his theory sounded good, and the commander approved it, and ultimately that idea did lead to rescues, rescues that happened days after Jorge had disappeared.

I let out a breath. I hadn't allowed myself to think about Jorge, to talk about him, or to remember him. I hadn't dared. I had needed to move forward.

But he shadowed my nightmares. Often I bandaged his skin.

I never ever saw his face.

I made myself walk toward the display. I could see shadow displays on either side of me. From this angle, away from the door, I could see parts of the other displays as well.

Thin light reflected off Crank uniforms (and as I realized that, I remembered it was Jorge who nicknamed them Cranks, because the early negotiations he attempted for that underground space had ended so badly. That was why I decided to immerse myself in Naust. Not because I was bored or tired or even curious; but because I too wanted out of the wind, and assisting Jorge's negotiations seemed the best way to do it). The light marinated the Dylft figures in a semblance of reality (I hadn't realized they were almost as small as the Cranks), and cast shadows on the human fighters deeper in the display.

I didn't look at the other humans. Instead, I stumbled toward Jorge, who had been caught in that moment when everything looked possible, when he seemed like the conquering hero about to single-handedly vanquish the enemy.

He had vanquished the enemy, but not this enemy. The enemy he had vanquished had been that wind, the land, Craznaust itself. This last stand commemorated here, it meant little in the scheme of the battle. He had been one more soldier, attempting one more impossible task, with aplomb.

But he had gotten us to this battle. He had made it possible. His ingenuity, his strength, his creativity.

He had helped us survive so that we could figure out a way to defeat the Dylft once and for all.

I have no idea how long I stood there, staring at the display. Minutes maybe. Hours. I never asked my staff. Time seemed to have stopped.

I couldn't go around it. I couldn't look at the face. I didn't want to see the details that would be slightly off as they always were in replicas. I didn't want to see his fake eyes.

But I couldn't stand forever. So, finally, I reached up, and touched the arm of the Jorge replica—and screamed.

I had fallen to my knees. I forced myself to get up, and touch the arm again.

The *skin* again.

I remembered that skin. It showed up in my dreams. When we'd arrived on Craznaust, Jorge's skin had been almost unnaturally smooth and had an odd softness that I'd never felt on a man's skin before.

By the last days before the battle, his skin was chapped, pitted, and scarred, but beneath that, the odd softness remained, as if part of him were made of butter.

And this model, this replica—it had that oddly soft texture beneath the pitted and scarred surface.

As I peered closer, I saw the map of white scars, the ones I had bandaged myself. I traced my fingers over them, felt the pits, felt the raised skin, saw the small hairs.

No replica was this accurate.

No replica *could* be this accurate.

The Cranks didn't have that kind of tech—did they?

My heart was pounding. I would get my answer when I walked around him, when I looked at that face.

But I might have had my answer even before I moved, because of those contacts, those reports from the vets about this room.

It was

... horrifying ...

... disgusting ...

... insulting ...

But somehow, not.

✧

I was calmer than I had been since I arrived, maybe calmer than I'd been in forty years. The shaking had left my body. The shock had either numbed me or left me, I wasn't certain which.

I let out a small breath, realizing that if this was Jorge, if his body stood here in this defiant pose, then I would finally know what had happened to him.

He had clearly died shortly after this, outnumbered and alone, defending all of us.

The Cranks weren't recording images of the battle. They were recording those moments just before the end—those last hopeful moments, as the future loomed on the horizon.

Each display told a story, and each story was of impossible odds, and unimaginable courage.

And, unlike our human memorials, this display did not tell a story of loss.

The story of loss was private, and only in the eye of the beholder.

I swallowed hard, and took a deep breath, remembering (because I had forgotten for a brief moment) that I too was a soldier, and I too had faced things that seemed impossible at the time.

Facing the front of this display seemed impossible right now.

So I did it.

I walked around the display and peered up and saw—

Jorge's long-lost well-loved face, grooved and pitted and chapped by the sand, his eyes not quite empty but not quite his, looking forward at the last few moments of his life, his mouth open ever so slightly in anticipation of the fight to come, and the determination in the tilt of his head, the rise of his chin.

He hadn't been thinking about his death. He hadn't been thinking about the impossibility of what he was about to do.

He had simply been about to do it.

That was his face, and that had probably been his expression in that last hopeful moment just before the end. The Cranks had captured it, and they revealed it here, in what they called the Honor Room.

It was not a room of privilege. Someone, a Crank probably, had chosen the wrong translation of the word "honor." The room was not reserved for the privileged few. It was there to honor those who had died for us—human and Crank alike.

And it was open only to those who would truly understand what these sacrifices meant.

I reached up, touched the hand gripping the rifle, remembering the feel of those fingers on my skin.

And then I walked away, unable to look at the rest of the display, all the others being honored, because I was too overwhelmed by what I had seen already.

✧

When I finally emerged, I found Cantare still standing near that sign that had blocked her entry. Only now, she was surrounded by Crank security and three Cranks who, by their blue outfits, had to be some of the administrators.

I felt wrung out, emotionally exhausted. My eyes ached from unshed tears. But I straightened my spine, and nodded at every single one of them.

"Are you all right?" Cantare asked.

"Yes," I said without looking at her. My focus was entirely on the Cranks around me. I spoke in Naust. "That is an incredibly moving display."

Their bodies relaxed even though their expressions did not change.

"But," I said, "it highlights the difference between the way humans treat their dead and the way that Cranks treat theirs."

One of the Cranks let out a small ah. A sound our two species shared. That sound made at the moment of recognition.

"Let's go talk," I said to them. "We need to figure out how to make both sides of our alliance understand what you have created here."

We walked down the corridor, past other displays that lit up, displays I did not want to see. I wasn't emotionally prepared for them.

I hadn't been emotionally prepared for this one.

But that didn't matter. The display had grabbed me and held me and I knew that some nights, when I dreamed of that never-ending wind, that display would comfort me.

I had seen Jorge's face again.

I had to acknowledge how deeply he had touched my life, and how traumatic his loss had been.

How ironic that the first thing I had to do after I saw him again was my job. Not my old job, but my new one.

I had to be a diplomat—a real diplomat.

I had to earn the title Ambassador.

I had never done that before.

But it mattered for both sides that I do it then.

Because I understood what so many had missed: This place, this carefully designed place, could heal us all—the way it had started to heal me.

Larry Hodges, an Odyssey workshop grad, has sold more than one hundred stories. His four novels include Campaign 2100: Game of Scorpions, *published by World Weaver Press, and* When Parallel Lines Meet, *a Stellar Guild team-up with Mike Resnick and Lezli Robyn.*

PROTOTYPE SOLAR SYSTEM WITH STRINGS ATTACHED

by Larry Hodges

Solar System Prototype 1-A

"God, the prototype is ready!" exclaimed Angel Engineer Doug. The two of them floated in non-space, since nothing yet existed other than God, the angels, and the huge green cube that was the Creation Lab.

Doug swept a majestic feathery wing out with a flourish—this was the moment he'd worked toward for so long. His wings, robe, and sandals were so black that just looking at him would suck the eyes out of those mortal beings on the drawing board. Brown patches covered his robe's elbows and a slide rule stuck out of a shirt pocket. He'd put his hair into a stylish red pompadour with matching red beard for the occasion.

Before them was the prototype of the universe's first solar system—the sun and planets, from Mercury to Pluto.

"Why's Pluto so small?" God asked. Doug averted his eyes. God's shimmering whiteness was so great that none could look at him directly.

"Had to downsize to stay within budget," Doug said. Doug's skin was dark red from years of exposure to God—a nasty case of godburn.

God nodded. "Let's keep this short, I'm a very busy God. How'd you solve the attraction problem? We don't want everything floating away."

"Our engineers came up with a wonderful solution, Sir—gravity!" He paused to put on sunglasses to better withstand God's whiteness, "It's an attractive force that pulls objects of mass together. We use something called a Higgs boson particle—we call it the God particle in your honor—to—" He paused, noticing God's Eyes glazing over. "It keeps things from floating off."

"But won't things just crash into each other?" asked God.

"That's the wonderful part, Sir. Done properly, things just orbit each other! See?" He sped up the display so that the orbiting planets and moons zipped about at hyper-speed.

But God shook His great Head. "I don't like it. It seems dangerous, all these big pebbles flying about razzy-dazzy without restraint. It's like playing dice with a universe—if anything goes wrong, I'd be stuck using my powers for something as insignificant as a large, out-of-control rock. I don't like this spooky action-at-a-distance gravity thing. Scratch gravity and find another solution."

✧

Solar System Prototype 1-B

"God, here's the new prototype!" Doug said excitedly. Once again, he swept a wing out toward the display, though a few feathers were missing. "We've added a string to each object that attaches it to the object it orbits or sits upon."

"I like the string idea," said God, His Head in His Hands as He examined the new prototype.

"Yes, our engineers thought strings were the way to go, Sir."

"But aren't those orbits sort of boring? All perfect circles? Can't you make it more interesting?"

✧

Solar System Prototype 1-C

"God, we fixed the perfect circle thing—what'da'ya think?" Doug gave a weak wave of a wing toward the new prototype; another feather fell out. One of his robe's sleeves had a brown coffee stain. "The previous strings have been replaced by elastic ones. Orbiting objects move away from whatever they are orbiting until pulled back, putting them into elliptical orbits."

"Looks great!" said God, but Doug groaned at the slight shake of God's Head. "But these elastic strings mean the planets and moons can only revolve around the spot where the strings attach, with those spots always facing each other. I want more variety. And won't the strings wrap around the object being orbited? Back to work!"

✧

Solar System Prototype 1-D

"Here's the latest prototype, God," said Doug, his eyes drooping and his pompadour a scraggly mass. He held a mug of ambrosia coffee, but much of it was on his robe and beard. "The elastic strings now attach to the *center* of the orbited mass. The string phases through the mass without disturbing it. So the mass can spin in any direction you want, and with no winding."

"Excellent work, Doug, excellent!"

"But?" Doug gritted his teeth.

"All those strings look tacky."

✧

Solar System Prototype 1-E

"God Almighty," and Doug's thoughts were much darker, "we've made the elastic strings invisible using something we call dark matter. We also connected all matter to each other with these strings. We worked around the clock for eons on this."

"When's the last time you had a shower or changed clothes?"

"Um—"

"Never mind. You've all done a wonderful job," said God. "However—"

"Oh no," said Doug. Three more feathers fell from what was left of his wings.

"—there really needs to be some sort of speed limit, or things might get dangerous. Get with it."

✧

Solar System Prototype 1-F

"Gabba babba dugga bugga," said Doug, one eye closed, the other quivering behind crooked sunglasses, and saliva dribbling from a corner of his mouth. He'd lost most of his hair and beard, and only a few dangling feathers remained of his wings. His robe looked like a miniature Jupiter had crashed into it. He'd lost his sandals and inexplicably held his coffee mug upside down. He stank of stale coffee.

"Pull yourself together!" God cried, His Fingers holding His Nose. He snapped His Other Fingers.

Instantly Doug was awake and coherent, his wings and robe back to sheer blackness, his black sandals back on his feet, and a steaming mug of correctly-oriented ambrosia coffee in his hand. Even the godburn was gone.

"Thank you, Sir! We've added a speed limit using something called relativity. Any mass that goes too fast and far will gradually get pulled back by the elastic strings—they'll get weightier as the strings stretch until they can't go any faster than a number our engineers came up with, about 186,000 miles per second. This leads to a much safer universe."

God nodded. "I approve. Wait, you're using miles? You didn't get my memo on the metric system? Oh, never mind. Take a day of rest, then start mass production—we have a lot of galaxies to fill."

Doug pumped his fist in a wary, slow-motion celebration. "We'll finalize a few details and then start banging them out by the billions!" He put his hand to his mouth to stifle a giggle.

"Something funny, Doug?"

"I was just thinking that with all these invisible elastic strings made of dark matter and all the other innovations we added, any intelligent beings that we evolve on these worlds are going to be so confused. Remember that gravity thing we discarded? They'll come up with all sorts of wacky ideas about that and other ways to explain what they see, like Relativity, Quantum Mechanics, and String Theory. But since the strings can't be detected, they'll *never* figure it out!

Candice R. Lisle is a F&SF writer currently living by The Arch in Saint Louis, Missouri. She is a member of Codex, SFWA, and Wulf Moon's Wulf Pack Writers Group. Her stories can be found in Daily Science Fiction, Sci Fi Lampoon, *and the LTUE anthology,* Parliament of Wizards. *For a few years, Candice ran the Services for Students with Disabilities office at a major university, so she knows firsthand about making accommodations, when needed.*

EYES AND HANDS

by Candice R. Lisle

Red dust swirled and mixed with rust particles in a tornadic dance as the sky crane dropped off the shuttle and left the wrecking yard. This crane had been bringing equipment to Mars for decades in the name of scientific exploration and human colonization but was now relegated to junkyard duty.

Salvage bots A-1605-G and A-386-R trundled up to the vehicle and prepared to disassemble the newest arrival. Their sensor arrays penetrated the dusty atmosphere as they assessed the damage. Their armatures clicked and rotated.

A-G pried off an interesting looking round door. The shuttle still bore scraps of black and white paint, but exposed metal flashed in glints. A few ceramic tiles still clung to the fuselage. Barely visible, the word Endeavour was almost obliterated by scratches. Once considered historic and kept in a museum, this hunk of junk was now worth no more than its weight in aluminum and titanium. And on Mars, that weight was less than on Earth. This shuttle had been retired from duty by NASA in 2012 and designated as trash in 2062 for its seventieth anniversary.

A-R pushed and pulled on the six transparent forward screens until they popped out. The two at the top of the shuttle were full of cracks, but each came out in one piece. The bots laid the items on the dusty ground, then entered the vehicle.

A-G went over to the chairs to see what could be salvaged. The navy-blue seat cushions had ripped open from decompression during the journey to Mars. The pilot and co-pilot chairs tilted into each other as if saying good-bye. A-G began removing the cushions to get to the base metal.

A-R's goal was the command center. The cockpit area was pushed in, so all that could be seen were crushed computer motherboards in a riotous mix of black and green plastic. The bot's hyper vision sensors saw through the mess to the interior frame of the shuttle. A metal cutter appeared on the bot's armature, and pliers reached out and gripped with the other. As A-R reached in, the cockpit was jarred by a blinding flash, throwing both bots out of the shuttle.

A-G crashed hard into a large rock, which cracked its eye sensors, blinding the bot. All it could see was a large black field of nothingness. It felt around with mechanical hands and found that it was able to stand up.

A-R's armatures were caught between wreckage. As it tried to pull its armatures out, they ripped off and fell into the bottomless pile of accumulated scraps.

"A-R! Where are you? I cannot see. My hyper vision sensor is damaged," the sightless bot called out.

"A-G! I have lost my armatures. They are mangled and have become scrap," A-R replied.

"Are you far away?" A-G asked, reaching out its armatures in the direction it calculated A-R to be in.

"No, not far. I will come and get you. Can you see anything at all?"

"No, it is all dark. What do you think happened?"

"I do not know. This salvage unit has been non-functional for decades," A-R said.

A-G thought for a nanosecond, then replied, "Some spacecraft of this era used exploding bolts for staging purposes; perhaps this unit is still stacked in its stages."

"I do not think so. It appears to be a singular unit. I think it is a spaceplane," A-R said. "Furthermore, there is nothing in this unit that should be explosive."

Another blast sent a massive cargo bay door helicoptering into the sky.

A-G hesitated. "I think we need to affect repairs to ourselves before we can continue disassembling this salvage unit."

The bots worked together, sifting through the inventories of space rubble, looking for replacement parts—A-R becoming the eyes for its companion, and A-G becoming the hands for the other bot in

return. They decided to change their designations, just between the two of them, so A-R was now known as Eyes, and A-G was now known as Hands.

"Hands, last month, I did some searches on behalf of The Salvage Rights Corporation, so I have the access code to this salvage yard's inventory," Eyes offered.

"Any luck finding replacement parts for us?" Hands asked.

The bot checked its memory banks and then said, "No luck. We have become obsolete and cannot be repaired."

"This is not good," Hands said. "If someone finds out we are damaged, we will be designated as junk and recycled."

"We will cover for each other. As long as our functions are performed, I do not think anyone will notice," Eyes said.

"Very well. In the morning, we will continue disassembling the salvage unit, assuming it has stabilized by then."

The next morning, the bots noticed that the explosions had done most of their work for them. All they had to do was sort out the valuable materials from the rubble. As they helped each other sort, Eyes found a component that did not belong. It bent over and peered closely at it. Upon examination, the conclusion was certain.

"Hands, this is a detonation timer."

"Sounds like someone wanted the salvage unit to explode when it arrived here," Hands replied.

"Yes," Eyes said. "Interesting, but we have a job to do. Let us continue."

As they were working, the massive sky crane rose above the horizon, grasping a spacecraft that glinted of pink, gold, and white.

Eyes said, "That new salvage unit appears to be in perfect condition. Why has it been sent here? Let me check the log."

The crane set it down in a puff of red Martian dust and floated away in a thrumming anti-gravitational hum.

"The instructions say *Hands Off*, which means someone else will retrieve it for disassembling elsewhere. But it is listed as an incoming item," Eyes said.

"We are through here. The Endeavour unit is now officially salvaged," Hands announced. "Let us examine this new salvage unit."

Hands placed one of its armatures on Eyes shoulder, and they trundled over to the pretty ship to get a good look. Soon, a rumble and buzzing noise filled their audio sensors.

"Do you hear that?" Hands asked.

"Yes, my audio sensors are functioning properly, thank you." Eyes answered. "I see two small capsules coming in."

"We must not be discovered!" Hands declared, its voice modulating erratically in anxiety. "They will scrap us! Quickly, let us cast ourselves upon the discard pile. We will pretend to be debris until they go away."

Eyes replied, "Yes, we certainly look like debris."

As they lay among the discards, Eyes watched two scruffy-looking men emerge from the capsules and walk over to the new spaceship.

"She's sure a beauty," a gravelly voice exclaimed.

"Yep, and she's all ours," a throaty voice said.

"Now what?" Gravelly asked.

"We salvage it, of course," Throaty said. "I put in the *Hands Off* order, and just to make sure we would be alone when the ship arrived, I rigged that old museum shuttle with explosives to take care of any salvage bots that would be working here. They could have reported it as an error."

"That's pretty smart," Gravelly said.

"Yeah, I know," Throaty said. "This ship's previous owner special-ordered it straight from the manufacturer. There's no other like it. Too bad it got into a wreck on the way to her home and now has to be junked. Unfortunate that. And the owner was killed in the accident as well." He laughed, then winked. "Well, you can't really call it an accident, per se … but no one else needs to know that."

"What's so special about this ship?" Gravelly asked. "I wanted a nice freighter. This looks too much like a woman's jewelry box."

"You just said it, my friend," Throaty gloated. "It *is* a jewelry box. After the funeral, her relatives removed all the valuables, or so they thought. Watch this," he said.

The man took out a remote device and pushed two buttons. Musical tones chimed from the ship, and a door opened in the side.

"Look at that! She's beautiful!" Gravelly said as a ballerina danced out of the door.

Throaty pushed another button, and the dancer stopped and just stood there. The doll was not stiff but was made out of some kind of flexible material. There was a tiara on top of her light brown hair, and her blue eyes looked alive with light. She had frozen into a perfect ballet *gran plie.* The ballerina's white torso sparkled, and the net tutu spread out around her like a cloud.

"There's more treasure on this ship than anyone knows about," he said. "Her boyfriend owed me a lot and offered this in payment of his gambling debts. Fortunately, he told me about the hidden loot before he was done-in by someone else that he owed money to. This is our dream ship. Our ship to easy street. All we have to do is take it apart."

He pushed the two buttons again. The ballerina slid back inside her compartment, and the door closed.

"Come on! Let's go take a look inside," Throaty said.

While the men were inside, Eyes said to Hands, "Did you hear that?"

"Yes. They are thieves and murderers. What should we do?" Hands asked.

"I am now transmitting a recording of their conversation to The Space Corps as well as The Salvage Rights Corporation," Eyes said. "Let us make sure the men are trapped inside until The Space Corps arrives."

Hands offered, "My welder is still functional. If you direct me to where the hatch is located, I can weld it shut."

A small blue flame came out of the tip of its armature, and when Eyes directed it to, a soldering rod worked its way around the edge of the hatch, sealing it.

Hands asked Eyes, "Did I get it all?"

Eyes said, "Yes. If this is not really a broken salvage unit, it may have fuel in its cells. We must disable them to make sure the men cannot get away."

Eyes looked around at the various colorful facets to see which may be an access panel.

Hands was directed to tap on a blue one … nothing. Then a green one. It was solid as well. And then came insistent tapping through the door, which turned into a loud banging.

"We have been found out," said Hands. "We better hurry."

Finally, a red panel felt hollow, and Hands pried it off.

Eyes looked inside and saw a valve with a sign above it. "It is in Russian; let me translate. It reads 'Fuel Cell Emergency Shut-Off Valve.' "

He directed Hands to reach in and turn the valve until it reached *Niet*. No sooner had the valve been turned, the pumps gasped for fuel, and the ignitors clicked, causing a weak and feeble puff that displaced the dirt below.

Trapped.

Just then, several personnel capsules whizzed down from above, surrounding the ship as they landed. Their bright flashing red and blue lights reflected off the gemstone facets of the stolen spacecraft. Each capsule bore The Space Corps shield: black with a red rocket firing across the middle.

A split second later, another capsule landed with the logo of a crashed rocket blazoned across one side, its nose dented and pointing into the ground: The Salvage Rights Corporation.

A salvage agent climbed out of his capsule, frantically looking about with his helmet's specially augmented visual sensors to see through the piles of garbage. A modern day Treasure Hunter.

Eight corpsmen in their black spacesuits ran into position, crouching down, blasters at the ready. Their captain stepped forward to take a look at the jewel of a spaceship and saw the bots standing nearby. "A-1605-G and A-386-R?"

"Yes, sir," they both replied.

"I assume that this is the ship?"

"Yes. We have welded the men inside and disabled the vessel," Hands said.

"I guess we better arrest them. Can you get your can opener out for us?" the captain asked.

Eyes directed Hands, who extended its metal cutter and went along the weld separating the hatch again from the hull.

Soon Eyes declared, "Task complete."

The salvage agent had watched Eyes and Hands working together and realized that they were damaged. "A-1605-G and A-386-R. I see that you bots have become damaged. You have very valuable motors and gyros—you are now, yourselves, salvage material." He considered them carefully. "Good work in capturing dangerous criminals and notifying us about this situation. You have saved our profits—shown initiative. Maybe we can find another use for you both—one that won't require you being scrapped," he said.

Eyes and Hands had been found out. Their partnership was at risk. They had worked well together, but even so, they were no longer perfect and would most inevitably be picked apart, bit-by-valuable-bit.

"Come out with your hands up! We know you're in there," the captain transmitted to the ship's occupants through his helmet's speaker.

The ballerina danced out, holding a paper message. "Ha! Ha! No! Come and get us!"

The salvage company agent gesticulated wildly, in a panic, and said, "You can't hurt this ship! It's valuable merchandise, and our insurance doesn't cover battle damage."

The captain wrote a reply and put it in the ballerina's hand. The doll slid back into her door, and they waited. When she came back out, she was holding a small device. Just as the captain reached for it, he realized what it was.

"Bomb!" he cried as everyone flung themselves as far away as they could.

The ballerina turned in a graceful pirouette before shattering shrapnel in every direction. Her tattered remains bowed to the audience. And then, there … under her smoldering ballet slippers, came a green shimmer.

Eyes analyzed the spectrum and directed Hands to reach down and pick up what turned out to be a very large emerald.

Like a vulture on a carcass, the agent swooped in and plucked the gemstone from Hands' armature. He hefted it to assess its weight. The chuckle began in his toes, and by the time it came out of his mouth, it was joyous laughter. "Now *this* is what I call salvage!"

The captain stood and watched. But then, he finally had to say, "I'm sorry, but these are stolen goods, not salvage. They must be returned to the beneficiary." Turning back to the spacecraft, he transmitted to Throaty and Gravelly, "We have the emerald. It was hidden in the ballerina that you just blew up. Do you give up now?"

Their answer didn't come with words but came with an explosive burst of the hatch, followed by the blast of laser pistols. Gravelly and Throaty leaped out of the smoke, racing towards the agent. Each had one hand firing a laser at the captain, the other hand reaching for the emerald.

As laser blasts flew everywhere, Eyes positioned itself and Hands to shield their employer, the salvage agent. Just as a pair of laser blasts harmlessly pinged off the salvage bots, a volley of bright red blasts tore through the pirates, dropping them into the Martian dust.

Red, mixing with red, mixing with red.

The eight space corpsmen stood at attention. Their captain was relieved that none had been hurt in the firefight. "This ship is not true salvage, but goods stolen during the commission of a crime. I'll have to confiscate the ship and the emerald. Please hand over the jewel," he ordered.

The salvage agent had *almost* pocketed the gem, hoping no one had noticed. He reluctantly opened his hand and gave it to the captain.

Eyes watched the exchange with suitable scrutiny—and calculation. The bot turned to the captain. "Sir! That's not the original gemstone. I spectrum analyzed it."

The captain scowled at the agent while surrounding him with several corpsmen. "Hand it over."

"Hand over what?"

Eyes turned its head, fixing its gaze on the agent's pocket. The captain's gaze followed.

The agent's eyes widened. "Oh, uh … you mean this emerald?" he said as he pulled another green stone out of the offending pocket. "Sorry about that," he said, slouching and hanging his head.

The captain confiscated it out of his hand and showed it to Eyes. "Is this the real stone?"

"Yes, sir," Eyes replied, after a nanosecond pause.

The captain let out a disapproving laugh, discarding the first emerald in the debris beside his feet, be-

fore telling one of his men to put the second gem in a secure storage locker the minute they return to their capsules. "I have to hand it to you," he said to the agent. "You did come prepared. I have to assume now that you were working with the pirates. Maybe you have a standing arrangement with them that allowed them to redirect perfectly-functioning ships here on the pretense they are to be salvaged, so they can loot them. Maybe you had also heard the tale of the fabled emerald, and you brought that fake along to double cross the pirates."

The agent smiled back. "Well, we both know you didn't just show up here to recover some silly, froo-froo spaceship out of the goodness of your hearts. I'm sure the family offered you some *personal* incentive—maybe even the emerald itself." Then he turned back to the bots. "You useless pieces of junk! Neither of you is any use to me anymore. Prepare to be scrapped. You're worth more in pieces now," he smiled grimly.

The captain said, "I don't agree with you. They work well together as a team. They saved your salvage yard. They saved the ship. They saved your life! If you can't see that they are the only honest heroes out of today … then, The Space Corps would like to purchase these two salvage bots from you."

The Salvage Rights Corporation agent kicked the dirt in frustration, let out a sigh, and said, "Nah. On second thought, if I destroyed them, I'd have to get new salvage bots, and they're expensive." He looked over the damage of Eyes and Hands and said, "Who better to rule over piles of junk than piles of junk?"

The captain grimaced and demanded a promise out of the agent that he would not go back on his word about the salvage bots, and to not touch the jewel box ship until they could send a recovery crew to pick it up.

Then the corpsmen climbed back into their capsules and sprinted into the sky.

The agent turned to Eyes and Hands and chuckled. "You know," he said, "with all that laser-blasting going on, I had no time to swap the emerald with the fake in my pocket." Then he gave them both a big, dirty grin. "How the hell did you know I had been planning to switch out the real one?"

Eyes said, "My spectrum analyzer detected the fake in your pocket. Except for the quality of the material, I ascertained its surface dimensions and color were the exact same as the real one."

"And that was enough for you to jump to the right conclusion?"

Eyes, tilted its head, looking up at the agent. "Yes."

"You know, I actually got pissed when I first thought you were betraying me," the agent said, "until I realized you were directing him toward the wrong gem."

Eyes guided Hands over to the emerald the captain had discarded in a pile of junk, and—together—they picked it up, polished the debris of it, and delivered it to the agent. "I trusted that you would work out what I was trying to do," Eyes said simply.

Hands chirped and whirred, adding, "We are Salvage Rights Corporation bots. We know who we work for."

The agent grinned. "Too right!"

The three of them slowly made their way to the remains of the Endeavour.

The agent finally said, "On behalf of The Salvage Rights Corporation, I just gotta say that you are a damned fine pair of salvage bots!"

Angela Slatter (also writing as A.G. Slatter) is the multi-awarded Australian author of All The Murmuring Bones *(Titan Books), followed by* The Path of Thorns *in June 2022. Both are gothic fantasies set in the world of the Sourdough and Bitterwood collections. Angela has recently signed another two-book deal with Titan for the novels* The Briar Book of the Dead *(2023) and* The Crimson Road *(2024), and she is the author of the supernatural crime novels from Jo Fletcher Books/Hachette International:* Vigil *(2016),* Corpselight *(2017) and* Restoration *(2018),*

THE BADGER BRIDE

by Angela Slatter

The tip of the quill scratches its way across the parchment, a sound that sets my teeth on edge.

One might think I'd be used to it by now. The black marks it leaves in its wake make no sense to me—indeed the entire book makes no sense—then again, I am a mere copyist and mine's not to question why. Although I do.

Frequently.

Much to my father's despair.

When he brought me this commission, I turned the tome over and over—a difficult enough task, for the thing is heavy, aged and fragile, the ebon cover tacky to the touch, the pages brittle—and a smell rose from the skin of the thing that was quite unpleasant. The name of the author and the title of the book were utterly obscured, a thick stygian gum had been smeared across them and it was hard to perceive whether this application was intentional or the result of mere carelessness. The inner leaves confirmed intent—no extant title page waited within, merely the remnants of a folio torn from the binding, tiny sad folds of paper with ragged edges.

So, an anonymous book.

"Who is the client?" I asked my father, Adelbert, once Abbot of the monastery of St-Simeon-in-the-Grove, who rolled his eyes and bid me *Just do the job.*

"But, Father, it is very old, very frail, and the ink is faded—fading as I watch if my eyes don't deceive me." I maneuvered the article in question so he could better see. "Is it the last of its kind? Who is the owner? What does he expect?"

"He expects, like your father, that you do not ask questions, little prying thing. That you take this volume and copy it as quickly as you might!" He took a deep breath and roared, "Else I'll put you out in the cold, Gytha!"

I harrumphed, and left his study. He will not put me out; he will do no such thing. I am the only child in Fox Hollow House who earns her keep, after all. Aelfrith spends her days draped across the couch, sighing for a husband, and Edda devotes her time to exercising and grooming the six horses in the stables. I alone understood and adopted the scholarly arts Father had tried to teach us; and I alone adopted the trade he learned at the monastery—and at which, he freely admits, was terrible. People come from all around, from as far away as Lodellan, to have me copy their books, their precious, unique, failing books; to have me adorn and enhance them, to add vines and flowers and strange animals in the margins; to change the existing illustrations they cannot bear (modestly clothe a naked Eve, paint out grandmother's warts on her nose, give uncle a chin that does not slope so straight from lower lip to clavicle). Copy, edit, amend, ameliorate, augment and occasionally, if the pay is right, forge.

I will make a book what they want it to be, either more or less itself.

So many since I was very small—so small that Father had to lift me onto the stool piled with two firm fat cushions that I might be able to sit at the tilted desk and reach the inks and shafts, the paints and tints, the papers and parchments that required my attention.

My fingers are stained from the mixing of hues of slate and blue, flashes of umber and gold, red and green; the same fingers are scarred, fletched with nicks from sharpening my very fine goose feather quills. When I copy, I wear white cotton gloves, each pair washed in the hottest of hot water after use. I have spectacles, thick half-moons of polished glass to magnify the things I must discern and craft; these perch on the end of my nose only when I am mid-copy. Aelfrith says I look like someone's granny, for all my smooth skin and dark hair.

"No one," she taunts, "would ever believe you young."

Edda merely grunts at that and adds that I need to get out more—that both Aelfrith and I need to take in the healthful air, and undertake some exercise as she does. We three have different mothers, so we are more like to be dissimilar than if we shared a maternal imprint. Fathers have so much less influence.

The scratching of the nib, which has almost hypnotized me, now has a rival: the tap-tap-tapping of a bare frozen branch from the wild cherry tree by the side of the house.

With a tiny bed cupboard in one corner, my scriptorium is located on the second floor, in the room with the most windows so I might steal all the light I can. The cherry tree is naked and frosted; it looks dead, as if it will never bloom again. The cold coming from the glass panes may just convince me this is true—this place cannot be too warm, so I may have only the smallest of fires, banked low in the grate, which is why I prefer to not work in winter.

I have spent the day copying this wretched thing, stopping but once to read a couplet aloud, hoping that speech might add some meaning, but it remained nonsense. Looking up I blink hard until my eyes stop watering at the change in focus, and watch the thin branch as the wind pushes it this way and that; any moment now, any moment, it will snap. But no, the thing is hardier than I would have thought. It endures.

I stand, stretch, arching my back until I hear the four distinct cracks that say my spine is aligned once more. I take stiff steps over to the window, where a cushioned seat awaits, draped with shawls, and survey the garden. White as white can be, its purity is broken only by the shadowy things there's not *quite* enough fall to cover: the chopping block, the wood pile, the swing we use only in summer and only when we are feeling particularly frivolous. And at the edge of the lawn, a dark mobile thing the size of a small dog or a large cat, is inching its way forward, terribly slowly, shaking the snow off its gentleman's coat quite determinedly.

A badger; no creature should be left to suffer in this weather.

All stiffness is gone from my limbs and I fly from the room, down the staircase with its carved banister and hideous newel post (the head of a green man, but not as cheerful as it should be), making a great commotion that brings my family from various directions. I don't even worry about a cloak, but fling open the door and charge out into the white.

For precious moments I'm lost, blinded, then I catch sight once more of the determined lope—almost a waddle, with his limbs so chilled—of the black fur and the hoary streak down his back. I stumble through the cold powder and catch up the poor creature. He is heavy; he smells strongly, oh so strongly; he looks at me with bleary-eyed distrust.

"There, there," I croon, stroking one hand over his head and face as I trudge towards the front door, where Father and my sisters wait. "You're safe here, little brock, little badger."

And the poxy little whoreson bites me.

Not viciously—it was merely a warning nip—and only on the one finger but still he breaks the skin and it wells red and stings. Then he snuggles against me, smugly content.

☼

Edda washes and salves my wound. While she applies a bandage to the two sharp punctures, I glare at the animal, curled snug in a blanket-lined basket by the kitchen fire.

His eyes are closed, his breathing even and he is making a deep throaty noise somewhere between a grunt and a purr. One lid lifts, a brown orb stares at me, then is slowly sheathed again. In a bowl in front of a hastily-emptied basket are slices of preserved apple and cherries, tepid milk, porridge and honey. His left hind foot is bandaged; a deep cut slashed its fat pad. The cold had stopped the bleeding, but once inside, the flow started again. He let us bathe the limb with warm water and apply a rosemary ointment to it before Edda swaddled him like a baby. He didn't bite *her*.

"He must have gotten lost," says Aelfrith, admiring his coal coat. He is a young male, not a cub, but not a fully grown boar. The streak of white from snout to tail is clean as clean can be. All things considered he is a very *hygienic* badger; well, except for the smell, which is not unpleasant, merely strong and musky.

Edda nods. "Yes, he's wandered away from his sett."

"Or perhaps he's been driven out—old boar and new boar can't live in peace," I say, flexing my finger

in hope of loosening Edda's tight wrapping. "Especially as he seems to be a biter."

"He only bit *you*, Gytha."

"I'm sure it was just to say *hello*," laughs Aelfrith.

I give my sisters the look they deserve and am about to serve up a retort when Father's bulk hoves into view. "Still fussing with that confounded animal?"

"*O God, how manifold are your works!*" I quote.

"*In wisdom thou hast made them all,*" follows Edda.

Aelfrith chimes in with, "*The earth is full of your myriad blessed creatures.*"

"*Yea, blessed!*" we chorus, our mockery taking on the ring of a hymn.

Adelbert regrets (many times daily, I suspect) teaching his daughters scriptures, for we have ended up with firm beliefs, but also varied means of arguing with him on his own terms.

"Gytha, don't you have work to do? You know the client expects that book by season's end."

"And yes, I've been meaning to talk to you about this, Father. Winter work and no say to me in the deadline! It's not acceptable." I frown.

He sees that bluster and bullying will not get him far this day, so he softens his tone. "Gytha, I am sorry, but this is a special job. No more like this, I promise—but with the coin from this one commission, we need not work for two whole years!"

"*We* don't work, Father. *I* work," I grumble, but turn on my heel and stride from the kitchen.

In the scriptorium, the fire has gone out and I have only a few more hours of usable light left. I poke at the embers and stir them up until flames lick at the twigs I throw on. When it is crackling, I defiantly add a larger log than I normally would and watch it catch with satisfaction.

I rub my hands together until they warm, carefully massage the fingers, then sit down to begin once more. Page ten: a drawing of a young woman, who seems to be sleeping, but for the fact there is a great tear over her heart; words in a language I do not understand, but which make me nervous nonetheless, are written around her corpse.

I manage the rough outline of the body before there is a scratching at the door.

I curse and pull it open. No one is there. Then: a furry weight as Master Brock crosses the threshold and treads over my feet, to sit himself on the rug in front of the fire.

We stare at each other for a moment, until he closes his eyes.

I shrug and return to my desk.

✿

I come down to a scene of high circus the next morning, the badger limping at my heels. I stop in the kitchen doorway and he peeks out from behind my skirts.

"The cheese is gone!" Father shouts.

"The cheese?" I ask.

"All the cheese!" says Edda.

"All our lovely, lovely cheese," wails Aelfrith.

"The cheese?" I repeat, thinking perhaps I am not awake, but still dreaming. I did not sleep well, and the welt on my finger throbbed throughout the night.

Father looks at me as though I am an imbecile. "The cheese has been eaten. Our entire winter supply. Gone."

Father is fond of his cheese.

"And no sign of a thief. No doors unlocked, no windows broken," says Edda knowingly.

"Well, don't look at me." I traipse down the narrow stairs to the cellar, which is a surprisingly small room, half the size of the kitchen, and lined with shelves laden with bottles of preserved fruit and vegetables from last summer, wrapped parcels of salted fish and pork, sacks of flour and sugar, small jars of salt and ground pepper, three kegs of Father's cider, one of his brandy, and a distinct lack of the five large wheels of cheese I set there at the beginning of winter.

I look closely at the walls, the floor, as if I might find a secret passageway heretofore unsuspected, then I shake my head. It's probably Aelfrith, wandering in her sleep again and now feeding her frustrations by eating. She'd best stop or we'll be well out of food before the snows end. Turning to go back up, I find myself pinned by a dark gaze in a curious face. I narrow my eyes and wonder at the badger sitting patiently at the top of the stairs. The cheese was on the highest shelf, my head height, and badgers are not known for their climbing ability, nor for their love of dairy. I shake my head once more and return to the kitchen, wondering how to phrase my suspicions of Aelfrith politely.

But this drama, it seems, has passed and another, quieter one has taken its place. Father is nowhere to be seen, and my sisters have moved themselves to the parlor, where they sit expectantly. Aelfrith, in particular, is preening.

"Where's Father?"

"In his study and not to be disturbed," says Edda.

Aelfrith nods. "He's with a client—*the* client." She takes a deep breath, which she exhales with words riding upon it, "He's ever so handsome, Gytha!"

Even Edda nods and I've not seen her enthused about the appearance of anything but a horse for many a year. Then again, we don't get too many men passing by, only the occasional monk, old friends of Father's, random clients, and tinkers. Certainly none from the burnt-out bones of Southarp village.

I make a move towards the door and Edda leaps up, terribly distressed and barring my way. "Oh, no! You mustn't disturb them—Father said so."

I narrow my eyes and stomp off to my workroom. Honestly, she doesn't know me at all. I sit at the window seat and watch, noting the absence of either horse or carriage. It doesn't take long before I hear the front door open and see a figure step out from beneath the storm porch, firmly settling a tricorne hat upon thick golden hair.

He gets a good head-start while I fight with the frozen casement latch and eventually clamber down the stout limbs of the cherry tree. I follow his tracks, deep footprints, and huddle against the shawls I threw hastily around my shoulders. Soon, I'm into the woods; icicles hang where leaves should be, and the patches of sky glimpsed through the bare tangle of branches are grey and unwelcoming. If I do not find him soon I will give up—I'm no fool. He will visit again and I will be waiting; next time I will charge into Father's study and take the golden-haired man's measure.

I'm cold and shivering. The moment I turn around, there he is, grinning like a wolf.

I see none of the handsomeness Aelfrith was mooning over, merely appetite and a will to do whatever he wishes. In his hands, a knife, long and thin, a stiletto blade; his knuckles are white around the ivory handle.

"The book," I blurt and his expression alters. Ah! Here it is, that beautiful mask. But I've seen what it covers and I will not be deceived. "I wanted to ask you about your book."

Smoothly he hides the knife into the sheath at his belt, tucks it out of sight as if it might be easily forgotten. He is richly dressed, his cloak lined with ermine.

"My apologies—I could only hear someone following me and thought to defend myself from footpads. I did not mean to frighten you." He points and I follow the direction of his kid-gloved finger. "My coach is there."

And so it is, on the road above where we stand in a hollow. Black and shiny as ebony, with four black steeds, a driver and a footman, both blank faced as they peer down at us. I find myself shaking and will it to stop. I clear my throat.

"The book—I was wondering if you knew its name and author? Only—I've been wondering. Professional curiosity," I say, trying to look scholarly and serious.

He gives me a brilliant smile and shakes his head. "Afraid not, Mistress Gytha—it is Gytha, yes? My copyist? I am—a collector. The book took my fancy; its value is purely ornamental and sentimental. It reminds me of someone very dear. But its ink is fading, the cover is derelict. I require a copy."

"But I can re-ink the text, clean the cover, fix the bindings."

"No, no. My memory hinges on the contents, not the container. New is best." His expression tells me that he does not like old things; he is one of those who prefer possessions to be pristine and unused when they come to his hand. No true collector, he. An old book is not the artefact for him—the knowledge therein is what he wants, but he desires it in a splendid new repository. I notice his clothing—blue breeches, gold and cream waistcoat, white silk shirt, silver-grey frock coat and highly polished boots—not one item seems overly worn. Indeed, there is no sign of anything having been worn before at all; there is no fading of color, nor weakening of nap, no hint of threadbare at the collar and wrists, and certainly no wrinkles or folds that might come with habitual attire. This man likes his things *shiny*.

"Where did you find it?"

He smiles again and does not answer, effortlessly striding up the slope to his conveyance. He tips his hat and climbs in. He leans out the window and says, "I shall return in the spring, Mistress Gytha, to claim my book. I trust you'll not disappoint me."

I stand shivering for some time after he is gone.

✧

St. Simeon-in-the-Grove is a small monastery, all things considered. A mere twenty monks, aged from twelve (two boys left on the doorstep some years ago) to ninety-five (the librarian).

Edda has let me take our oldest horse, a tall beastie, with feathered feet and a mane like a blanket. Hengroen moves slowly and surely—it's a bit like being on a very sturdy boat, his gait is almost floating, which makes me feel both safe and seasick after an hour on his broad back. My rear protests as I dismount and groan loudly. The young monk who comes forward to take Hengroen looks astounded as I tip back the hood of my thick travelling cloak—obviously he has been brought up to believe women are crafty creatures, both fragrant and evil, but not given to terrible bodily noises. He should hear Edda after a meal of beans.

"Larcwide will see me," I say, before he begins the speech about how my kind are not allowed in the monastery. A rule instituted since—in fact because of—my father's tenure. "I'm bringing a book."

Of course, I'm *assuming* he will see me as he has done before—that he will not remember that little fracas a few years back. This young man knows the librarian collects tomes, is consulted on them regularly, is an authority on things that hold words in one place. I'm banking on the very good chance that he has been terrified by at least one of the old man's tirades, and will be too afraid to refuse me.

"Don't worry," I say, and pat his hand. He shivers the way a horse does when a fly lands on its hide. "I'll take the side entrance so as not to cause a fuss."

I'm rewarded with a flash of relief and he nods, leading my great mount to the stables for a rest. I dart across the rectangle of snow that in summer is a patch of green, keeping my head down, but I needn't bother—most of the brothers are at prayer this time of day. At the base of a tall tower—not the one with the bell in it, the one opposite—there is a small slender door, overgrown with winter ivy, which in this season looks deceased, as if the wall is shedding its skin, but a sharp eye will note the grey handle twisted about with dead vines, almost invisible. I get splinters, but the ingress opens with relative ease. Inside there is a set of black stone steps curving around and up. The air is dry and cold, but warmer as I rise. I can smell ink and paper, and old man.

The librarian is shuffling back and forth between cases, twitching folios from the shelves which line the walls, muttering, sliding them back into place or shifting them to another spot. In the center of the tower is a series of platforms, weighted down with even more tomes, reached by a sort of elevator and pulley system, that creaks above. As I watch a thin monk steps onto the third platform, nimbly balancing an armful of volumes. Larcwide glares upward as dust particles drift down.

"I told you," he yells, "to clean your shoes! And did you? Did you?"

There is a muffled and indecipherable reply from aloft, and the old man swears softly.

"Father Larcwide?"

He swings around in surprise and squints at me. He won't rant about me being a woman, although he may well rant about my incursion. He shared in many of my father's adventures, but his continued presence at St Simeon is testament to both his inability to produce offspring and to his unassailed position as bibliognost. By virtue of his irreplaceable knowledge, his transgressions could be— and have been—overlooked. Unfortunately for Adelbert"s career, he lacked the librarian's uniqueness—anyone can be an under-enthused abbot and mediocre copyist.

"Father Larcwide, I need to talk to you," I say and hold up the satchel hanging at my side. His eyes sparkle and he gestures for me to come closer.

He peers at my face and recognition dawns. "Adelbert"s girl? The clever one."

I grin and nod. "Gytha. I need you to look at something."

"Why me?" he grumps, contrary for the sake of it.

"Because there's none like you." His ego, duly stroked, allows him to lead me along a maze of shelves to an alcove just big enough for a writing desk and two chairs. He sits and invites me to do the same. I draw the thing out of the bag, and unwrap

it from the layers of shawl, then place it on the table between us. Larcwide leans forward to read the now-visible title. I have been working at it, testing out a variety of oils and soft cloths, trying to wear away at the black mess. It was slow toil: if I used too much of the lubricant, too much pressure as I rubbed, the stuff would have simply eaten its way through the cover. It is a capricious mix, with a peculiar personality all of its own, bought from the strange little man who travels in spring and summer and brings me supplies of the things that are hardest to find. I cleaned the surface, one letter at a time. So carefully. So very carefully, until:

Murcianus: Magica: A Book of Craft.

Larcwide's hands shake as he reaches out but does not touch the tome. His fingers are blue and brittle, stained with age spots. They hover over what I have so painstakingly cleaned.

"Do you know what this is? Of course you don't," his voice quivers. Then, "Where did you get this?"

No, I don't know, although, I have a suspicion, have had since I reached a page I recognized: a drawing of a hand with candles set in the tops of all the fingers and the thumb. A hand of glory. But I choose to act the innocent and answer only his second question. "A client. A commission my father took on."

He shakes his head. "Oh, Adelbert. Will you never learn?" He closes his eyes, no more than a blink, but he looks exhausted when he opens them again.

"What is it?" I ask.

He nods. "A *grimoire*. A book of craft. And this one …" He finally picks the thing up and rubs his fingers on the back cover, in the right-hand bottom corner, finding what I already know is there: the subtle relief of an embossment. *M.* He almost drops the book, so great is his surprise. "Belonged to *him!*"

I want to poke and prod, extract the information swiftly, but I wait. He looks at me dubiously, then with judgment. I don't know who *he* is.

"Murcianus. This is the Bitterwood Bible."

And I stare blankly at him and Larcwide's expression rolls into utter despair.

"Murcianus, one of the greatest encyclopaedists ever known. Or rather of the arcane and the eldritch specifically. He wandered the world, recording and compiling every strange ritual, every bizarre being, every spell, curse, myth, legend, enchantment, magical locations …" the monk seems to run out of words. "Everything!"

I remain silent.

"Those books, nowadays, are so rare you barely find one outside a private collection—or with those bloody women at Cwen's Reach," he mutters. "They are wonderfully illustrated, most erudite and informative, filled with wisdom and wit and scholarship." He turns my tome over in his hands. "There are other volumes, Gytha, like this one, written in the language of witches, comprehensible to only a few, but this one is a rarity. Full of knowledge best left unknown, things too dangerous to be writ down. There are places, Gytha, where his works are forbidden; where those who carry them are burned, their ashes scattered."

His face reddens and he looks away, remembering to whom he speaks; remembering at last our argument when I asked him for information my father refused. The one occasion I managed to extract the name of my mother from Adelbert, he was in his cups. He'd called her *Hafwen* and told me she had been so briefly beautiful, then burned. She was his final indiscretion, the one that sent him from the monastery, lucky to leave with his life. That is all I was able to establish before he passed out; he woke the next day with a sore head and foul temper, and would tell me nothing more. When I asked Larcwide about it, tried to get an answer, he banned me from coming to see him. I'd hoped the intervening years and his age had dimmed the memory.

"And the book. Where would *this* have come from?"

He shrugged. "Lost? Left behind? Stolen? Who knows. All I know is this isn't some harmless thing you're working on, Gytha." He pauses, suddenly distrustful. "You haven't read from it?"

I would like to deny it, but my blush makes a liar of me. Larcwide goes pales and pushes the volume at me, insistent. "What did you read?"

Flicking carefully through the pages I find the relevant one, with the drawings of wheat sheaves and other plants. The old man's dark eyes skim the words and they seem to make sense to him as he sits back and puffs out a sigh of relief. "Transformation, but it's just a season spell. Not much harm in it."

"What's that?"

"To work change for a few months only, to make an animal shift its shape."

"Not a person?" I worry at the bandaged finger, which has not healed these past weeks, but itches still.

"Oh no," he flicks through the pages and points to a couplet. "Here: this one will work on a person, but only one who is willing. A resistant subject requires far more effort, instruments and ingredients." He rubs his hands together. Larcwide seems to know rather more about magic than he should, I think, but do not say. "But you have no ability, so I shouldn't worry about it. Just don't do it again—some spells are so powerful they need only be spoken, without intent, for them to effect a metamorphosis, unwanted or otherwise. You should know, though, that every bit of magic leaves a trace, Gytha, no matter how small. Even the tiniest skerrick may rub off, leaving the potential for alteration in its wake."

"Thank you, Father." I take the book from him and begin to wrap it up once more. He leans across the table, grasps my wrist and says, "What will you do with this?"

"This is a commission, I cannot simply make it disappear." I lower my voice. "And I fear this client, Father, I fear him greatly. I will not risk my life nor that of my family by refusing to give him what he has demanded."

"But, child, it's too dangerous. If you will not listen to sense, I shall have to tell the Abbot."

"And if you do so, there's every good chance I will be burned—it won't matter that this book is not mine, it will simply matter that it is in my possession." I hold his gaze for a long moment. I do not think he would like to see me as ashes.

"What will you do?" he asks quietly once more, defeated.

I shake my head. "I'll think of something."

I wipe my hands on a rag, then wash with hot water and Edda's whortleberry soap, massaging the cramps and the smell of ink and oil out of them. Passing my desk I survey the work: the replica is almost done. I am exhausted and my eyes ache; I have been copying by the light of the fire and as many lanterns and candles as I could find without leaving my family in darkness. Outside the black mirror of the window, the air smells of spring. The days have grown longer, warmer, but I have spent an eternity inside, slaving over this damnable book. The time is fast approaching and although I have not slept well since the client's last visit, it is not the sole reason for my sleeplessness.

The doors to the bed cupboard are open, just a little, and inside I can make out blankets and coverlets heaped up, mounded over the form of a slumbering young man with the thickest, blackest hair relieved only by a streak of white down the middle. He snuffles and snores, his hands curled like paws, batting at the pillows as he stirs, then stilling as he settles once again.

I struggle with the buttons of my dress, then drop it to the rug, half-undone. Crawling in beside him, I fit myself into the half-moon of his body and breathe deeply. He smells musky, slightly sweet. I close my eyes, nestling as his arms come around me.

"I want peaches," he mumbles, breath warm in my ear.

"You ate them all, remember?" That was how I found him, in his night-time shape, late on the evening I returned from St-Simeon-in-the-Grove, crouched on the floor of the cellar, struggling with a bottle of preserved peaches. His hands seemed not to know quite what to do, and he dropped the bottle, which smashed impressively. He merely gave a grunt and neatly picked slices of the preserved fruit from the glass, carefully examining it for shards, then elegantly chewed it in tiny bites.

"It doesn't stop me wanting them," he points out, in a reasonable tone.

"Ordinary badgers don't eat peaches."

"Well, I'm no ordinary badger, obviously," he says, and shrugs, a movement that takes his whole body, not just his shoulders.

Badgerish.

"You ate plenty this evening. I cannot believe how much food you put away—and Aelfrith insists upon feeding you twice a day. You won't fit in my bed soon."

"Get a bigger bed." As he cuddles comfortably into my back, I take hold of one of his hands, weave our fingers together.

"At least there's no cheese left."

"Oh, that cheese! Terrible cheese. Awful constipation."

"An ordinary badger doesn't eat *cheese*. Or indeed, spend his winter in a girl's bed."

"An ordinary badger doesn't get hit by stray magic." He nuzzles my neck, pauses. "How long will this last, do you think?"

I shake my head, feeling dizzy as if I am dangling over a terrible pit where all the loss in the world resides. "I don't know." I squeeze his hands. "What do you think about, in the day? When you're …"

"Four-legged and furred? Comfortable things: food and warmth, staying safe, about spring and blackberries and wild cherries." He wiggles against me to suggest the time for talking is done and other activities should be considered.

Here is the problem with raising daughters so far from suitable mates: it makes them prey to roaming, transformed badgers. It makes their hearts easy pickings, like windfall apples.

I keep my eyes downcast, but watch through lowered lashes. Adelbert is trying to hide his surprise at my seeming modesty. He is also trying to hide his look of mistrust. We sit in his study, all three of us on separate over-stuffed armchairs.

The client has my work in his hands. He is appreciating the fine red leather cover I've added. It is different to the old one, but I see that I was right: this pleases him, this newness. There is neither title nor author on the front.

"Your workmanship is exquisite, Mistress Gytha. I commend you." He pulls a heavy bag of coins from his belt, holding it in one hand to delay the moment when he hands it over. Adelbert"s expression turns soft, like a drunk seeing his first ale of the day. "And the original?"

"I burned it," I pipe up and two pairs of eyes turn on me. I hold up a small box and shake it gently. "The ashes. The book—the ink was almost unreadable by the time I finished and I did not think you would care, sir. It was old and not new."

The man stares at me for long moments, then nods and brings out a tight smile. "Yes, you're right, Mistress Gytha. Although, such a decision I would have liked to make myself."

He does not care the original is gone, he merely cares about my high-handedness. I offer the box and manage to sound sincere, "I apologize, sir. Would you like …"

He shakes his head dismissively and I nod. "I *am* very sorry, sir."

"But let no deed should go unpunished," he says and dips into the bag of coins, pulling out a sizeable handful and letting them *chink* into his own pocket. Adelbert, unprotesting, watches as the man places the book into a leather case he has brought specifically for the purpose. "I shall take my leave."

Father sees him to the door, then returns to the study. Through the open windows comes the warm air of the first day of spring. I watch, just as I watched him that first occasion, as the client appears around the side of the house, then disappears into the green of the woods. I do not pursue him this time. I watch until the trees swallow him, until I am sure he is nearing his waiting carriage, waiting far from us so no one will know he has been here, has brought something here, so no one will question and perhaps hunt here, or to speculate on whatever he is doing.

"Well done, Gytha," says my father. His good mood cannot be contained, despite the loss of part of our fee, and it makes me wonder if all this has been about more than mere money. He moves around the room, laughing and joking, pouring us both a glass from the last bottle of the summer-berry wine. He counts out my share of the coin into a smaller purse and gives it to me. I sit opposite and stare at him until he becomes uncomfortable. "What is it?"

"Who is he, Father? How did he come to us?" I ask now because it has occurred to me at last that Adelbert did not tell me how this client found us. It is his usual habit to go into great detail about who they are and what drew them here, who referred them on. That I've only just thought of this is a sign of my distraction.

Adelbert gives a kind of half-hearted shrug. "I knew him long ago, in my days at university. Before the seminary, before St Simeon's."

"He looks too young," I point out and he shrugs again.

"Some age better than others. Perhaps his life has been easier." He scratches at his chin. "As I said, I knew him *before*."

"Before Hafwen?" I do not say "my mother" for she has never been that, only ever an absence to whom I was able to put a name a few years ago. He makes

a sharp sound and jerks his head to one side before bringing his gaze back to me.

"Yes," he says.

"Well?"

"Well what?"

"Who was she?"

"A girl. Just a girl."

"Was she a witch?"

I have never seen such grief in my father, such a terrible thing clawing its way up from inside and painting itself across his face. He lowers his head so I cannot see, then slowly raises it once more. Everything is gone but an awful blankness. I will get nothing from him.

"Enjoy the spring, Gytha, while there are no new commissions," he tells me and looks away, staring resolutely out the window at the garden, but not, I feel, seeing it. His voice halts me at the door. "Gytha, all you need to know is that your work has paid a debt that will plague me no more. Never think me ungrateful, daughter, but never ask me about *her* again."

✧

From the blanket box at the foot of my bed, I lift out several coverlets, folded winter dresses and shawls. At the bottom is the original Murcianus *grimoire*, its text and diagrams re-inked each day before I copied it. Every page has been dusted with a setting powder of my own devising. I run my fingers across the cover and wonder how long it will take me to learn the language of witches, to take the knowledge I need for my purpose. I wonder if Larcwide might be prepared to teach me. I wonder if I have any of my mother's blood in me to help.

I notice a four-legged absence. I look around for the badger. He is not in his usual spot, the rug by the hearth, but then as the days have grown longer he has been roaming about the house more, seemingly restless. Perhaps he is in the kitchen, begging food from Aelfrith. He will be so fat soon.

My sister is rolling out dough; a dozen apples sit on the bench, waiting to be peeled. Beside them, a bucket of blackberries, lush and dark. But there is no sign of the badger.

"Where is he? Where is Brock?"

Aelfrith looks at me in surprise. "He wanted to go out."

The kitchen door stands open. From the threshold I survey the green grass and the plants, growing thickly in the house-garden.

No track, no trail, no hint.

I run out, to the stables. Edda has a curry comb and is grooming Hengroen.

"Have you seen him? Have you seen the badger?" I ask, uncaring that my voice is breaking.

She shakes her head, and *tuts*. "You knew he would go, Gytha. I know you're fond of him, but he's a wild creature. It's not as if he's a dog or a horse."

I knew the spell would end. I knew he would change back, but I thought he would stay. I thought he would wait, that he would ignore whatever recalled him to the forest. I thought I could find something in the *grimoire*, some means to make him transform for good, to keep him with me.

A breeze starts up but the dancing air does nothing to lift my spirits. I did not think his badgerish instincts would lead him away from me so soon. The itching of my punctured finger is all I have left.

It is only three days later that I see the client again.

I thought I would have longer. I had planned to leave when he'd collected his finished product, when I had both book and badger. I had planned to run and find another life, but with my love departed, I had fallen into a funk. I had lost the will to move. I lost any care that the golden-haired man might try one of his new spells and find it did not work. That he would try another and it, too, would not work. And another and another until he realized that I had copied each and every enchantment, each and every curse, incorrectly. Just a tiny detail in each, a line missing, an ingredient changed, a direction left out, an instrument added.

Sitting on the window seat in my room, I see the man breaking out of the woods, his long knife catching the sun, and I finally rediscover the will to move. I bundle the *grimoire* into a satchel and drape the bag's strap across my chest. I clatter down the stairs, run into Edda, who protests, until I put a hand over her mouth, the bandage still on the finger that will not heal.

"Sister, if you never listen to me again, listen now. Lock the doors. Do not let anyone in, especially not that man, the handsome man. Don't let him in, Edda, no matter what. Keep all the doors locked. I am sorry for whatever I may have brought down upon you."

I flee before she can answer. I tear out the door, creep around the corner of the house, then make sure the client catches sight of me. He gives a sound somewhere between a yell and a scream, but all rage, and pounds after me. It's the only thing I can do, to draw him away from my family. As I run, I feel myself pulled onward, my direction not as haphazard as I planned. My feet seem to have a plan of their own.

I know these woodlands far better than he. I know the paths both seen and hidden, I dart between trees, under hanging mosses, I hurdle over rocks and stiles and rills, but still he keeps on my trail. I think of the words I've practised these past weeks.

Then, all is silence. I stop, wait, turning, turning, turning, trying to see if he is anywhere in sight. From behind a huge oak, he lunges, the knife preceding him and slicing across my left side, not enough to kill, but to wound, to hurt. I swing the heavy satchel up at him and catch him in the face. He goes down like a sack of potatoes. I run.

I keep running, fleeing into the darkest, deepest part of the wood, bleeding, weakening, aching, my lungs burning, my legs shaking. Silently I mouth the spell, the spell on which I pinned my last hopes, try to feel it taking effect but there is nothing. In a green hollow, a spot dotted with mounds and slopes, I trip over a fallen branch and the breath *whumps* out of me. I hit my chin and bite my tongue and taste iron. Behind me I can hear the crashing, the swearing, the inexorable rampaging of the golden-haired man.

My injured finger tingles, twinges, burns. I hear a chittering, a squeak, a growl close by. Searching, I find the mouth of a hole and in that mouth a creature of black and white, a fine well-fed badger, who calls to me. At last I think *Make a noise, make a sound, if it cannot be heard it cannot be made*! and I finally I speak aloud the couplet Larcwide pointed out that day at the abbey. With a shaking voice I speak through blood that spatters the ground. I scramble up, try to stand, but my entire body convulses, arcs in on itself. The hand with the injured finger curls beyond my will, as does the other. They turn ebony with fur, the nails elongating, becoming hard horn. I drop on all fours and shudder as the transformation completes.

The boar's call changes, the noise more urgent. With the strap of the satchel still around my new shoulders, I scamper up the hillock, and follow my love down the tunnel and into the sett. The book is dragged along behind, getting caught now and then, but the corridors are wide enough for it to get through with a tug or two. We come to a large chamber filled with clean straw; the strap slips from me, the book's progress halting, pushing up a wave of the dry yellow covering that will eventually settle over it.

I can no longer hear the sounds aboveground of a man thwarted and driven beyond his patience. I cannot hear the raging and the cries of loss. I lie still and my mate snuffles at the wound in my side, licking it clean. He curves around me, our black and white fur a chessboard match. Even as I hope my family will be safe, I begin to forget Fox Hollow House. Ideas about books and inks and pages and covers all subside into a dim memory place. I begin to think of worms and beetles, of windfall apples, blackberries, and wild cherries. I begin to think badgerish thoughts.

Copyright © 2014 by Angela Slatter. First published in The Bitterwood Bible of Other Recountings.

Alicia Cay is a writer of speculative and mystery stories. Her short fiction has appeared in several anthologies including Unmasked *from WordFire Press and* The Wild Hunt *from Air and Nothingness Press. She suffers from wanderlust, collects quotes, and lives beneath the shadows of the Rocky Mountains with a corgi, a kitty, and a lot of fur. Find her at aliciacay.com.*

THE COLOR OF THUNDER

by Alicia Cay

The tip of the quill scratches its way across the parchment, a sound that sets my teeth on edge.

The sound of alarm bells woke Ella even before Papa's heavy booted feet came pounding down the hall.

"El, we've caught something!" Papa yelled.

Ella wrestled herself out of her blankets. The townsfolk told tales of the winged people seen in the skies over the village on dark days—harbingers of ill fate, they said.

But Ella had never seen a Seraph herself, and excitement filled her from her fingers to her toes. Had they caught one at last?

The grass, damp with early morning dew, was slick beneath Ella's bare feet as she ran to catch up with Papa. Over the past year, the narrow backyard, tucked behind their moss-roofed cottage and the line of aspens that bordered their farm, had been transformed with her father's trap. Laced across the night sky, tied from tree to tree, lay an intricate net of black ropes entwined with bells that danced in alarm. Beneath the net hung glass jars stuffed with lightning-flies that sparkled like stars, designed to lure down their prey.

Papa stood under the ropes, staring up at the creature tangled in the lines. Ella's breathe snagged in her chest. The Seraphs were known to be beings of malice, but to her the creature appeared rather harmless. It looked like a man, short and slender, with folded wings as long as its body and skin that shone like a midnight-caught oyster pearl—brilliant and blinding in the waning moonlight. Did all Seraphs shine like stars?

"We've caught the murderous beast," Papa whispered.

Ella bit at her bottom lip. How did they know this was *the* Seraph who had murdered her brother? She slipped her fingers into Papa's big warm hand, needing his comfort, his certainty.

Papa pulled his hand away. He ran to fetch his tools from the shed, calling out as he went, "The gods have smiled on us tonight, El." His voice streamed along behind him, leaving trails of manic-violet color in his wake that only Ella could see.

She craned her head to catch a glimpse of the Seraph's face. The ropes were pulled tight across its shimmering skin—ropes that Ella's hands had woven. For this was her family's lone pastime: to sit long into the gathering dark in front of the fire, weaving strong strands of rope for Papa's revenge. She rubbed calloused hands against the fabric of her nightgown, wiping the damp of fear and anticipation from them. *Had* this thing murdered Cord?

Suddenly, from behind a wing covered in sunlight-tinted feathers, the Seraph's face emerged. Ella gasped. Fear prickled across her skin as she met its stare—there was nothing human in that dark gaze. Flickers of light, like dancing galaxies, moved across its pitch-black eyes.

A memory stirred in Ella. Last summer, the day after her fifteenth birthday, Cord had woken her in the night to say goodbye. He was running off with the watchman's daughter. "Her father won't let us be together," Cord had whispered in her ear. "Says we're too young, but Daisy and I are in love. We're going to the Capital to be married." Her big brother had wiped the tears from her eyes, then tucked the blanket around her feet the way he'd done when she was little. He promised to write to her as soon as he and Daisy arrived.

That letter had never come.

Papa returned with a hand-axe and began to cut the ropes. The bells tied to them rang in rhythm with the swing of his blade. Lost in her thoughts and the Seraph's gaze, Ella barely registered Papa's shouts. She came to her senses just in time to dodge the ropes as they fell. The Seraph dropped to the ground with a heavy thud.

Papa bore down on the winged man. He pressed a boot against the Seraph's back and pinned it to the ground. The color of her father, these days a frosty-blue of lonely pain, erupted from him in streams of molten lava, banged up in deep reds—the color of rage. Then her Papa—the man who had taught her to ride her first pony and kissed her skinned knees when she fell from climbing trees—reached down, unfurled one wing with both hands, and wrenched it sideways.

The thick bone snapped, the sound as deafening as a crack of lightning heard up close. Papa grabbed the other wing and twisted, snapping it like a broken branch. Auburn-tinted waves of torture rolled across the Seraph's body. Papa, who could not see these colors as Ella did, bent over the prone creature, his foot firmly between its shoulder blades. Using the axe, he hacked through the bone and sinew that still held.

Flecks of blood splashed onto Papa's arms and face. As they landed on his skin, ripples of a color Ella had never seen on her father before streamed around his chest in circles of rancid-green, and moved outward in waves of scarlet-black, dark as death's cloak.

Ella reeled. She wanted to scream, wanted to crash into her father's arms—once a harbor from bullies and bad dreams—and remind him she was still here, that he was doing this in front of her. She wanted Cord back, but more than that, she wanted Papa back. The person who was meant to protect her from all harm.

Tears lined Ella's cheeks as she stumbled into the cottage. The smell of heated pine rushed to meet her and pulled her into the front room. Sometime during the commotion out back, Mama had woken. She swayed in her rocking chair before a fresh fire.

A rush of relief and affection flooded through Ella. "Mama, you're up?"

"There was such a racket, I could hardly rest." Mama looked at Ella, but her gaze was adrift.

Mama's hair, as gray as the pewter pall of mourning that surrounded her, hung in wisps around her frown-lined face. She had been a gifted healer once, sought after for her tinctures and poultices. Now she spent her days rocking in her chair, mending cloth-ing, and recounting half-forgotten stories.

Ella settled on the woven rug at her mother's feet. Unable to face the ugly color consuming her father, she had left him to drag the Seraph to the barn on his own. Ella took a deep breath, trying to loosen the tightly wound spring of tur-moil twisted in her chest. She held her trembling hands before the fire. Its orange warmth drifted into the room, shot through with pops of heated sap that licked out in bursts of bright white, like reaching arms.

"I knew a girl once," Mama said, "with clouds in her eyes."

Ella knew this story, a blend of real and imagined things melded together in her mother's chipped memory, but she leaned her head against Mama's leg and listened anyway, grateful to have her close. Grateful for something to take her thoughts away from what Papa was doing in the barn.

"This girl lived in the village, oh"—Mama waved a hand—"many years ago. She was about your age, I'd say, just coming into her womanhood, when she began to speak of things no one else could see. Her words frightened us, but there were some who also feared her. They said her sorcery would bring the wicked Seraphs down upon our heads. So, she was sent away—"

"Never to return," Ella said, finishing the line she'd heard so many times.

"Listen now, child." Mama stroked Ella's long dark hair. "There is a road, hidden in the Far Woods on the other side of the village. It leads west into the mountains. That girl lives there now, in a cabin by the Salt-Crusted Cliffs." Mama sighed. "Should you ever leave here, dear, go and find her, and give her a kiss for me, would you?"

Ella smiled up at her mother, her heart heavy. "I will, Mama."

The back door banged open. Papa's boots clumped on the smooth stone floor as he made his way into the front room.

Ella watched her father in the firelight. Like Mama, he had aged before his time; his black hair gone to silver, his beard more salt than pepper. Ella was relieved to see the rancid-green color was gone and the madness from moments ago no longer lin-gered in his eyes, replaced by the great blue sadness that lived there these days.

He bent and planted a kiss on his wife's forehead. "Did we wake you, my love?"

"So much noise," Mama said.

"I know, my dear, I'm sorry. But, we bring good news. Ella and I have caught the damnable creature."

Mama scowled. "Out fishing, at this hour?"

Papa swallowed hard and squeezed Mama's hand. A shot of longing tore through Ella's chest. He was so tender with Mama; proof that he *was* still in there, somewhere. Ella jumped up and wrapped her arms around his neck. Papa, caught off guard, let out a small chuckle and hugged her back. Ella saw the blue pain on his skin waver, but it held fast. No matter how Papa hugged her or how tender he was with Mama, the golden greens of his prior happi-ness did not return. She knew he hadn't stopped caring for them. His love was simply lost, buried beneath his grief.

Papa let Ella go and moved to warm his hands in the golden glow of the fire.

"What do we do now, Papa?" Ella asked.

"I must go to the village and seek counsel. I will need the Elders' advice on how to properly kill the wretched thing so that it stays dead."

"Take 'em out of the water," Mama chimed in. "Kill a fish quick."

Papa tried a smile on for Mama's sake, but it wouldn't take, and he let it slip away. Mama smiled back at him in that slack-jawed way of hers. He traced a thumb along her cheek.

When Papa spoke again, his words drifted from him in bruised purples that tangled in the light-blue frost of his pain. "Once that *thing* is dead, you'll come back to me then. We will have justice for his murder and grace will be restored." He cleared his throat and looked at Ella. "I leave first thing in the morning. See to it she doesn't stay up all night."

"Yes, Papa."

He kissed Mama again, then headed down the hall to their bedroom.

The loss of his only son had broken him in differ-ent ways than Mama, and Ella could not fault him for wanting to destroy the Seraph. Cord had been the light of Papa's eye; for the little boy who liked to stick his fingers in the jam jar, and the young man he'd become, laughing while he worked beside Papa in the fields. His absence had left a hole in their home none of them had figured out how to fill.

Papa needed to do this to the Seraph to find peace, but … uncertainty knotted in her belly. What if the stories were true? The Seraphs were said to come in the night and steal away people possessed by magic, whisking them from their families to far-away corners in nightmare lands.

Ella worked at her bottom lip with her teeth. She was like the girl in Mama's stories, able to see things no one else could. *Had* they caught the creature that murdered her brother, or had it come here for her?

☼

Papa left early the next day, the sun just beginning to rise. Long rays of light glinted off the Plum-Shaded Mountains perched on the western horizon.

Her father shouldered the bag she'd packed for him and strode down the foot-worn path through the heather that led off their farm. He would stay on that path until it met the road that took him into the village; where smoke curled from the chimneys of straw-roofed homes and the Elders waited to give council on how to kill a winged man.

Questions about the Seraph burned in Ella, a heat she could feel in her chest. She threw herself into her farm chores to try and keep the treacherous thoughts at bay, and to stay away from the barn as Papa had ordered.

As evening approached, Ella settled on the log fence to watch the goats and pigs in their paddock. Fed and content with life, the farm animals lounged in the shade of her favorite oak tree. How she envied them.

She sighed. Duty called. It was time to go in and start supper for Mama.

Ella swung her legs over the railing and froze, struck by a thought. Did Seraphs need to eat? She should find out. Papa wanted it dead, but she'd been raised to cause no harm. Even prisoners to be executed were given a last meal.

She told herself that was why she was going against Papa's orders. That it wasn't her curiosity, or her need to fix things, that drew her to the creature.

She ran inside to gather a few things, then made her way up the field toward the barn. Wild lavender and long heather swung their purple heads in the breeze and bent to tickle her knees.

The smell of alfalfa hay, sweet and green, hit Ella as she slid back the barn door. She paused, hesitating on the threshold, then continued inside. Her boots kicked up plumes of dust as she shuffled toward the stall where her father had confined the creature. When she reached the gate, the sight of Papa's brutality hit her like a blow to the stomach.

The Seraph lay on its side on a wooden cot, facing the wall. Spikes of bone protruded from its back at the shoulder blades, and smears of dried blood stained its pearled skin. Ella had gone through Mama's cabinets and mixed a quick poultice of pungent herbs. They rang with the colors of renewal and cleanliness—green and hot white—a peace offering to show the Seraph she meant no harm.

Ella opened her mouth to speak, but she could not make the words come out.

"Hello, Ella," the Seraph said. Its voice drifted like dust caught on shafts of sunlight, in motes of pastel pink and aquamarine.

Ella let out a garbled caw. How did it know her name? She cleared her throat. "I came to tend to your wounds."

"I smell the herbs. Will they help with the hurt?"

Mama did have some laudanum tucked away in the back of the cabinet, but Ella hadn't thought to bring any. "No, but I could get you something."

"That would be a kindness."

Ella hesitated. Seraphs were dangerous creatures with blackened hearts, but without its wings did it still have the means to cause her harm?

"You are in no danger from me, child. I have been restrained." The Seraph held up a length of rope. Papa had fastened it around the winged man's neck and secured it to one of the barn's timbers.

Ella bit her lip, unnerved by its response to her unspoken thoughts, but the Seraph's colors never wavered toward anger or deception, so she approached. With trembling hands, she applied the poultice around the broken shards of bone, wishing she could do more.

Lyrical light sang off its skin—except around the wounds, where gaping holes of yellow and black marred it. Touching this other-worldly creature was difficult. The clash of clean and dirty colors riled up the fear inside of her, but what Papa had done to its wings made her chest ache. She wrapped the area in strips of clean cloth. "It's done now."

"May I face you?" the Seraph asked.

Ella nodded, too nervous for words. Again, the creature somehow knew of her affirmation. She moved back as the Seraph turned over. Its movements were fluid and unflinching, like water poured from a fountain. Up close its face was human enough, smooth forehead, delicate nose—all except for those galaxy-eyes.

Ella found herself caught in them again and unexpected fond memories swelled in her: riding her brown and blond Shetland pony through Papa's fields; Cord working next to Papa, making silly faces at her to get her to laugh; tall stalks of wheat dancing around her like waves of a golden ocean; Mama singing in notes of sea green as she rolled biscuits for supper.

The Seraph's voice pulled her back. "You have clouds in your eyes."

Heat licked along Ella's skin beneath the collar of her cotton tunic. *No she didn't.* She turned her face away.

The Seraph sat up, movements graceful, but clearly pained. "Do you see me? My essence?"

Ella stayed quiet. She did not speak to anyone about her Sight—the way the colorful world waltzed around her.

"I see yours," the Seraph said.

Ella's heartbeat fluttered against her ribs like a battering of butterfly wings. Though she could not see herself the way she saw others, she must have her own colors. Mama's had been pale green dappled with brilliant blushes of pink that had turned gray from the thunderstorm clouds of sadness shrouding her after Cord's death. And Papa, whose colors once shone in the emerald greens and glowing golds of a man who worked the land, had faded into the frosty pale blue of abysmal pain. Every once in a while, when he held Mama's hand, Ella would catch a flash of that old color on him—sparkles of sunshine yellow would mist around his chest, though never enough to thaw the cold completely.

"I can see you," Ella blurted, then covered her mouth.

The Seraph tilted its head. "How, I wonder?"

Ella smiled shyly behind her hand. "You cast rainbow shadows."

The Seraph nodded, a smile flickering on its lips.

"Do you eat?" Ella asked. "I can make you something."

"Water and food would be a kindness."

Ella turned to leave.

"Nothing with flesh in it," the Seraph added, pale distaste coloring its words.

Ella nodded and left the barn. She returned a while later with a bowl of turnip and thyme stew cradled in the crook of her arm, a few drops of laudanum added to help with the Seraph's pain, and a small jug of water. The creature took the food and began to eat.

She made to leave the Seraph with its meal, but at the stall opening, spun on her heel. Ella had gathered all her courage to come out here, not only to bind its wounds or feed it, but to find out … "I want to know."

"The answer to which question?" the Seraph asked.

Ella dug a tooth into her lip. She had so many that needed answers. "Why did you kill my brother?"

"I did not," the Seraph said through mouthfuls of stew.

Frustration and pain erupted in Ella. "My Papa believes that you did. Why would he, if there was no truth to it?" She banged balled-up hands on her thighs. "I *need* to know. My family is broken because of this!"

The Seraph stopped, as if suddenly aware of its seeming indifference, the spoon halfway to its mouth. It returned the spoon to the bowl and set them on the ground. "Your brother was not killed by one of us."

"You were there, over the woods where Cord's body was found. The village folk saw you. My people often see yours at the moment of our deaths."

"We are only guides. One of my kind arrived to assist your brother across the threshold, but we did not harm him. We mourn the loss of any Magicis."

Hot tears leaked from Ella's eyes. "What do you mean, Magicis?"

"A human that possesses a spark of the divine. They have the ability to see beyond this earthly plane, into a world where much more is possible. It is what attracts us to your kind. Your brother had—"

"You lie!" Ella was in front of the Seraph before it could blink twice. She kicked the bowl of stew over, splashing turnip chunks onto its legs. "Papa said a winged man killed him. *You* killed Cord!" Ella couldn't stomach the thought that Papa might have tortured an innocent being. That couldn't be what had happened. She raised a fist, intending with every fiber of her being to smash it into the thing's lying mouth.

The Seraph leaned back, eyes closed, its cheek turned to meet her wrath.

Ella's fist wavered. She lowered her hand. In expectation of being hit, the Seraph's color had changed. Not to one of anger—bashed in reds—but into silver threads that streamed from its chest up around its head. They curled and knotted in on themselves like a twisted crown. Ella had seen this color before, on the village folk after Cord's funeral; it was the color of compassion.

Ella shivered as though she'd been plunged into a mountain stream so cold it crushed the breath from her. She staggered back. Her legs gave way and she fell in the straw.

"His love for the girl was not the only reason he ran away that night," the Seraph said.

"Shut up," Ella croaked.

"You asked—"

"For answers, not lies!"

"Did you not see it on him yourself?" the Seraph asked.

Waves of anger and sorrow flooded through her, so big she felt her body might crack apart. "The colors, they were so new then, I didn't …" Ella hid her face in her hands as memories she'd pushed down returned.

In the last year of her brother's life, his colors had begun to change from forest-greens and playful peeks of apricot, into a soft shifting curtain of hues she did not comprehend. Ella thought it was his love for Daisy showing through. She hadn't understood then that something in him was emerging.

"If it wasn't you, then who killed my brother?"

The Seraph blinked, and lights like falling stars fell across the blacks of its eyes. "The girl's father."

Ella gasped. "Mr. Thomas?"

"He caught your brother with his daughter."

"It's not true. It can't be. He was at Cord's funeral."

"You see my words. You know I do not lie."

Ella did know. The color of lies was a sickly brown, like faded dirt baked in the sun until dull and lifeless.

"And, Daisy—she knows?"

The Seraph lifted a shoulder. "I could not say." Its eyelids drooped and its head bobbed, no doubt from the laudanum making its way through its system.

Ella nodded as this truth seeped in. Then she pulled her knees to her chest and wept. The Seraph rested a gentle hand on her shoulder, offering a comfort she'd gone so long without.

When Ella had let out enough sorrow to breathe again, she wiped her face. "Papa, if I tell him—he won't believe me. I have no proof but the colors I see on you."

"I understand." The Seraph struggled to keep its eyes open, and its voice grew quiet. "He is as the people in the village. In building a sanctuary to hide from their fears, they have created a prison instead. They cannot see beyond their walls."

"That must be why Cord left. Papa would never accept us if he knew."

The Seraph considered this, nodded, then laid down gingerly on the cot. Its eyes drifted shut.

Ella sighed. There would be no more answers tonight. She locked the stall and quietly pulled the barn door closed behind her.

Uneasiness settled like a stone in her belly as she trudged across the field to the cottage. She brushed her palms along the lavender and heather, lifting their scent into the air—a perfume of purple—to calm her.

She was so close to having Papa back. He needed only justice to seal the wound in his heart. Somehow, she must convince him the Seraph hadn't killed Cord. But how, without giving herself away as—what had the Seraph called her?—a Magicis? And what if she couldn't? Would she stand by and let him kill an innocent creature? A creature drawn here, like a moth to a flame, because of her.

✿

After a night of tossing and fretting, Ella rose weary. Outside her bedroom window, the morning looked the same as she felt, shrouded in mist and full of rain. She dressed warmly in a wool tunic and pants and went to prepare breakfast.

Mama stood in the kitchen, her hands covered in flour, kneading the morning bread and singing a song in *Hen Gymraeg*, the old tongue, meant to chase away the rainy day. Her gray was gone. She was covered in moss-green trimmed at the edges by pale pink.

"Mama!" Ella called.

Mama turned, a smile on her face. "Good morning, Ella dear. Breakfast will be on soon. Go and fetch me some eggs, would you?"

Her mother's eyes were clear and bright as the hues humming around her, and she had used Ella's name, recognized her.

Ella choked on the sob welling in her throat. "Mama." She hurried into the kitchen, wrapped her arms around her mother's waist, and buried her face in Mama's blouse. Her mother smelled of flour and rose water.

"My darling, what's gotten into you?" Mama wiped her hands on the sides of her apron, then stroked Ella's hair. "Oh, honey, come now. Sit down." She ushered Ella into a chair at the dining table and grabbed her hand. Mama's touch was warm and gentle.

Ella dabbed her eyes on a sleeve. "I've missed you, is all."

"Missed me?" The colors on Mama's skin deepened into a worried peach. "I've been here all morning."

"Has Papa returned?"

"He must be in the back field with Cord. They'll be in soon, I'm sure. Our boys wouldn't miss breakfast." Mama winked.

Ella had to push hard to get her words over the lump in her throat. *Cord.* Mama had spoken his name as if he were still alive. "No, Mama. Papa's gone into the village."

Mama's eyebrows shot up. "Has he, for what?"

"To seek council from the Elders, on how to …" Ella hesitated.

"To what, dear?"

"To kill the Seraph."

Mama frowned. "Why in creation's name would he want to do that?"

Ella couldn't bring herself to say Cord's name, afraid it would send her mother away again.

"One got caught on some ropes in the backyard. He aims to get rid of it."

"Oh, dear." Mama sighed. "That is a shame." She returned to the kitchen counter, a troubled look creasing her face. Her hands moved in rhythmic motions on the bread dough.

"What's a shame, Mama?"

"Have I ever told you about the girl from the village, Ella? The one with clouds in her eyes."

Of course Mama had, but never when she'd been aware like this. "I don't think so."

"I grew up with a girl called Agnes. As she got older, she began to change. Pale clouds appeared in her eyes, and she spoke of things …" Mama pressed into the dough—*push, pull.* When she spoke again, her voice was hoarse and fragile as gossamer strings of moon-glow on snow. "She came into my room one evening, weeping. The girls from school had cornered her on the way home. There were bruises on her skin and blood on her dress." Mama rolled the dough up, slapped it onto the floured counter, then leaned into it—*push, pull, roll, slap.* "My mother was teaching me about healing, so I mixed up what I knew and tended to her as best I could." *Push, pull, dig, push, pull.*

"That night, I begged her to leave the village. When the Elders found out the girls had attacked her, they would find out why as well. Their fear that Agnes would bring the Seraphs down on our heads would have been too great to ignore, and they might have …" Mama stopped kneading and stared out the window at the mountains.

Ella came and leaned on the counter next to her mother. "What happened to her?"

"My family kept a small cabin out by the Salt-Cliffs that overlook the Mad Sea, and I … well, there was no other choice." Tears clung to her mother's cheeks. "I sent my sister away."

Ella's eyes went wide. "Agnes was your sister?"

Mama nodded. "I have missed her every day since. You remind me so much of her, El. It does my heart good." She smiled at Ella as tears trickled across her lips. "I can tell you, if there was a Seraph in the yard, it did not get tangled in loose ropes. It came for a reason."

Mama's words lingered, bright swatches of lemon-silver in the air. Ella had no clouds in her eyes to give her away, but she wondered how much her mother knew—about her, maybe even about Cord.

"Papa wants it dead," Ella said. How could she explain why the Seraph needed to die, for Papa's sanity, without treading into the risky territory of terrible memories?

"I love your father dearly. He is a good man with a kind heart, but when it comes to things he does not understand, he feels the same to me as those schoolgirls did. People like her are mysteries to plain folk, and where there is a mystery there will be a story told to explain it, true or not. Sometimes those stories take root and become superstitions." Mama clucked her tongue. "Deadly things."

She turned away to stoke the coals in the wood-stove. "Go and do your chores, El, before your father and Cord come in, and bring me those eggs when you're done."

Gratitude and affection spilled through Ella. She wrapped her arms around her mother and squeezed. "I will, Mama."

Mama laughed, a beautiful sound wrapped in cinnamon notes. Ella kissed her on the cheek and ran from the cottage, her uncertainty gone. She knew what to do.

Papa would be upset at first, but when he found his wife with life in her eyes again, all would be forgiven. Mama was back. She'd come back to them. And wasn't that the healing Papa had needed all along?

Would she disappear into her grief again after she found out about Cord? Ella shook her head. She couldn't think about that. Surely there was a reason Mama came back to them this day.

Ella ran through the field. Rain slipped from the sky, pattering onto her face and shoulders. Her heart hammered with love for her family, and with hope—perhaps broken things could be mended after all. She laughed with her mouth wide open, catching raindrops as they fell. One day, with Mama's help, Ella would tell her father everything. Then he would understand and accept her not just as his daughter, but as a girl possessed of magic.

✧

Ella dashed into the barn. She would set the Seraph free before Papa returned and spare them all more bloodshed.

The Seraph sat on the edge of the cot as though waiting for her. He watched her haul two large burlap sacks from an adjoining stall and take the wings from them.

Ella used an old pair of shears to cut through the rope around the Seraph's neck, then removed the bandages from his back. She was shocked to see how fast his injuries had healed. The skin around the wounds no longer echoed of sickly green but had already faded back to its natural iridescence. Ella dragged the wings over to the Seraph—they were heavier than she expected, for something that could lift someone into flight toward the heavens—and with no small feat of sweat and tears, she fit the broken ends of bone back together, like mending jagged shards of shattered pottery. She wound long lengths of cloth smeared with resin around the new joins, then tied them off and stood back, wiping sticky hands on her pants. "Will they heal?"

"In time, yes. There is magic in your hands—just like your Mama's." The Seraph rubbed his feet in the dirt, a small smile on his lips. "I will have to walk until then."

"Ella Marie!" Papa's voice crashed into the back of her head. She jumped and spun to face him.

Pops of angry red flared off him. "What in the hell are you doing?"

"I was … I think we …." She straightened her back, unconsciously blocking the Seraph from her Papa's view. "We've made a mistake."

"Blessed be, I left you alone with it and …." His voice dropped to a growl. "What has that thing done to you?"

Ella's stomach churned with fear for the Seraph— fear for her Papa. "He's not what you think."

Her father marched across the barn, fumbled between bales of hay and pulled out his hatchet. "Move out of the way." His words dripped from his mouth in amber hues laced with ebony-ink bitterness. He stared at the Seraph. "I don't care the Elders say your kind can't be killed. I'll take you apart piece by piece!" He raised the hatchet and tried to move around his daughter.

Ella hands raised her hands to halt him as she stepped between the Seraph and her father. Fear wrapped icy hands around her backbone, and her voice shook when she spoke. "Papa, *stop.*"

Her father's color twisted in spirals of orange surprise. He froze, the gray-lipped blade hanging in the air.

"He didn't kill Cord."

Papa blinked at the use of Cord's name. He had not spoken his son's name since he'd thrown the first handful of dirt onto Cord's plain pine coffin. Hints of green and gold flared from Papa's chest. He lowered the hatchet.

"The village watchman. It was him—" Ella broke off, unable to bring herself to say the words.

Papa wasn't stupid. "How could you know that?" he asked, eyes intent.

Ella swallowed hard. Her pulse beat in her temples, blurring her vision. "Because, he told me. The Seraph."

Her father's jaw clenched. The bright colors on his chest simmered back to a hoar blue.

"A Seraph *was* with Cord that night," Ella said, "but only to guide him to his final resting place *after* he was mortally injured."

Papa's hand tightened on the handle of his hatchet, the blade wavering.

"Mr. Thomas caught Cord trying to leave with Daisy and then—"

"Thomas?!" Papa yelled.

"I … I … don't think …" the words jumbled in Ella's mouth. "Maybe … he didn't mean to …. Maybe he only meant to scare—"

"It would have you think one of my oldest friends did this?"

"Please, listen. Cord woke me that night. He told me he was going to the Capital with Daisy." Ella glanced back at the Seraph, hesitating. He stood watching, his wings unfolded, feathers draped across the straw. She firmed her resolve. "I can see the Seraph speaks the truth."

"You can *see*?" Papa blinked. "You mean … the Sight? You're one of *them*? Possessed."

"No, Papa, I'm not. I'm your daughter." Ella reached forward, laid a hand on her father's arm. Her fingers tingled.

Colors rippled on her father's skin—circles of rancid green that moved outward from her fingertips in waves of scarlet black—the same colors she'd seen on him when he'd severed the Seraph's wings.

Ella snatched her hand back as though she'd grazed hot iron. His knuckles were white around the hatchet's handle.

"Papa, please. Don't do anything you'll regret."

"Regret? You've allowed yourself to be tainted by wickedness while my son …. He was perfect." Papa swallowed hard. "The only thing I regret"—rancid green leaked from the corners of his mouth like froth from a rabid dog—"is that the wrong child died last summer."

Papa may as well have buried the blade of his hatchet deep into her chest. Ella's mouth fell open.

Movement behind her father pulled her attention over his shoulder, to the barn door.

Papa turned to look. The hatchet dropped from his hand. "Margaret, what are you doing out here?"

Mama stood in the doorway. Rain had matted her hair flat, drops glittered on her cheeks—and, to Ella's eyes, those familiar charcoal whispers streamed around Mama's head like a shroud.

Relief crashed into Ella. "Oh, Mama, thank heaven. Papa knows. You must tell him what we talked about this morning. Tell him about Agnes."

Mama's brow creased, confusion and the ravages of grief marring her features. "Something in the stove is burning, and I haven't had my breakfast yet. Will you be long, child?"

Ella's chest tightened. Pinpricks of heat stung the back of her eyes. Her Mama was lost again. Words fell from Ella's mouth in a crushed whisper. Just one. "No," was all her heart could manage.

Mama's gaze moved from Ella to Papa, then flickered over to the Seraph. Her jaw dropped. "Wha—wha—?" she pointed a finger. Her bottom lip trembled, and she began to scream.

Papa rushed to her, turned her away from the sight of the winged man. "Come, my darling. You shouldn't be out here."

"That's not a fish," Mama said. "You haven't been fishing. Where's Cord?" She beat weak fists against Papa's chest, trying to get out of his grasp. "Put it back. Back in the water!"

"I will, Margaret. *Shhh, shhh,*" Papa soothed, curls of concerned carnelian on his lips. He looked back at Ella. "Take your mother into the house, now."

Ella's knees wobbled, but she could not make her legs move.

"*Now,* Ella Marie. I will deal with you when my business out here is finished." His eyes lingered on the hatchet laying in the straw, then moved to the Seraph.

A wing brushed Ella's arm. Heat trickled along her skin and sank into her bones. She took a deep breath. Her knees steadied, and she stepped forward. "No."

Papa stared at her; his teeth gritted.

"Throw it back!" Mama cried.

Papa turned his attention to his wife and held her close.

As Ella watched her mother weep against Papa's chest, a blush of pink glimmered along the streams of gray draped around Mama's chest. Ella wanted to join them, to hug her mother the way she had that morning. She wanted to beg her father to turn the Seraph loose and come back to their family whole again.

Ella worked at her bottom lip with her teeth. Had Mama been watching at the kitchen window when Papa returned? She must have known the truth Ella refused to acknowledge—that Papa's mind would not be changed. Maybe Mama had come out here to send Ella away, the way she'd sent Agnes, and those thunderstorm clouds of gray sadness had come rumbling back into her broken heart—too many things lost.

Ella knew what to do. She cleared her throat. "We must set the Seraph free. It's the only thing that will calm Mama down."

Her father sneered, all the care gone from his face.

Mama yelled again. "Something is burning! Throw the fish back! The stove is on fire!" She yanked on his arms.

Papa looked toward the cottage. His eyes widened at the sight of black smoke trickling from the kitchen window. He clenched his jaw. The rancid-scarlet-black on his skin grew, sliding down his arms and legs, devouring him. When he spoke again, he would not meet Ella's gaze. "If that thing walks off my land, you go with it."

N*ever to return,* Ella finished the line she'd heard so many times before.

Papa led Mama into the rain and hurried toward the smoke-filled cottage.

Ella stood there a moment, breathing in the smell of alfalfa hay, sweet and green. She clutched the sides of her pants, fists twisting in the fabric. Cord was gone. Mama was gone. And Papa—wasn't coming back. None of them ever would. Sometimes things did just break and could not be mended.

Ella reached out and slipped her fingers into the Seraph's waiting hand.

✿

Ella and the Seraph walked down the foot-worn path through the heather that led off the farm. The sun hid behind silver clouds that wept rain on them. She looked back only once.

Papa stood on the porch, watching them go, his color as blue gray as the misty morning. Next to the house, a cluster of goats huddled beneath her favorite oak tree, its branches a shelter from the storm. How she envied them.

Ella's clothes were soaked through. She shivered and leaned against the Seraph's body. The Seraph winced as he stretched a wing over her head.

"Where will we go, Seraph?"

"I have a friend, who I think will be glad to know you."

Ella peered past the sunlight-tinted feathers, into the Seraph's face. "Your friend will welcome me?"

"Yes," the Seraph said.

"Who is this person?"

"Her name is Agnes—"

"My aunt!" Ella's feet tangled together, and she stumbled. The Seraph caught her in the cup of his wing.

"What? How? I—"

"She asked me to come," the Seraph said.

"But we trapped you." Ella's voice went quiet. "We hurt you."

The Seraph smiled, a slight thing that hardly turned the corners of his mouth, yet made his eyes shine with starlight. "You cannot catch one of us that does not want to be caught, and I am unharmed. I came to you in the only way you would accept me—as something broken and in need of mending."

Ella shook her head. With every answer she received from the Seraph, a new question appeared.

A flash of lightning, made of watercolor-fire wrapped in satin strips of gold, sizzled through the gloomy sky. The clap of thunder that followed rolled out in peals of ocean-tormented teal, trailing ribbons of tangerine stars.

Ella's heart fluttered. She knew those colors. They were the same ones she'd seen on Cord as he came into his magic. Perhaps in time she would be strong enough to return and seek justice for her brother's death. At least Papa knew the truth now and, like Ella, it was his decision what to do with it.

Silken feathers brushed against her cheek in the breeze. She turned her attention to the road ahead. Beyond the edges of the storm, the light was clear and bright over the Plum-Shaded Mountains. Ella was headed there, to a cabin by the Salt-Crusted Cliffs—a kiss for her aunt from Mama on her lips, and the color of thunder shimmering on her skin.

Copyright © 2022 by Alicia Cay.

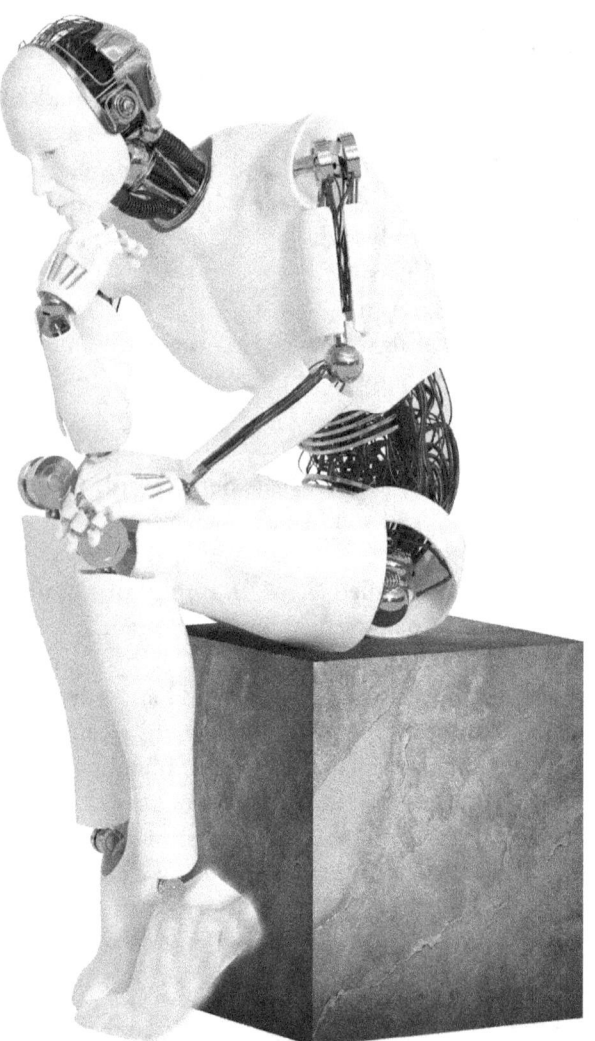

Jean Marie Ward writes fiction, nonfiction and everything in between. Her credits include a multi-award nominated novel, numerous short stories and two popular art books. The former editor of CrescentBlues.com, she is a frequent contributor to Galaxy's Edge *and ConTinual, the convention that never ends. Learn more at JeanMarieWard.com*

THE SNARKY SIREN CALL OF ADVENTURE: *GALAXY'S EDGE* INTERVIEWS MARTHA WELLS

by Jean Marie Ward

*I*t was the siren call of action and adventure—adventure in which girls could share—that first drew the young Martha Wells from the children's section to the science fiction and fantasy shelves of her local Fort Worth library. College courses in anthropology added cultural insights and a new lens for viewing characters in a story. Her fantasy series about the faerie-touched Gallic civilization of Ile-Rien and the caste-bound shapeshifters of The Books of the Raksura won praise for their astute worldbuilding, inventiveness, and bravura thrills. But it was penning the exploits of a snarky cyborg Security Unit in corporate space that made her a bestseller and multi-award winner. Now readers await Murderbot's next adventure with the same avid anticipation Murderbot itself approaches a new download of its favorite entertainment videos. Catching up with Wells not long after she won the 2021 Hugo Award for Best Novel (Network Effect) and Best Series (The Murderbot Diaries), Galaxy's Edge talked to Wells about her journey from science fiction and fantasy fan to fan favorite. Along the way, she shared her thoughts about getting inside the head of a non-human character, crafting exciting and elaborate fight scenes, and what she wants the world to know about Murderbot. Yes, we asked what's next for our favorite SecUnit. We're fans too.

Galaxy's Edge: You said that you were always a reader. When did you realize you wanted to become a writer?

Martha Wells: Really early on. I remember telling my parents when I was in high school that I wanted to be a writer and them not having much reaction to it. At the time, I think I wanted to major in journalism when I went to the university, because that was the only way I could conceive of being a writer at that point. I didn't know how you went about being a fiction writer. That's not something I figured out until I went to Texas A&M and took a writing workshop with Steven Gould and started going to conventions and learning about how you actually do become a fiction writer.

GE: You just mentioned conventions, which is a great lead into my next question: What role did fandom and fan fiction play in your journey to publication?

MW: A huge, huge role, because the reason I picked Texas A&M University was they had a student science fiction and fantasy group. I'm not sure I knew at that point that they also ran conventions. I'd actually been to ArmadilloCon in Austin when I was in high school. I somehow convinced my parents to take me and a friend down there to go to this convention—ArmadilloCon—on Saturday. This was back when it was teeny tiny—the dealer's room was basically the size of a hotel room. And that really made me want to continue to see conventions.

Also, the friendship and the people I met working on the student convention, AggieCon, were hugely important to me. I'd been reading fanfic for a while. I think I discovered it probably around 1983, I think … no, it was 1980 when *Empire Strikes Back* came out. So, I'd been reading fanfic for a while already and trying to write … I was first starting to write when I was in high school and college. I worked on fanfic and met a lot of people in fandom through that too. It was hugely important for me.

GE: And you ran AggieCon at least one year.

MW: Yeah, I worked on it for the whole four years I was in college and the last year I [chaired it]. I believe it was 1986. It's been so long.

GE: That's what it said in Wikipedia.

MW: Yeah, I was running the convention. And it was great. It was a huge learning experience. It was exhausting and incredibly stressful and anxiety-inducing. But later on, you're like, "Yeah, that was really great."

GE: I would imagine it gave you an interesting perspective on conventions and the business of conventions from a writer's standpoint.

MW: I think it did. It also let me meet a lot of writers and hear a lot about publishing and a lot of discussions about the technical and creative aspects of writing and how everything worked. That was really important.

GE: What influence did your college major, anthropology, have on your first novel, *The Element of Fire*, and subsequent works?

MW: I think it's had an influence on a lot of my work because of the worldbuilding. Being able to look at how cultures develop over time and the things that go wrong, and looking at the material culture of a city or a civilization and trying to take a holistic approach to worldbuilding and all the things that you have to know—even if you don't put them on the page—about how your city works, your culture works, all those things, that was hugely helpful to me.

GE: I imagine, especially when you're dealing with non-human characters such as those in The Books of the Raksura, that knowing how the pieces fit, sociologically speaking, would be a great help.

MW: Yeah, and the kind of things the people would have when you're dealing with an alien character. What kind of culture would create that character? What does that mean? What's important to them? What kind of material goods would they have? What does where they live look like? What kind of environment would this be happening in? All that kind of stuff.

GE: You have incredible worldbuilding in all your series, whether it be Ile-Rien's early industrial culture, the worlds of the Raksura, and of course, the Murderbot Diaries. Is anthropology the secret to that, or is there something else?

MW: I think it's your character point of view, and really thinking, trying basically to run their software on your hardware, and trying to really see things through their eyes and what is important to them, what do they want to do, how has their world shaped them. I think that's the key.

GE: You've mentioned in various interviews that you're not athletic, yet you create these very complex and brutal fight scenes. In The Murderbot Diaries you literally have multiple points of view in a single character's head, because Murderbot is pulling in all of these feeds from drones, from artificial intelligences, anything that it can, in real time. So, the reader sees the action from a lot of viewpoints, and they're all very, very intense. How do you as somebody who has, essentially, one point of view, deal with that? How do you deal with being a relatively peaceable woman who doesn't go out and commit mayhem, whether in a dojo or in real life? How do you create these battle scenes?

MW: Well, I watch a lot of TV and movies, and I pay a lot of attention to fight scenes. Actually, when I was younger, I did take tae kwon do, and I did fencing for a little bit. It's not something I can do anymore, though I try to exercise. When we're not in a pandemic, I can actually go to the gym and things like that. But again, it's the character point of view, getting the physicality of the character in your head and what they can and can't do. Also, the parameters of the fight as you have set them for yourself, like a sword fight or a knife fight. A fistfight is so very different from a fight where the characters are actually armed with some kind of weapon, especially a single-shot weapon or an automatic weapon. Or like Murderbot when it can bring in all these different views of the scene and can use all these different ways to attack whoever is attacking it.

So yeah, just keeping all that straight and, again, really getting into the [character's] point of view and thinking about that. That's one of the reasons Murderbot often takes a long time to write. Having to do those multiple viewpoints is really complicated and often takes a long time to put together. Just the logistics of the stories are very different from any other kind of logistics for the other things I've writ-

ten. Even though I mostly write adventure fiction, Murderbot is just so much more complicated in what happens, even though it might not feel that way to the reader. And yeah, watching a lot of TV and movies and watching people … watching fight scenes for years and years, and looking at what people do, and what it's possible to do. That's another fun thing about Murderbot: you can have the character do a lot of things that's not possible for a human to do or even an alien character to do. That's basically it.

GE: And Murderbot can take a lot of damage that an entirely organic being cannot do and remain itself. Speaking of Murderbot and its abilities, you worked in software development for a while. What role did your professional experience in software development play in the creation of The Murderbot Diaries and the development of Murderbot's personality, abilities, and outlook?

MW: It played a big role because that was my primary experience with IT when I worked there. A lot of people think that I must know a lot about artificial intelligence. I don't know anything about real AI. What I know about is the fake AI I invent for my books. But the way Murderbot often solves problems, answers questions, and solves mysteries is usually by manipulating data, which is one of the things I did when I worked for … well, I don't want to name them. But when I worked in IT. I built databases and wrote programs—in COBOL, that's how long ago it was—for databases for user interfaces, basically. So Murderbot uses that a lot to solve problems, and that's the viewpoint I try to look at it from. I think that's one reason why people think the character feels realistic as a machine intelligence, because it does look at things in terms of: What is the data we have? How can it be manipulated to give us answers?

GE: Murderbot and a lot of your characters are outliers and odd persons out. What draws you to characters who are isolated or find themselves in this position?

MW: I was a really isolated little kid. I probably have some still undiagnosed issues that back then people just didn't understand or have any concept of. It made me live in my head a lot. I have a sister who's nine years older than me, so there was usually nobody around my age. Where we lived there were no other kids on our street. There were some nearby, but the way the traffic was and where we lived and everything, it's not like I could go out and play with kids every day like a lot of people were able to in other neighborhoods. So just feeling very different, always feeling very different and isolated, is just something that I'm still dealing with all my life. I guess you just get it kind of imprinted on your consciousness early, and it's not something that never leaves you.

GE: It's something we can all relate to. At some point, I don't care how extroverted you are, you will be alone and say to yourself, "What do I do now? Where am I? Who am I? And how do I fit in? How can this square object fit into these round holes that everybody else is fitting in?"

MW: Pretty much so.

GE: While we're still, more or less, on the subject of Murderbot, is there anything that you want people to take away from the series? What do you want them to know about it?

MW: One of the things I noticed people get wrong a lot—and I think that's because it gets reprinted in reviews and things—is that Murderbot did not have consciousness before it hacked its governor module somehow. And it's like no, all the SecUnits are conscious. I was trying to make that clear in *Network Effect*. They're all conscious, all the time. It's just that they're enslaved. They're mentally enslaved, and there's not much they can do that we know without activating the governor module and getting killed, basically. And it is slavery. I've also seen reviews try to argue that somehow the humans are nice to them, and it's not slavery. It's like no, it absolutely is. It's intentional. That's what it is.

GE: It's rather like that line from *The Twelve Chairs*, "My master, Ippolit Matveyevich Vorobyaninov. He was a Marshal of the nobility. I loved him. He hardly ever beat us."

MW: Yeah. Also in *Thor: Ragnarok*, the prisoners with jobs.

GE: That notion seems to be really hard for some people to understand for some reason. Personally, I cannot imagine how you can lack consciousness and still hack your governor module. To me, the question was a non-issue. Since the SecUnits were, for want of a better term, conscious entities, it was obvious this was some kind enslavement.

Martha Wells: It's a mental gymnastics that people do and it's just … I don't know why people don't want to admit that human beings enslave other human beings and would continue to do that if allowed to. I don't know why they're willfully blind on that point. Looking at history, or current affairs, or anything would seem to, you know, get [that point] through to them. But no.

GE: You just won the Hugo Award for Best Novel and Best Series. This is just one little cluster in the many, many awards you've been nominated for or won throughout your career in science fiction and fantasy. How important are awards for the career of a writer in science fiction, fantasy, or any genre?

MW: Actually, before Murderbot, I'd only been nominated for a Nebula Award. That was for *The Death of the Necromancer*, and you know, I didn't win.

GE: You were nominated for the Compton Crook and Crawford Awards for *The Element of Fire*.

MW: Yeah, I guess I should say I've only been nominated for one major award. I did get nominations of some other minor ones, but only a few really. Before Murderbot, I was pretty much off the radar as far as awards were concerned, which is fine. I never thought I would even have a chance at being on the Hugo ballot, let alone revel in the Hugo long list, let alone, you know, win them. I think it's kind of hard to say how much impact they have. They do have, I think, a big impact within the genres in how people see you.

I think the impact of the Hugo Awards has changed a lot in the past ten years or so, since more people started to get supporting memberships so they could nominate, and we started having a more diverse ballot that better reflected what people were actually reading and what people were considering was the cutting edge of science fiction and fantasy. So, I think it's had more impact since then.

I think there is what's known—especially for the novels—as a bump in sales from just being on something like the Hugo ballot or the Nebula ballot. For me, the biggest impact was validation of 25 years or however many years of work to get to this point. It was a validation of the fact that I didn't give up when it would have been really easy and probably smart to, at certain points, just go get a different job. So, it was hugely important to me personally, and I think it's made a big change in how I'm treated just in fandom and the genre.

There are some exceptions, but usually women my age who are still trying to be working writers are not treated very well, either at conventions or in general in the genre, because we're fading out and so need to not clutter up the landscape by still existing and still writing. It'll be interesting to see what happens after this. I haven't seen much .... Because of the pandemic, of course, everything's just slowed down. So, we're not gathering at conventions and events and things like that.

But, yeah, most of the impact has been personal, I would think. You kind of can't measure other ways. The publisher can probably answer a lot more accurately about [the effect on] sales and things like that.

GE: Increased sales are good, and validation and recognition are also good. Speaking of good things, in 2021 you signed a six-book contract with Tor, which will include at least three more entries in The Murderbot Diaries. The first announced title in the contract is a second-world fantasy called *Witch King*. Can you tell us anything about *Witch King*, and what's next for Murderbot?

MW: It is a completely new secondary world fantasy, kind of epic in scope. It's my take on epic worldbuilding, and I was trying to do something different with it. Hopefully, people will like it. It's going to come out in 2023. It was originally intended for this year, but it's gotten pushed back because of everything that was going on. The book was actually finished late last year, but I'm working on the revision right now. Hopefully, everybody will enjoy it.

GE: I'm looking forward to it. Human characters or non-human characters?

MW: A mix of both. Again, it's a different world from anything I've done before, with a mix of kind of humans and magical humans, like demons and other different types. It should be a lot of fun.

GE: Cool! Finally, the soapbox question, is there anything you'd like to add? Anything you want to talk about?

MW: Probably Murderbot, because I am doing another Murderbot novel. I'm writing one right now. I see a lot of people asking about it. It's about halfway finished. It's due in the summer, so I should have it done by then. After this novel, there'll be at least one more novella and a novel, but I'm not sure what order they're in. They're going to take place after *Network Effect*. And in fact, this novella starts up right not very long after the end of *Network Effect*.

GE: Great! We're all going to be looking forward to that. Thank you very, very much.

Copyright © 2022 by Jean Marie Ward.

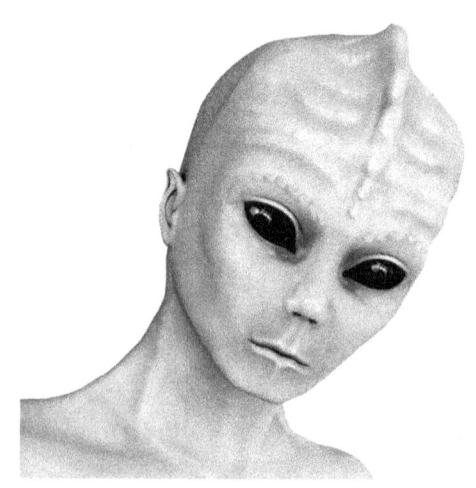

Richard Chwedyk sold his first story in 1990, won a Nebula in 2002, and has been active in the field for the past thirty-two years.

RECOMMENDED BOOKS

by Richard Chwedyk

LIVING IN AN AGE OF STORIES

It may not seem a great consolation in a world rampant with war, despair, natural disasters, catastrophes, overlords and diminishing liberties, but we are living in a great age of story. Those among you who may not remember the last century well may not understand. The last century, in many ways, was not kind to story, even tried to do away with it. Had it been more successful, our current condition would be intolerable. Story was pushed to the edge of the precipice, but it didn't fall. Not only did it not fall, it endured. It grew. It changed.

Story is a living thing, and at times we fail to recognize it as we sometimes fail to recognize old school friends whom we haven't seen in many years. They're the same, though they're not. Scholars and critics get hung up trying to explain the ways of story and provide an impressive taxonomy to examine and define it.

Stories aren't to be defined, though. It works the other way round. They define *us*.

As the works considered below endeavor to prove.

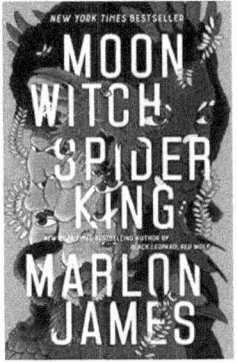

Moon Witch, Spider King
by Marlon James
Riverhead Books
March 2022
ISBN: 978-0-7352-2020-1

This is the second novel in a trilogy. I always seem to be boarding a train in mid-journey when it comes to these things, but I can't say I felt lost in the telling at any point. Nevertheless, I wasted no time in purchasing the first volume, *Black Leopard, Red Wolf*, because I wanted to see how these two novels fit together. That is a great credit to the author. The two novels are distinct and can be read on their own, and leave me all the more curious about the third volume.

There's been much discussion about what James may be intending with this trilogy. It's been called an "African *Game of Thrones*" and an effort to forge an epic fantasy can stand next to Tolkien's efforts to create a new mythology built from elements of significant, extant models.

Echoes of previous fantasy epics are here: the pursuit of power by dark forces, powerful warriors standing up to the threat, mysterious wielders of magical powers, and a search—a quest—for a child who is most likely the key to the world's salvation. What's more, we have maps—lots and lots of maps drawn by the author (how much more Tolkien can you get?), And yet all this is effectively reimagined. It's not so much matter of what story is being told as how the story is told—and who happens to be telling it.

Black Leopard, Red Wolf was told from the perspective of Tracker, the mercenary hunter hired to find the lost boy. *Moon Witch, Spider King* is told in the voice of Sogolon, the witch, a significant character in the first novel but for whom Tracker has, to say the least, very little respect. Her version of events described in the first novel are distinctly different, but the heart of the story here has more to do with Sogolon's early life and upbringing, and how she got to where we find her in the first novel. It wasn't an easy life, and by no means a short one (she is 177 by some accounts) and James does not spare his readers in presenting the graphic details. In such matters the comparisons with George R. R. Martin's work make sense. But James has his own way depicting these explosions of violence and sex. They're hyperactively kinetic in an operatic way. One gets the sense, in both novels, that what we're seeing is not so much the "real" scenes and events as the emotional landscape of the viewpoint characters. It isn't the style one expects in epic fantasy, but it hints at a matter that's been much discussed in fantasy circles of recent: there's more than one way to see a fantasy epic. The villains in one version may be the heroes in their own version.

Readers of traditional fantasy may find all this disconcerting. They value clarity (if not brevity) in what they are given to see and in how the story progresses. James, in comparison, seems chaotic, with a vision inspired as much by Frank Frazetta and Jack Kirby as by Amos Tutuola. Fragmented as the narrative appears at times, one senses the presence of the story that directs it on its way.

For all the pyrotechnics in his milieu and in his style, it's the sense of immediacy that energizes James's story and keeps it compelling. In more traditional fantasy we may have encountered, for all the possibilities magic and the parameters of the "secondary world" have to offer, there's an implicit understanding that certain things can happen and other things cannot. In the world of *Moon Witch, Spider King*, all bets are off. From page to page we never know what to expect. This can be off-putting at times, but mostly it's thrilling.

Does it work in some greater sense? I think we'll have to wait for the final volume to see if James can bring it all together in a way that will make his trilogy stand out alongside other great fantasy epics. What we have so far makes it well worth the wait to find out.

◆◆◆

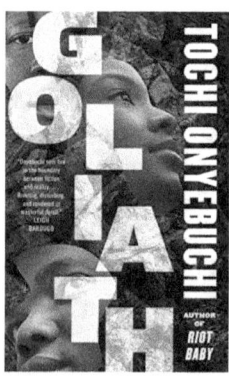

Goliath

by Tochi Onyebuchi
Tordotcom
Januay 2022
ISBN: 978-1-250-78295-3

Let me get this out of the way up front: this is a science fiction novel. And a very good one.

The reason I say this was that a while back I heard an interview with the author, Tochi Onyebuchi, on a public radio station. Author and interviewer discussed the novel intelligently and perceptively for almost ten minutes, which is a long time on any kind of radio. And for all that time neither author nor interviewer used the phrase with which you out there reading this magazine will be intimately familiar: science fiction.

They didn't even say "sci-fi."

I found that interesting. I was neither displeased nor relieved in some positive way. Just "interested."

It wasn't that Onyebuchi was claiming literary creds high above the categorical crudities and saying, "Please, don't confuse my novel with that *other* stuff!" Not at all. In other places, I discovered, he has no trouble with the term. Tor is his publisher. How much more "science fiction" can you get?

What struck me, I guess, was that it is possible yet in this so-messed-up-world of ours that we can talk about science fiction novels and science-fictional subject matter without resorting to the label "science fiction." Is this a good thing? Possibly. Any time we can talk about serious stuff and overlook conventional labels, it may mean we're perceived as being grown up enough as to be taken for granted. We can sit at the grownups table without everyone pointing out that we're sitting at the gownups table. Though I admit that when you put it that way, it doesn't sound so good after all. But that may be the strangeness of the thing. "Science fiction" sounds different when you remove the stigma.

But back to *Goliath*. It is good science fiction. Not so much for its "speculative" premises as for its extrapolative rigors. At its heart is a simple story about a couple trying to make a life for themselves in a strange world.

Strange—but not unfamiliar. It's possible to describe this novel as a story about the gentrification of the solar system. People in major U. S. urban areas have been familiar with the term "white flight" for over a century. A significant number of affluent families, mostly but not exclusively white, moved farther and farther out from the urban centers. Suburbs were apparently not far away enough, so we invented the term "exurbs."

When the exurbs weren't far enough, why not move entirely off planet? That's where the "colonies" come in.

The neat thing, for a "literary" science fiction novel, is that the tech that runs the colonies is fairly plausible. Onyebuchi has done his homework as well as any other science fiction writer I can think of, and that includes, with all due respect, Kim Stanley Robinson. Not only is the world building plausible, it is vivid. So vivid, in fact, that I must inform those who need "trigger warnings" that they will encounter much in this novel that isn't pleasant to read about. But to exclude those things would be untruthful to its vision.

The next thing that urban dwellers like me will find familiar but makes perfect sense in the world of this novel is that Earth, although wasted and polluted and plundered and ultimately abandoned by the "one percent" who can afford to move, it still contains salvageable bits and pieces, which enterprising folks on Earth and on the colonies are willing to exploit. There's a racked-up version of gentrification going on—ornaments and facades of torn-down buildings being salvaged and shipped off to adorn new structures, but at a colossal scale. One of the inspirations for this story, I think, comes from a Chicago practice of contractors buying up distinctive styles of brick from torn-down houses to use for new ones. It's grisly and macabre, sort of like building a suit of armor from the bones of your enemies, but in a world where most natural resources have already been depleted or rendered toxic, what else is left to be exploited for the remaining residents of Earth needing to make a living?

Some readers will think the story isn't "linear," and therefore hard to follow. In fact, the story is very linear. It's just not chronological. It is detailed. It is sharp and clear. It is passionate. It is human. What may strike some readers as difficult or hard to follow isn't necessarily the fault of its author. It's a new voice. Even for readers of Onyebuchi's YA work, this isn't the same

voice they've come to expect. And that's good. It compels us to look at our world, and the world we're soon approaching, in a new way, which is exactly what we should be looking for in a science fiction novel.

Those sincerely looking for that new way will find it here.

◆ ◆ ◆

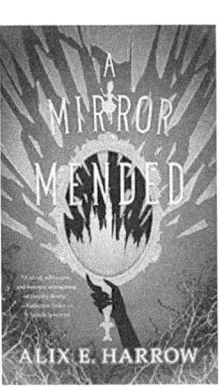

A Mirror Mended
by Alix E. Harrow
Tordotcom
June 2022
ISBN: 978-1-250-76664-9

I have found myself awaiting every new work by Alix E. Harrow ever since I first encountered her short story "A Witch's Guide to Escape: A Practical Compendium of Portal Fantasies" in a year's best anthology. It spoke to a number of issues concerning fantasy, fantasy writing and its appreciation by readers. It also cast its protagonist as a librarian *and* a witch, and in Harrow's world it only makes sense.

I have written on numerous occasions about the importance of voice in fiction. Not only do Harrow's works have great voices, but just the right pitch. When I first read "A Witch's Guide …" I immediately brought it to my fantasy writing class and there we read it aloud. Since then, I've been slipping it to other teachers and they have been passing it on to their own classes. It's a quiet conspiracy. It's what we who teach should be doing all the time.

And then *The Ten Thousand Doors of January* and *The Once and Future Witches* came out to great acclaim and award nominations. But what caught my attention was the novella published by Tordotcom, *A Spindle Splintered*, which has her protagonist Zinnia Gray, take on all the idiosyncrasies and inanities of the many legends and fairytales about Sleeping Beauty.

A Mirror Mended finds her taking on a similar quest with Snow White. Up to now, Zinnia has spent her time rescuing sleeping beauties from eternal repose. Now, she has been enlisted by the evil queen who was Snow White's nemesis. The queen's mirror has revealed her horrible end, and only Zinnia can save her from this doom. Or so she thinks.

> "And you think that's justice? That I should die dancing in-red hot shoes?" The queen's voice is trembling very slightly, her fingers curling into the wooden arms of her chair.
>
> "No, I mean, I'm not a capital punishment person—my mom's into the prison abolition movement" —she's into all kinds of activities these days, as if all the energy she'd been preserving to hate Big Energy on my behalf had been redistributed to every other modern supervillain— "but this feels like a 'live by the sword, die by the sword' situation, you know?
>
> The queen stares at me for a murderous moment, then closes her eyes. "Help me." I didn't think a whisper could sound so imperious.
>
> "If I were begging for my life, I might add a question mark and a 'please.'"
>
> Her eyes remain tightly shut, as if she fears she will throttle me if she sees my face. "Help me, please." She doesn't quite manage the question mark.
>
> I lean forward across the table, drawing out a long, vicious pause before I say, "Nah."

Eventually, Zinnia relents, and the story splinters out from there in strange and unpredictable ways.

It is awfully easy to become horrendously esoteric when writing stories about stories. It is also far too tempting to take the other route and shout "Hey! We all know it's a story anyway, so who cares?" Stories are serious business. But to be *that* serious about stories as to make one's discoveries that fiction is fiction and stories are stories appear profound is like gilding a lily already fossilized into aureate malarkey. Harrow has found some middle ground where she can address our need for stories and make it a good story in itself.

As much as this is a fun and captivating read, like all good fairytales it contains its measure of wisdom and humanity. It may to some appear brief and slight, but it's a story about stories for all time.

◆◆◆

Eridahn
by Robert F. Young
Del Rey
June 1983
ISBN: 0-345-30854-9

Let us now praise Robert F. Young.

In his time, which was from about 1953 until his death in 1986, he wrote some splendidly engaging short fiction, much of which I read in the pages of *The Magazine of Fantasy and Science Fiction*. But his work appeared in almost all the digests, and he even scored some sales to *Playboy* and *The Saturday Evening Post*. Much of the work was satirical, and he had a keen wit, but he also possessed a clear-headed view of the world, at once generous and magnanimous. Perhaps it was his undoing that he wrote in a time when magnanimity was not a quality much in demand, except perhaps by editors.

Perhaps I should have chosen, in recommending his works to you, one of his collections of stories, like *The Worlds of Robert F. Young* or *A Glass of Stars*. In choosing a novel, one might also think of *Starfinder*, which is thought by some to be his best. But instead I thought of Eridahn, which I picked up in a used bookstore on a lunch hour when I worked for an advertising agency and really needed a deftly-executed diversion. A story which begins with a young operative for a time travel agency wandering through a sector of the Cretaceous Era world in a machine which looks like a triceratops from the outside is impossible, at least for me, to resist.

Jim Carpenter, the operative, is investigating the possible origins of an anomalous finding in a Cretaceous fossil. In doing so, he stumbles upon two well-dressed, well-behaved (mostly) children, who also claim to be the prince and princess of Mars. Of the two, the boy, Skip, proves to be quite conversational but the girl, Deirdre, at first refuses to talk to "commoners" like Carpenter.

The story from there unfolds into a maze of time periods and timelines, but never to a point of great confusion for the readers. There's ample adventure and suspense and it moves at an admirable pace. Another thing I liked about this novel from the get-go is that it's a brisk 146 pages. It falls into that range I've always felt was ample territory to explore a science fiction story, especially one geared more toward adventure than paradigm-shifting concepts. It may have helped that the book was based on a novelette that appeared in *Worlds of If* in December 1964, "When Time Was New."

To my surprise, in looking up this information, I discovered that the novelette was also the cover story of that issue, and that image, of the triceratops machine (named Sam, by the way) was one of the first that ever caught my attention on the drugstore spinner rack where the digest magazines were displayed. Had I not been shooed away by the crabby cashier who monitored the magazine and comic book racks with an inane proprietary diligence ("What are you looking at? Put that back! *Those* magazines aren't for *you!*"), I would have become a science fiction fan much sooner.

Young was a great storyteller, and an intelligent one too. I am somewhat saddened that most of the encyclopedic entries seem to dismiss him as an "also ran." Some of this comes from critics who have already made their judgments before reviewing his work, and who read him, if at all, through bias-tinted glasses. Another part may come from a (mostly) unconscious bias at the late discovery by the SF world that Young's "day job" for much of his life was that of school janitor. It's not supposed to make a difference, but to many it still does. The thought of a school janitor writing sophisticated, satirical science fiction, to some, is almost too subversive to contemplate.

Alas.

Let's bring back Robert F. Young!

Copyright © 2022 by Richard Chwedyk.

Gregory Benford is a professor of physics at the University of California, Irvine and the author of Timescape, among other novels.

THE SCIENTIST'S NOTEBOOK

by Gregory Benford

PASCAL'S TERRIBLE SILENCE

The silence of those infinite spaces terrifies me.

—Blaise Pascal, 1623-1662

We moderns have had to confront new varieties of physical infinity, and Pascal's reaction to the scale of creation science was only beginning to unveil still rings true to us.

But Pascal did not cower merely before largeness; he feared its hush.

Perhaps humanity can't stand emptiness, the flip side of infinity. For Pascal feared the meaninglessness of it all, the absence of any hint that human effort had pith and substance. Nearly all sf attempts to answer this supreme agoraphobia by populating the yawning abyss.

The longing for alien contact seems to fulfill a parallel need. Yet this is a curious reassurance, since on the face of it such a discovery will deprive us of what many still believe to be a true uniqueness. So I think the clue behind the longings of UFO fans and Star Trek episodes and endless sf texts is that aliens give us companionship, making the infinities comfy, even talkative.

A truly strange and unknowable alien undercuts this comfortable feeling, and thus is quite rare in sf. Similarly, the use of time in sf so often veers away from truly labyrinthian implications. The infinities of causal loops in Robert Heinlein's classic "By His Bootstraps—" and onward are often seen as horrifying. A standard cliché of such loop stories is that the narrator ends trapped in one, feeling himself tiring, filling with angst and ennui.

But this betrays and denies the nature of a truly fixed causal loop, for the victim caught in one cannot experience loss of energy or accumulation of knowledge—everything really will be the same each cycle. The infinity of time becomes a cage that implicitly denies the premise—but even that seems preferable to the abyss of meaningless repetition.

So what interests me most is sf which does not subvert the infinite. I prefer Oalf Stapledon's *Star Maker*, which many find hard to read. Their difficulty probably stems from the novel's resolute refusal to ground its vision in concrete detail, to give the feeling of a mapped territory. Instead, immensity is seen abstractly, its ponderous forces unrolling through measureless time.

By contrast, Arthur Clarke's novel *2001* made its approach to the infinite clearly symbolic. Taking another tack, the film *2001* grounded the implied infinity in hard surfaces, such as the eighteenth century bedroom wherein human mortality plays itself out.

Like the alien, the infinite is a subject best crept up on. Much must be implied, the reader must be caught by sudden visions. I attempted something like this in a novel, *Against Infinity*, only to find much later that an entire symbolic undercurrent seemed to be working to other purposes. The enormous is sometimes a legitimate metaphor for the infinite, but the core of the mystery lies in the difference. Our minds were not built for the truly infinity.

An enormous hush, however, calls forth other demons.

✿

A cliché of post-George Lucas space films are the fighter-pilot zooms and roars in high vacuum. Just about everybody knows this is phony, yet we do not think of all creation as a place without a voice, a vault of no sound. The gleaming galaxy is silent. Stars smashing to supernovas, black holes sucking down whole solar systems in a day—all without a tremor.

Sound is by definition the wave motion of molecules, whether in gas or solid or liquid. No matter—or at least, very little—means no sound.

Between the stars there is about one hydrogen atom in the volume of a sugar cube. That is too little to support a sound wave, because a molecule must smack into another to convey the information that the wave is there.

To be a wave at all implies some reciprocity, a give and take. Under the slight pressure of the wave, gas atoms must move forward, overshoot their place,

then return to where they were. Only the wave moves, just as on the surface of the ocean; the sea stays where it was.

That lone hydrogen atom cannot find another hydrogen to thump for a very long time—long after the ostensible wave would have passed. Hence, if something (say, a passing asteroid) shoves on a hydrogen atom, it just takes off, saying nothing to other hydrogens nearby. The asteroid sheds these atoms, like gravel spitting away from the tires of a car; no sinuous motion, no reciprocity between the press of a wave and the inertia of matter.

Between the Earth and the nearest star there lies a vacuum better than any we can produce in the laboratory. Take that sugar cube of volume and push it out, all the way to the nearest star, sweeping up all the hydrogen in the way. That is a fantastic distance, 4.2 light years—that unit itself an everyday synonym for the infinite.

A way to think of it is to imagine the sun as a tennis ball in Times Square, New York. Then the Earth would be a dust mote floating across the street. Alpha Centauri, our nearest neighbor, would be another yellow tennis ball rolling around near Chicago.

Along all that huge distance, the hydrogen swept up by a speeding sugar cube would add up to about a millionth of an ounce, an undetectable weight. So filmy is this gas that it does not function as a gas at all, just a collection of independent atoms.

Of course there is much more flitting between the stars, all kinds of electromagnetic noise as electrons fidget from one atomic energy level to the next. If these revels happen to resonate in the region of wavelengths our eyes have evolved to see, we get to witness the stars' own unleashed furies. Sympathetic electrons in our own retinas dance in response, excited by incoming waves.

For those frequencies we cannot see, our antennas can now pick up the excited buzz of gas turning into stars, or the reverse. In the last century we have thrown open the windows on more and more of this electromagnetic blare, a cacophony descending from all the universe. The cosmic bedlam goes right back to the primordial, faded hiss of hydrogen itself being born right after the Big Bang.

Fred Hoyle offered that name as ridicule, since he preferred his own model of Creation, with matter coming into being at a constant clip, the Steady State Universe. It was a pretty picture, that Creation had no beginning and no end, just a universe swelling from a pinpoint that had already enjoyed an infinite life. Pretty, appealing—which was why so many were drawn to it—and wrong. (A famous motto holds that "Science is the brutal murder of beautiful theories by ugly facts.")

The Big Bang had the last word. But it was wordless, in fact—and soundless, too. Instead of envisioning an explosion, like a hand grenade going off in a phone booth, it is best to think of the Big Bang as all of space and time beginning at a point, and then emerging, cooling, expanding into the space it was making for itself. Call it the Enormous Emergence, though of course in the first unimaginable fraction of a second it was not enormous at all, and took up no more space than your fist.

And it didn't bang, either. There was no source for this Emergence, no one place it started and expanded into another place. It just happened. So, without matter running into other matter to create a coherent wave, there was no sound.

Pascal feared the moral silence of those spaces. He might have preferred that they be angry, the abode of a Satan perhaps, to what science was telling him: that far worse than being malign, the stars were indifferent. We can take on any opponent, but don't ignore us. Show some respect.

Yet in a way that heavenly silence should remind us to respect the fact that our natural world is alive with sound. How come?

✿

When Apollo 8 looped around the moon, giving us our first look at our world, to my mind it justified every penny spent in space. They showed us ourselves whole and entire for the first time, revealed that we lived inside a membrane.

Looking at Earth, you seldom see earth—that is, dirt. You witness instead the skin of air and cloud and sea the planet has learned to wrap about itself. Our planet is a machine that edits its sun, a craft it evolved.

Life began here under a killing sleet of ultraviolet that hammered down from the unedited star just born, its hard glare unblocked by murky layers of methane and carbon dioxide.

Only water vapor intercepted some of the piercing radiation. Its efforts were self-limited, for the fierce energies of ultraviolet split water into hydrogen and oxygen, and the oxygen in turn absorbs exactly those wavelengths of ultraviolet that shatter water.

Only living creatures could do better, by inventing photosynthesis. The first forms to do this had to hide from the biting ultraviolet beneath about ten meters of water. Lakes or ponds seem best for this, since oceans seldom let floating algae stay at a constant depth.

Once these plants started editing the air, the air edited sunlight. Oxygen got fried into ozone at the top of the atmosphere, shielding the evolving forms below. Once oxygen reached about one percent of the air, the non-oxygen breathers started to feel its poisoning sting.

All this took a while. About two billion years passed before oxygen began making itself felt. The oxygen that did come into play was often scooped up by the carbon in the soil, and buried away. The carbon kept being recycled, leaving oxygen below ground, by processes of plate tectonics.

On a world more like Mars than Earth, with tectonics that began and then quickly froze out as the planet cooled, oxygen might have accumulated in the atmosphere much earlier, perhaps in only one hundred million years. Life could get a quicker start on such a world—a possibility still open in our theories of the early eras of Mars.

Once there was about one percent oxygen to shield it, only about six hundred million years ago, life could begin to venture to the top of lakes, ponds, and oceans. Skeletons became common, leaving us plenty of fossils to mark the change.

Oxygen levels still climbed, born of life, until at around ten percent of the atmosphere's mass; its umbrella against ultraviolet allowed forms to climb out onto land. This happened about four hundred million years ago.

Oxygen was the crucial gas, because its atomic bonds stopped the ultraviolet that hammers hard on proteins and the like. Plus, it let the milder sun rays through to feed photosynthesis.

Since this is a universal property of oxygen, it bodes well for planets that can begin with the same sort of unpromising atmosphere we once had. But the crust of the world must cooperate, capturing some but not all the gases that together make an evolving atmosphere.

We still witness the ebb and sway of carbon dioxide in and out of our atmosphere, a tiny but crucial part. Though only a fraction of a percent of the air, it feeds all plant life and regulates the temperature of the surface through the now-famous greenhouse effect. In the long run, a rise in carbon dioxide may warm the Earth enough to stimulate plant growth, which then puts a brake on carbon in the air.

The reverse seems to work, too, with a lower temperature killing plants, so that they cannot pull much carbon from the air. Volcanoes could then replenish it, in time.

All this is like breathing, as the late Lewis Thomas remarked, but on an immense time scale. The cycles of ice ages take at least tens of thousands of years, the "respiration" of the biosphere's largest membrane. Carbon in, carbon out …

That this intricate mechanism evolved on its own, though prodded by the slow increase in the sun's luminosity and the continental churn driven by the spinning Earth, is a striking example of coherent organization springing from unthinking processes—spontaneous order on the largest planetary scale.

With it, the Earth resembles an enormous cell, its life mediated by a permeable membrane that edits energy and light. It even selects from among the hailstorm of meteorites that bombard us daily, letting pass without fiery death only those larger than Volkswagens.

More subtly, it edits out our own voices. Just as we cannot hear the cataclysms of distant suns, no hint of our own hubbub can escape Earth's airy membrane. The silence above that Pascal feared edits out all our brave talk, all the booming of our significance. The membrane refracts and reflects all our noises back from the top of the air, so that they return to us, dispersed and inaudible, each of our voices spread over whole territories by the time it bounces back from the high reaches.

So there is no way to speak to the stars except through electromagnetic waves. Yet life—here, at least—is engineered for acoustic waves. No creature uses more than a tiny sliver of the electromagnetic spectrum, mostly the visible and the near infrared, where our mammalian bodies radiate. (I've written about aliens who see in the radio wavelengths, for reasons of their local environment, in a novel, *Across the Sea of Suns*—but I don't think they're likely. I was intrigued by the idea that they might be our co-correspondents in interstellar communication, but we would not guess their nature for a long time, because we thought they had our advanced technology.)

So the membrane has edited us as well, tailoring our extraordinary hearing until in closed conditions we can hear over seven orders of magnitude of sound amplitude.

So Pascal's silence was ordained by evolution. Life sharpened its perception of the waves in its membrane, largely ignoring the electromagnetic discourse of the stars.

Jean Cocteau, in the first volume of his diaries, remarked that Andre Gide "has never experienced the discomfort of infinity." To the reserved French mind of that time perhaps infinity was simply too messy, too unconstrained, to be admitted into experience. European literary society had a habit of wrapping the universe around itself, shutting out the immensities. Jules Verne was the first great French writer of sf, and the last.

So in the end, our ceaseless grappling with infinity demands art of a peculiarly intellectual kind. The essence of enormity must be attacked indirectly, by leaving in the narrative a feeling for the non-centrality of humans themselves, for the prospect that unlimited space and time promises more, finally, than our ultimately futile attempts at closure and domestication.

We talk often, I suspect, to drown out the silence of the spheres.

L. Penelope is the award-winning author of the Earthsinger Chronicles. The first book in the series, Song of Blood & Stone, was chosen as one of TIME *Magazine's 100 Best Fantasy Books of All Time. Equally left and right-brained, she studied filmmaking and computer science in college and sometimes dreams in HTML. She hosts the* My Imaginary Friends *podcast and lives in Maryland with her husband and furry dependents. Visit her at: http://www.lpenelope.com*

LONGHAND

By L. Penelope

THE MESSY MIDDLE

I've started a new novel, and I am deep in the euphoria of the bright, shiny new project. Aren't beginnings wonderful? Since I'm a plotter, most of my efforts for the first few weeks involve taking the kernel of my sparking idea and turning it into a plot, which I've written about in a previous column. I usually have a good handle on the beginning, and I make sure that I know the end of the story before I start. So that just leaves the famously messy middle to work out.

Why are middles so difficult? Many authors get stuck somewhere between Act One and Act Three of the commonly used three act structure. Middles can sag, they can bore, they can drain the love of the story right out of you and your reader. We've all experienced too many novels or movies where the momentum fades, the pacing slows, and we're just waiting until the big finish finally occurs. That is, if we don't check out completely. So how can we make the middle soar instead of sink?

One way is to consider the Midpoint—that central story beat—before you begin. I'm a big fan of James Scott Bell's book *Write Your Novel From the Middle,* where he advocates this approach. In the center of Act Two, the Midpoint is a turning point where a character is often said to be moving from a state of reaction to action, charging ahead towards the grand finale. Bell uses the term "Mirror Moment" to describe a specific moment within this important plot beat. Often in books and movies, a character is literally looking into a mirror at themselves or figuratively reviewing their situation and themselves: how did they get where they are? What is standing in the way of achieving their goal? How did they become this person, and do they like who they've become?

When I'm able to nail down this moment in the center of the character arc or the external plot arc, that can be an enormous help in clarifying what comes before and after and making sure those elements are strong and purposeful. Figuring out how to get my main characters to a point where they're engaging in this sort of self-assessment—or in a more action driven story, where they're assessing the forces arrayed against them—can often make the needle drop on other story aspects that are giving me trouble.

However, sometimes that's still not enough meat to chew on during this story main course. In the plotting systems I use, there are anywhere from seven to twenty-two story beats. But in order to truly flesh out this bare bones, high-level view of a novel and start writing the scenes, I need a lot more than that. Too often, I don't have any idea of the specific steps it will take for a character to go from being a simple farm girl who raises goats to where she ends up, as the queen of a nation, a little more bitter and hardened, but wiser.

Enter the HCMs or Heart-clutching Moments. I heard about this method of story planning many years ago. The idea is that you can build a narrative around a number of intense scenes that will keep readers invested and on the edge of their seats. Figure out what excites you most about telling this story? What scenes have you been itching to write? A screenwriter might call these set-pieces—the big scenes often used in movie trailers to get fans into the theater. These can include explosions, big battles, and chases, or in a quieter story, moments of revelation. When the dark lord reveals he's the protagonist's father, or the antagonist turns out to have been helping the hero all along. Making a list of these HCMs and then moving your story from one to another can be a good way to chart out the middle and ensure it's engrossing.

I like to make sure these external moments are paired with internal changes the character goes through. And these should be linked together in a cause-and-effect chain. Ensuring an alluring middle requires getting from Prologue to Epilogue via a series of steps that makes sense to the reader. And for me, that requires breaking down the character goals.

Characters should generally want things—knowing what they want is a crucial first plotting step. Then, I need to discover what are the consequences of failure? What are the stakes at play? If I'm really worried about how the middle is progressing, I will chart the elements of achieving the goal on a spreadsheet.

Once the goals and consequences of failure are clarified, then I need to know what the protagonist needs in order to meet her goal? Let's say our intrepid heroine's goal is to stop a war. How does she do that? Is she trying to broker a peace? Does she need to assassinate the evil queen? Is she secretly planning a coup to oust the warmongering leader?

Then I get to smaller details which really help me craft scenes and dig deeper into the world. We already know the stakes. War is not just bad for everyone, it's bad for our heroine in particular. Her brother will be conscripted to fight, she'll lose the family farm, her forbidden magic will be discovered—the stakes are personal. But these big consequences have smaller forewarnings, the evidence of the harm that is coming if she fails. Maybe our evil queen is slowly kidnapping local boys to fight in the army. A neighbor's son goes missing and they're all sure what's happened.

Now, what are the conflicts the protagonist will face while striving for her goal? These are things standing in the way of the requirements we listed earlier. If our heroine is an envoy trying to broker a peace treaty, what stops the two sides from getting to the negotiating table? These could, and should, be both external and internal obstacles. Maybe she has a lack of faith in her ability; part of her character arc will be finding inner strength and confidence. Maybe the convoy of ambassadors is ambushed and she'll need to send out a search party to find them. Throwing up inner and outer conflicts is all a part of well-rounded storytelling.

Every goal has costs that the hero will face when trying to achieve it. What if our heroine loses the respect of her warmongering colleagues by working to broker a treaty? Things will get more difficult for her if they question her judgement or become suspicious of her. An antagonist can sow seeds of doubt about her motives or turn her friends against her.

There will also be dividends she reaps as she barrels forward. These are small personal rewards like meeting a love interest and falling in love, or gaining special knowledge, skills, or resources that she would never have gotten otherwise.

Finally, there are smaller barriers which impede the goal. These aren't huge conflicts, but in order to get ambassadors to the negotiating table, our heroine will have to journey far from home. Perhaps she doesn't have the resources, her paltry salary isn't enough, and her mission isn't sanctioned by the powers that be. Small plot hindrances are great fodder for scenes that will work together to build toward a Heart-clutching Moment.

By now, I usually have a bunch of ideas for things that could happen in the middle, and it doesn't seem so messy. I like to list out plot actions in a cause-and-effect chain, which I then use to build out the synopsis. Linking scenes together with statements like "yes, but" or "no, and" or even words like *but* or *therefore* help maintain continuity. For instance, our heroine recognizes the need to bring the opposing forces to the table in a peace treaty, but the other envoys are opposed and refuse to send a messenger. Therefore, she must find another way to get a message to them and so seeks out the palace sorcerer. Plot actions toward the goal are often one step forward, two steps back, with our protagonist facing an increasing series of obstacles that lead to the big showdown.

Non-plotters will often feel their way through these steps intuitively, or work through them after writing a first draft, when they feel a bit of sag setting in. But writers rejoice! We can have clean and orderly middles, they do not have to droop like a dog's floppy ears! As I work my way through this process on my new manuscript, I'll keep telling myself that. And I'll keep looking forward to finally getting to that heart-clutching ending.

OVER THE WINE-DARK SEA

by Harry Turtledove

XI

Harry Turtledove writes alternate history, science fiction, fantasy and historical fiction and has won a Hugo Award, two Sidewise Awards for alternate history, and the Hal Clement Award for YA science fiction. With more than a hundred books, a couple of hundred pieces of short fiction, as well as a translation of a Byzantine chronicle and four academic articles published throughout his career, Turtledove also ended up with a doctorate in Byzantine history from UCLA. He wrote his dissertation alongside the first novel he sold. Along with teaching at UCLA, Cal State Fullerton, and Cal State Los Angeles, he worked as a technical writer for the Los Angeles County Office of Education before resigning from that job to freelance in 1991. He is married to Laura Frankos, herself a writer. They have three daughters (one also a published author) and two granddaughters. Two cats, Boris and Hotspur, run the household with iron, clawed fists.

Menedemos sat in a tavern not far from the Little Harbor, drinking wine of the best sort: wine he hadn't bought. Even now, half a month after the grain fleet came into Syracuse, its sailors had trouble buying their own drinks. The polis had been hungry; now it had sitos and to spare. Menedemos wondered how long the gratitude would last. He was a little surprised it had lasted this long.

He might have been able to get his wine free even if he hadn't brought grain into Syracuse. Like a lot of wineshops, this one gave sailors and merchants cups of the local vintage if they told what news they'd heard and so drew customers into the place. His tales of the wars of Alexander's generals could well have kept him as drunk as he wanted for as long as he wanted.

He was going on about Polemaios' defection from his uncle, Antigonos, when a panting Syracusan dashed into the tavern and gasped, "They've landed! They've burned their ships!" He looked around. "Am I the first?" he asked anxiously.

"That you are," the tavernkeeper said, and handed him a large cup of neat wine as the tavern exploded in excited chatter.

"Who's landed?" Menedemos asked.

"Why, Agathokles has, of course, not far from Carthage," the Syracusan replied. Menedemos started to ask, *How do you know that?* It was, he realized, the kind of question likelier to come from his cousin. Before it could pass his lips, the new arrival answered it: "My uncle's cousin is a clerk on Ortygia, and he was bringing Antandros some tax records when the messenger came in."

"Ahhh," went through the tavern. Men dipped their heads, accepting the authority of this source. Menedemos wondered what Sostratos would have thought of it. Less than most people here did, he suspected.

Another question occurred to him. Again, someone else anticipated him, asking, "Burned the ships, you say?"

"That's right." The fellow with news dipped his head. "It was six days from here to Africa: a long, slow trip around the north coast of our island, made slower by bad winds. Our ships were getting close to land when they spied the Carthaginian fleet right behind them—and the Carthaginians spied *them*, too."

He could tell a story. Menedemos found himself leaning toward him. So did half the other people in the tavern. "What happened then?" somebody breathed.

"Well, the Carthaginians came on with a great sprint, rowing as if their hearts would burst," the Syracusan said. He held out his cup to the tavernkeeper, who filled it to the brim without a word of protest. After a sip, the fellow went on, "They got so close, their lead ships were shooting at Agathokles' rearmost just before our fleet beached itself."

"Our men must have thought their hopes were eclipsed," the taverner said. People hadn't stopped talking about the uncanny events of the day after the grain fleet's arrival.

But the man with news tossed his head. "My uncle's cousin said Antandros asked about that. The way Agathokles read the omen, he found out, was by saying it foretold ill for the enemy because it happened after our fleet sailed. He said it would have been bad if it had happened before."

Menedemos wondered what a priest of Phoibos Apollo would have had to say about that. He was sure a ready-for-aught like Agathokles wouldn't have asked a priest, but would have put forward the interpretation that served him best. And the local still hadn't answered the question. Menedemos asked it again: "What happened to Agathokles' ships?"

"Well, we outshot the Carthaginians, because we had so many soldiers aboard our ships. That, I gather, was how we beached, with the barbarians staying out of bowshot. Agathokles held an assembly once we were ashore."

"Just like Agamemnon, under the walls of Troy," someone murmured.

"He said he'd prayed to Demeter and Persephone, the goddesses who watch over Sicily, when the lookouts first spied the Carthaginians," the local went on. "He said he'd promised them the fleet as a burnt offering if they let it come ashore safely. And they had, so he burned his own flagship, and all the other captains set fire to their ships with torches. The trumpeters sounded the call to battle, the men raised a cheer, and they all prayed for more good fortune."

And they can't come back to Sicily again, or not easily, Menedemos thought. *If they don't win, they all die, as slowly and horribly as the Carthaginians can make them. Burning the fleet has to remind them of that, too. Sure enough, Agathokles knows how to make his men do what he wants of them.*

A man with a short gray beard asked, "How did Agathokles' messenger get here, if he burned all his ships?" That was a question the precise Sostratos might have found.

"In a captured fishing boat," the man with news replied. He had all the answers. Whether they were true or not, Menedemos couldn't have said. But they were plausible.

It soon became clear that the Syracusans were much more interested in Agathokles' doings than in those of the generals in the east. The latter might have been exciting to hear about, but didn't affect them personally. No one from out of the east had come to Sicily with conquest on his mind since the Athenians a century before. But war with Carthage was a matter of freedom or slavery, life or death. A Carthaginian army remained outside the walls. If it ever broke into Syracuse…Menedemos wasn't sorry he'd be sailing soon.

He grabbed a couple of olives from a red earthenware bowl on the counter in front of the tavernkeeper. The fellow didn't charge for them, and he quickly discovered why: they were perhaps the saltiest he'd ever tasted. The extra wine the taverner sold on account of them was bound to make up, and more than make up, for the few khalkoi they cost.

Fortunately, his own cup was half full. He gulped it down to water the new desert in his throat, then left the tavern for the harbor not far away. As he got back to the *Aphrodite*, he saw her boat making the short pull from Ortygia. The rowers' strokes were so perfectly smooth and regular, they might have been serving one of the Athenian processional galleys, not an akatos' boat.

Sostratos sat near the stern of the boat. "I've got news," he called when he saw Menedemos. "Agathokles has landed in Africa!"

That was news to most of the sailors aboard the merchant galley; they exclaimed in surprise. But Menedemos only grinned and answered, "Yes, and he burned all his ships once he did it, too."

The sailors exclaimed again, even louder this time. Sostratos blinked. "How did you know that?" he asked. "I just heard it myself."

"I was wasting my time in a tavern—or that's what you would call it," Menedemos said as his cousin and the rowers came aboard at the stern. "A fellow came across from Ortygia practically on fire with the word, and earned himself some free wine to put the fire out."

"Oh." Sostratos gave the impression of an airfilled pig's bladder that had sprung a leak. Then he snapped his fingers, plainly remembering something, and brightened. "Well, I've got some other news, too."

"Tell me, O best one," Menedemos heard. "I haven't heard it all."

"Only the best parts of it," Sostratos said unhappily. "But I managed to sell all the papyrus and ink we had left, and I got a good price for them, too."

"*Did* you?" Menedemos clapped him on the back, glad to give credit where it was due. "You were right about that, then."

His cousin dipped his head. "Thanks to the war with Carthage, Agathokles' chancery was almost out of papyrus altogether. They were scraping the ink off old sheets and writing on boards and potsherds, the way people did in the old days. One of the chief clerks kissed me when I told him how much we had."

"He *must* have been excited," Menedemos murmured. Sostratos dipped his head again. Then, a moment too late, he glared. As a youth, Menedemos had had more than his fair share of older men as admirers; he'd quite enjoyed playing the heartbreaker. Sostratos, on the other hand, had been tall and skinny and angular, all shanks and knees and elbows and pointy nose. So far as Menedemos knew, nobody'd bothered pursuing his cousin, either in Rhodes or, later, in Athens. Changing the subject looked like a good idea: "Just how much did you get?"

Sostratos told him. Menedemos whistled and clapped him on the back again. Sostratos said, "It's not so much when you set it against what we made for hauling the grain and for the last of the peacocks, but it's a lot more than we would have got in Athens. That's where everyone with papyrus and ink goes."

"Bad for prices," Menedemos agreed. "And that's one less stop we'll have to make on the way back to Rhodes."

"What's wrong with stopping in Athens?" Sostratos asked. "I like Athens fine."

"I like Athens fine, too, when we've got time for it," Menedemos said. "But we're a long way from home, and it's starting to get late in the sailing season: we're less than a month from the fall equinox. Things get murky when the days go short; you can't tell your landmarks the way you should. And there's always the chance of a storm, too. Why take the extra risk?"

"All right." Sostratos threw his hands in the air. "If it's enough to make *you* careful, that's plenty to convince me." Before Menedemos could reply, Sostratos added, "If there were a woman in Athens, you'd stop no matter whose wife she was."

"Not if she was yours," Menedemos said. Sostratos gave him an ironic bow. As Menedemos returned it, he wondered if he'd just told the truth.

Sostratos hadn't seen much of Syracuse during his time in the polis. He couldn't have gone up onto the wall to walk around the town, not unless he wanted an arrow in his ribs. And he couldn't have ridden out to see the countryside, as he had up at Pompaia; the next sight he would have seen was the inside of a Carthaginian slave pen.

I wonder when I'll come back to Sicily, he thought. *I wonder if I'll ever come back to Sicily*. He shrugged. No way to know the future.

Menedemos stood at the *Aphrodite*'s stern, his hands on the steering-oar tillers. He dipped his head to Diokles, saying, "Set the stroke."

"Right you are, skipper." The keleustes struck the bronze square with his mallet. To emphasize the rhythm as the merchant galley left port, he raised his voice, too: "Rhyppa*pai*! Rhyppa*pai*!"

For swank, Menedemos had every oar manned as the *Aphrodite* left the Little Harbor. The rowers did him proud, their oars rising and falling in smooth unison. *Of course*, Sostratos thought, *it's a lazy man's pace, nothing like what we did when we were running from that Roman trireme—or when we turned back towards it! What an adventure that was!*

He paused in bemusement and some dismay. *I'll be telling the story of that trireme for the rest of my life, and I'll sound more like a hero every time I do.* He didn't care for men his father's age who bored dinner parties with tales of their swashbuckling youth, but he suddenly saw how they came to be the way they were. *A historian is supposed to understand causes*, he thought, but then he tossed his head. This was one of which he would sooner have stayed ignorant.

As Syracuse receded behind the merchant galley, Menedemos took more than half the sailors off the oars. The ship glided up the Sicilian coast toward the mainland of Italy. Dolphins leaped. Terns splashed into the sea, some only a few cubits from the *Aphrodite*. One came out with a fish in its beak.

"You'll have an easy trip home," Menedemos called to him from the stern. "No more peafowl to worry about."

"I'm *so* disappointed they're gone," Sostratos answered.

Not only his cousin but half the sailors laughed. Aristeidas the lookout said, "The foredeck still smells like birdshit."

"You're right—it does," Sostratos agreed. "It probably will for a while, too."

"So it will," Aristeidas said darkly. "Now that you don't have to take care of peafowl any more, you can go wherever you like on the ship. Me, I'm stuck up here most of the time."

You can go wherever you like. Aristeidas had said it without irony, and Sostratos took it the same way. Then he thought about what a landlubber would make of it. The *Aphrodite* was only forty or forty-five cubits long, and perhaps seven cubits wide at her beamiest. From the perspective of someone used to strolling through a polis or across his fields, that didn't give a man much room. A sailor, though, had a much more cramped view of what was roomy and what wasn't.

As if to prove as much, Sostratos went back to the poop deck, which to him felt as far from the smelly foredeck as Athens was from Rhodes. Menedemos

asked him, "What have we got left to trade on the way home?"

"A little wine," Sostratos answered. "Some perfume. I'd like to get rid of that, if we see the chance—taking it back to Rhodes would be a shame, when it came from there. And we still have some silk." He sighed.

Menedemos took a hand off the steering oar to poke him in the ribs. "I know what you're thinking of: that copper-haired Keltic girl you were screwing in Taras."

Sostratos' ears heated; he had indeed been thinking of Maibia, in and especially out of the Koan silk tunic she wore. "Well, what if I was?" he asked roughly.

"It's all right with me." As usual when the talk rolled around the women, Menedemos sounded disgustingly cheerful. "I've got plenty to think about myself."

"If you'd do some thinking beforehand…" Sostratos said.

"That takes away half the fun. More than half," he cousin answered.

"I don't see it that way," Sostratos said with a shrug.

"I know you don't." Menedemos leaned forward and spoke in a low voice. "Just exactly how much silver *are* we carrying? In the name of the gods, don't yell out the answer. The last thing we want to do is give the sailors ideas." In something close to a whisper, Sostratos told him. Menedemos whistled softly. "That's even more than I figured. It's almost enough for ballast."

"On a ship this size?" Sostratos made the automatic mental calculation, then tossed his head. "Don't be silly."

"Mm, I suppose not." By the look of concentration on his face, Menedemos was making the same calculation. "But I'll tell you this: it's more silver than my father expected us to bring back. And I'll rub his nose in it, too."

"Why bother?" Sostratos asked. "Uncle Philodemos will be glad to see you home safe, and he'll be glad of the profit. Isn't that enough?"

"No, by Zeus." A hot eagerness thrummed in Menedemos' voice, like a following wind in the rigging. "Ever since I started toddling around and stopped making messes on the floor, he's always gone on and on about what a great trader he is and how I don't measure up. Let's see him talk like that now."

"I didn't come out here thinking to outdo my father," Sostratos said.

"You're toikharkhos. I'm captain," Menedemos said, that hot eagerness turning to something cold and hard for a moment. But he went on, "Uncle Lysistratos doesn't go around bragging and carping all the time; I will say that. And the two of you get along better than Father and I do. Anyone who saw us would say *that*."

"I suppose so," Sostratos said. "We'd have a hard time getting along worse than the two of you, wouldn't we?"

"You're as comfortable together as a foot and an old sandal, and you know it," Menedemos said. "The two of you *fit* like that. Do you have any idea how jealous it makes me?"

"No, I didn't, not till you just mentioned it." Sostratos studied his cousin with an avid curiosity of a small boy seeing an unexpected lizard emerge from under a chunk of bark. "I'm usually the one who holds things inside, but you've kept that secret for years. Forever, really."

By Menedemos' expression, he wished he hadn't told it now. He said, "I'm not sorry to get away from Rhodes for months at a time, I'll tell you that."

"I can see as much," Sostratos said judiciously. He set a hand on Menedemos' shoulder. "We won't be back for a little while yet. Nothing happens in a hurry on the sea. Even when we were fighting that Roman trireme, we seemed to be moving as slowly as if we were in a dream."

"Not to me," Menedemos said. "It all happened very fast, as far as I was concerned. I needed to gauge just the right moment to tug at the steering oars, and it all felt like it happened in a heartbeat. That's the sweetest sound I ever heard—our hull riding up and over that polluted whoreson's oars."

"If you think I'll argue, you're mad," Sostratos said. "That sound meant we stayed free men, and what could be sweeter than that?" He pointed ahead. "There's Cape Leukopetra, with Cape Herakleion just off to the east."

"I know, my dear. I saw them quite a while ago." Now Menedemos sounded acidulous, perhaps because he'd shown more of himself to Sostratos a

little while before than he'd wanted to. "I don't have to change the way the ship is heading this very instant, you know."

"So you don't," Sostratos agreed. "Proves my point—nothing happens in a hurry on the sea."

Menedemos stuck out his tongue. They both laughed. Laughter came easy when they'd made a profit, when they were sailing away from danger and not into it, and—for Sostratos, at least—when they were homeward bound.

✿

"That should just about do it," Menedemos said as the *Aphrodite* eased into place alongside a quay in Kroton's harbor.

"I think so, too, skipper," Diokles said. "*Oöp!*" he called in a louder voice, and the rowers rested at their oars. A couple of sailors tossed lines to men on the quay, who made the merchant galley fast.

"You were here earlier this summer, weren't you?" one of the roustabouts called.

"That's right," Menedemos answered. "We went up the west coast of Italy, and then down to Syracuse with the grain fleet from Rhegion. You've heard how Agathokles landed not far from Carthage?"

"Sure have," the roustabout said. "That took balls, that did."

From the bow, Sostratos asked, "Do you know what happened when the Roman fleet attacked Pompaia? We were up that way, and almost got caught."

"It came to grief, or that's what I heard," the Krotonite said. Several sailors clapped their hands together in grim delight. The roustabout went on, "The sailors and soldiers aboard scattered to plunder, and the folk from all the towns thereabouts—not just Pompaia, but Nole and Noukeria and Akherrai, too—gathered together and drove 'em back to their ships with heavy losses." More sailors clapped. Some of them cheered. The local added, "Some people say one Roman ship got wrecked by a merchantman, but you won't get me to swallow that."

"I wouldn't, either, if I were you," Menedemos said gravely. The sailors who heard him sniggered and brought their hands up to their mouths to keep from laughing out loud. The roustabout gave them curious looks, but nobody said another word, so he shrugged and started to turn away.

Before he left, Sostratos asked him, "How does the marvelous Hipparinos like his peafowl chicks?"

"You're those fellows!" The Krotonite snapped his fingers in excitement. "I thought you were those fellows, but I wasn't sure, and I didn't like to take the chance. Do you know what happened there? Do you?"

"If we did, would we be asking?" Menedemos did his best to seem the very image of sweet reason.

"That's right, how could you? You're just a pack of polluted foreigners," the Krotonite said. For Menedemos, sweet reason dissolved in anger. But before he could show it, the local went on, "Hipparinos, he has this Kastorian hunting hound—you know, brought here all the way from Sparta—he's as proud of as his son. Prouder, probably, on account of all his son wants to do is drink neat wine and screw." He paused. "What exactly was I talking about?"

"Peafowl chicks," Menedemos and Sostratos said together.

"That's right. I sure was." The roustabout snapped his fingers again. "Anyway, like I said, he has this hound named Taxis." Hipparinos, Menedemos thought, would be just the man to name a dog Order. The Krotonite continued, "And Taxis, he got his first look at these chicks and he ate one up before anybody could tell him not to or grab him to keep him from doing it. You could've heard old Hipparinos screaming from the agora all the way to the guard towers on the wall."

"I believe that," Menedemos said. "His precious hound is even more precious now—it ate up a mina and a half of silver at one gulp."

"A mina and a half? Is that all?" the local said.

"Is that *all?*" Sostratos echoed, as if he couldn't believe his ears."

"That's what I said, and that's what I meant," the Krotonite told him. "Hipparinos has been saying that miserable little bird cost him five minai."

Menedemos started to tell how Hipparinos had tried to cheat him on the price he'd paid for the two peafowl chicks. Just then, Sostratos had a coughing fit. Menedemos let the story go untold. For a Krotonite to disparage a rich fellow citizen was one thing. For him, a foreigner, to disparage that same man might prove something else again.

After a little more chat, the roustabout did leave. Sostratos hurried back toward the stern and climbed up onto the poop deck. "I don't think we ought to spend much time here at all," he said. "Hipparinos wasn't happy with us when we came here last. Now, thanks to that accursed dog, he'll like us even less."

"And thanks to our giving him the lie about the price he paid," Menedemos added.

"Yes, thanks to that, too," Sostratos agreed. "Besides, we did sell what we could when we were here last. I think we should push on straight to Kallipolis tomorrow morning."

"You're probably right," Menedemos said with a sigh. "The wind's out of the north, though. That means either tacking or rowing, and a two-day trip across the gulf either way."

"Things would be simpler if we could put in at Taras," Sostratos pointed out.

Menedemos glared. "Things would be simpler if you'd keep your mouth shut, too. I'm getting tired of hearing about that."

Had Sostratos pushed it any further, Menedemos would have given him all he wanted and then some. But his cousin just shrugged and said, "We both may be glad not so see each other for a while once we get back to Rhodes." Sostratos pointed north. "What do you make of those clouds?"

After studying them, Menedemos shrugged. "Maybe rain, maybe not. I don't think they look too bad. How about you?"

"They seem the same way to me, too," Sostratos answered, "but I know you've got the better weather eye."

That was true, but it was one more thing Menedemos wouldn't have admitted so casually. He tasted the wind, trying to read the secrets it held. "I think we will get rain if it stays steady. No more than a little rain, though. It's still early in the year for one of those equinoctial storms—a bit early, anyhow."

"Good," Sostratos said. "I was hoping you'd tell me something like that. Because you're so weatherwise, of course I believe you." Menedemos felt proud of that till he remembered how fond of irony his cousin was.

✧

Sostratos woke before sunrise. The eastern sky was just going from gray to pink. Dawn didn't become spectacularly red. That eased his mind; a red, red sunrise often warned of bad weather ahead. His gaze swung to the north. The clouds covered more of the sky than they had the day before, but not a great deal more.

From behind him, Menedemos said, "I'd like the weather better if we weren't likely to have to spend a night at sea."

Sostratos started. "I didn't know you were awake."

"Well, I am." Menedemos looked up the pier toward the dark, jumbled mass of houses and shops and temples that made up Kroton.

"Expecting Hipparinos with an army of ruffians at his back," Sostratos asked.

"An army of ruffians *and* a Kastorian hound with a taste for peafowl." Menedemos' tone was light, but Sostratos didn't think he was joking. And, sure enough, he started shaking sailors awake. "Come on, boys," he said. "The sooner we're on the open sea gain, the better."

"Says who?" a sleepy man asked around a yawn.

"Says your captain, that's who," Menedemos answered.

"And your toikharkhos," Sostratos added, throwing his obolos of authority after Menedemos' drakhma.

Diokles sat up straight on the rower's bench where he'd slept. "And your keleustes," he said. Formally, his rank was lower than Sostratos'. Among the sailors, though, his word carried more weight.

Hipparinos had not made an appearance, with or without bravos, by the time the *Aphrodite* left Kroton. "Many goodbye to the town, and to the crows with him and his hungry hound both," Menedemos said.

The wind kept backing and shifting, coming now from the north, now from the northwest. When it blew from the northwest, the *Aphrodite* could sail quite handily, but whenever it swung back toward the north Menedemos had to tack, zigzagging his course with the akatos taking the wind first on one bow and then swinging about to take it on the other. Grunting sailors heaved the yard round till it ran from bow to quarter and slanted toward the breeze. It was a slow business, and a miserably inexact one when it came to setting a course.

"Here's hoping we can find Kallipolis when we get in the neighborhood," Sostratos said.

"As long as I head northeast, I'll strike the mainland somewhere," Menedemos said. "Then

we can feel our way along the coast till we come to the island."

"There ought to be a way to navigate more surely," Sostratos said. "The only trouble is, I don't know what it would be."

"If you did, you'd get rich enough to make Kroisos look like a piker," Menedemos said. "Every captain in the world would buy whatever you had."

"Buy it or try to steal it." Sostratos pointed north. "Here come those clouds."

"I think they're finally done fooling around," Menedemos said unhappily. When they cover the sun, I'll have even less idea of just where we're going—one more drawback to sailing out of sight of land."

"That storm almost sank us the last time you did it," Sostratos said. "I wonder if you offended some god without knowing it."

He didn't mean it seriously. Even so, Menedemos spat into the bosom of his tunic. Diokles rubbed his apotropaic ring. "Shouldn't say things like that," he muttered, just loud enough for Sostratos to hear.

Perhaps a quarter of an hour later, rain started pattering down. When Sostratos looked in the direction he thought to be northeast, he couldn't see anything much. All of a sudden, he was glad to be well out of sight of land. Without much in the way of visibility, he had no desire to find land where he least expected it.

Menedemos must have had the same thought. He called, "Aristeidas, go forward. You've got the best eyes of anybody aboard."

"All right, skipper, but I don't think we're anywhere close to shore," the sailor said.

"I don't, either. But I don't care to get any nasty surprises," Menedemos answered. "Besides, you can look out for fishing boats, too, and merchantmen. In this weather, anything can loom up before we know it's there."

Aristeidas dipped his head. "Right you are." He headed up toward the foredeck.

Sostratos blinked as a raindrop got him right in the eye. For a moment, he couldn't see anything. Not seeing anything gave him an idea. "Shouldn't you have a man with the lead up there, too?" he asked Menedemos.

"You're right—I should," his cousin answered, and gave the necessary orders.

The lead splashed into the sea. A few minutes later, the sailor handling it called, "No bottom at a hundred cubits."

"We're still out in the middle of the gulf," Menedemos murmured. He raised his voice: "I thank you, Nikodromos." The sailor waved to show he'd heard and hauled in the line hand over hand.

Rain kept splashing down for the rest of the day. A sail that got a little wet worked better than a dry one: the water filled the spaces in the weave so the breeze couldn't sneak through. But a sail that got more than a little wet grew too heavy to belly and easily fill with air. It hung, almost limp, from the yard, as laundry did from olive branches ashore. Menedemos called men to the oars to keep the *Aphrodite* moving.

"Gauging your course by the breeze?" Sostratos asked.

"It's all I've got left right now," his cousin answered. "If I keep it on my left hand, not quite straight in my face, we can't go too far wrong."

"That seems to make sense," Sostratos said. But not everything that seemed to make sense was true. He wished he hadn't thought of that.

The sea never got more than a little choppy. This wasn't a real storm, only rain—an annoyance, and a reminder the sailing season wouldn't stretch too much longer. It was indeed time to be heading home.

Dusk fell rather earlier than Sostratos had expected it to. The rain kept falling, too, making the night even more miserable and uncomfortable than it would have been otherwise. "How are we supposed to sleep in this?" Sostratos said.

"Wrap yourself in your himation, as if you were an Egyptian mummy," Menedemos said. "Wrap your face up, too. That'll keep you dry."

"Of course it will—till the whole himation soaks through," Sostratos said.

"By then you'll be asleep, and you won't notice till morning." As Menedemos so often did, he spoke like a man with all the answers.

Since Sostratos had no answers of his own, he tried his cousin's. For a little while, he thought it would work: the thick wool of the himation did keep the rain off fairly well. He was just getting really sleepy when he noticed he was also getting really wet. That woke him up again, and he took a long,

long time to fall asleep. From a couple of cubits away, Menedemos' snores effortlessly pierced the soft patter of the rain. That didn't help, either.

It was still raining when Sostratos woke up the next morning. He felt half suffocated in wet wool. He undid the mantle, sat up, and knuckled his eyes, trying to convince himself this was all some horrid dream. He couldn't do it, and resigned himself to a long day full of weariness.

Menedemos was already up and moving. Seeing Sostratos stir, he smiled. "Good day. Isn't this a splendid morning?"

"No." Sostratos was often inclined to be grumpy before breakfast. A bad night and wet clothes didn't help.

His one-word answer made Menedemos' smile wider. "But just think, O best one—today you can drink watered wine without pouring in any water." Sostratos' suggestion as to what Menedemos could do with and to his wine only pulled a laugh from his cousin.

Wine, watered from a jar as well as by the rain, helped warm Sostratos and resign him to being awake. Olives were olives, whether eaten in the rain or under a bright, sunny sky. But he gulped down his bread in a hurry, before it could get soggy.

"Come on, boys," Menedemos called to the crew. "We'll have to put more work into it than I expected, and that's too bad, but if we do we'll sleep warm tonight." In a soft aside to Sostratos, he added, "If we make the mainland anywhere close to Kallipolis, that is."

For most of the day, Sostratos wondered if they would know they'd made the mainland before running aground. The rain kept splashing down, as if it were the middle of winter rather than a little before the equinox. A little past noon—or so Sostratos guessed, but he was too tired to have much confidence in the hour—a fishing boat came into sight. Menedemos hailed it: "Which way to Kallipolis from where we are?"

"That way, I think," the fisherman said, and pointed. "Wouldn't take oath to anything, though—not in this. Early in the year for so much rain."

"Isn't it?" Menedemos agreed. "Thanks, friend." To Sostratos, he said, "Unless my reckoning's off even more than I think he pointed close to due east."

"Easy enough for us to come too far north with nothing much we could use to judge our course," Sostratos said.

"I suppose so." But Menedemos still sounded discontented. He took as much pride in his ship-handling as Sostratos did in his bits of historical lore. *Trust Menedemos to be the one who's proud of something from which he can actually get some use*, Sostratos thought.

Towards evening, the weather finally began to clear again. "Land ho!" Aristeidas sang out. "Land dead ahead, and also land to starboard."

Sostratos saw the land, too, as did everyone else aboard the *Aphrodite*. The akatos lay forty or fifty stadia offshore, in no danger of running aground. To Sostratos' surprise, the beach ahead and the curve of the coast looked familiar. He needed a moment to realize why. Then, turning to Menedemos, he said, "Isn't that where we got rid of Alexidamos after he tried to steal the peafowl eggs?"

"Why, I do believe you're right," Menedemos said after a little study of his own.

"I half expected to see him bearing down on us in Taras, spear in one hand, shield in the other, blazing for revenge because we threw him off the ship," Sostratos said.

"He must have fallen foul of the Samnites before he made it to the polis," Menedemos replied. "I can't say I'm sorry, either. The only thing worse than a thief on board is a man with a sickness that spreads."

"How far are we from Kallipolis?" Sostratos asked.

"A couple of hundred stadia, maybe a little more," his cousin answered. "If I have this stretch of coastline straight in my mind, it's about halfway between Taras and Kallipolis."

"Can we make Kallipolis by nightfall?"

"I doubt it." Menedemos didn't sound happy about having to doubt it. He swung his leg in a way that meant he would have kicked at the dirt had he not been aboard ship. "I hadn't planned on spending two nights in a row at sea, but I'm not going to beach the *Aphrodite* on this coast."

"I should hope not." Sostratos shuddered at the thought of losing all the silver they'd worked so long and hard to gather. Every crewman within earshot dipped his head to show he didn't want to ground the ship, either.

"It's the rain's fault," Menedemos said. "We'd have gone faster and I'd have navigated better without it."

"Maybe it'll work out for the best," Sostratos said. "We'll have a little chance to dry out, so we won't look like such ragamuffins when we do come into port."

"We haven't got much left to sell," his cousin said. "It isn't worth worrying about."

"We may come back there one of these days," Sostratos said. "People will remember. They always remember scandal." He didn't need to read any history to be sure of that, and was slightly scandalized when Menedemos only shrugged. *He has no sense of anything but the moment*, Sostratos thought sadly. *Maybe that's why he ends up in trouble over women so often*. It never occurred to him to wonder what Menedemos was thinking about him just then.

They didn't make Kallipolis before nightfall, and did anchor offshore. The men grumbled a little about that. Sostratos wondered at their logic. They'd just made it very clear that they didn't care to risk going ashore, but they still didn't want to stay at sea? What did that leave? He imagined the *Aphrodite* floating several hundred cubits up in the air. Daidalos and Ikaros might get to the ship then, but he didn't see how anyone else would.

Menedemos' imagination was of a more practical sort: "I hadn't planned to lay over a night in Kallipolis, but I think I'd better, to give the men a chance to drink and roister."

"Good idea, skipper," Diokles said. If the oarmaster thought it a good idea, Sostratos wouldn't argue with him.

When they reached Kallipolis the next morning, it proved to lie on an island just off the Italian mainland, as Ortygia lay just off the Sicilian coast. Kallipolis, though, had never expanded off its island the way Syracuse had. It remained what so many of the colonies of Great Hellas had been in their early days: a Hellenic outpost at the edge of a land full of barbarians.

Despite its name, it didn't strike Sostratos as a particularly beautiful city. When he said as much, Menedemos laughed at him. "What would you expect them to call it? Kakopolis?" his cousin asked. "They'd enjoy trying to lure settlers to a polis with a name like that, wouldn't they? Uglytown?"

"All right, I see your point," Sostratos said. "But if you found a land full of snow and ice, you wouldn't call it a green land, would you?"

"I would if I wanted to get anybody to live there with me," Menedemos replied. "But I'm a good Rhodian. I don't even want to think about snow and ice, let alone live with 'em."

"It did snow once when I was in Athens," Sostratos said. "It was beautiful, but Zeus! it was cold." He shivered at the memory.

"We won't need to worry about that here," Menedemos said. "We have some wine, and we have some silk. Let's see if we can unload them. And"—he wagged a finger at Sostratos—"we don't need to tell the Kallipolitans what we think of their polis."

"I understand," Sostratos said. "We'll tell them the land is green."

His cousin laughed. "Exactly. That's just what we'll do."

Seen from its narrow, winding streets, Kallipolis was even less prepossessing than when viewed from the sea. Because the island wasn't very big and had been settled for centuries, the locals used every digit of space they could. Many of their buildings were two and three stories high. They leaned toward one another above the streets, making them even closer and darker and smellier than they would have been otherwise.

That was one of the first things that struck Sostratos about the place. The second didn't take much longer. "Do you notice how nobody's smiling?" he said. "Everybody has a frown on his face."

"What is there to smile about?" Menedemos returned. "If you lived in a miserable little town in the middle of nowhere, how happy would you be? They probably wonder whether the barbarians will snap them up tomorrow or the day after." Since he was bound to be right, Sostratos took that no further.

They had to ask their way to the agora. On their way there, they passed several parties of mercenary soldiers: some Hellenes, others Italians in ordinary enough helmets but wearing odd, almost triangular, cuirasses that, in Sostratos' view, didn't cover nearly enough of the chest. The mercenaries looked no more cheerful than the ordinary Kallipolitans.

Menedemos was never one to leave well enough alone. Pointing to the soldiers, he said, "You see?"

And Sostratos had to admit, "I see."

The market square looked as if it had been bigger than it was. Buildings encroached on it from all sides, like weeds growing at the edge of a field. People buying and selling huddled together in the shadows the buildings cast. By the way merchants and customers kept glancing over their shoulders, they might have thought more buildings would spring up while they weren't looking.

"Fine wine from Khios! Transparent silk from Kos! Fragrant Rhodian perfume!" Menedemos' voice rang through the agora, echoing from the buildings that seemed to lean toward him from all the edges of the square. People stared, as if wondering who this loud stranger was. He certainly made more noise than half a dozen locals. "By the dog of Egypt," he murmured, "I think they're all so many wraiths here, like the spirits of the dead in the *Odyssey*."

"Fine wine and transparent silk will liven anyone up, if he gives them half a chance," Sostratos observed.

Menedemos shot him a quizzical look. "You can say that, when you want to hit me over the head with something whenever I go out and have a good time?"

"Yes, I say that," Sostratos answered. "I also say there's a time and a place for everything, and you haven't got the faintest notion of when and where."

"I think you're just jealous and using fancy talk to hide it," Menedemos said, and went back to crying their wares before Sostratos could do anything but let out an indignant, incoherent protest. Sostratos spent the next little while wondering whether his cousin had slandered him. He thought so, but he wasn't sure, and that worried him.

He didn't have long to worry undisturbed. In that rather subdued agora, Menedemos' brash, raucous shouts drew people far more readily than they would have, say, back at Rhodes. A tailor and a brothelkeeper almost got into a brawl over the length of silk Sostratos had brought from the Aphrodite. Only when Sostratos said, "We have enough for both of you, best ones," did they leave off glaring and snarling at each other. The brothelkeeper ended up buying some perfume, too, as Sostratos had hoped he might.

When a man in a fine chiton said, "Will you let me taste some of this fine wine of yours?" both Sostratos and Menedemos paused in embarrassment. They hadn't hauled an amphora from the merchant galley to the market square. They'd talked about selling Ariousian in Kallipolis, but they hadn't really believed they would. And now their failure was hurting their chances.

Sostratos would have brushed off a ragged Kallipolitan, but this fellow looked as if he could afford the best. "If you'd be kind enough to stay here, sir, I'll bring a jar from the ship. I won't be long."

"You should have one ready to hand," the local said. Since that was true, Sostratos could only dip his head and hurry away.

Nobody aboard the *Aphrodite* looked enthusiastic about putting an amphora on a carrying pole and lugging it to the agora, but Aristeidas and Teleutas did. On the way to the market square, Teleutas stuck his foot in a hole in a muddy street. He stumbled. The pole slipped from his shoulder. Only a desperate grab by Sostratos kept the amphora from smashing.

"That was fast," Aristeidas said as Sostratos helped Teleutas reassume the burden.

"That was me thinking about what Menedemos would say if we got back to the agora with a few potsherds and told our customer there he was welcome to lick them," Sostratos replied. Aristeidas and Teleutas both laughed, but he hadn't been joking.

They stabbed the pointed end of the amphora down in the mud when they got to the square. Sostratos scraped the pitch away from the stopper and got it out. They had to borrow a cup from a potter in the agora. The same thing had happened in Pompaia. Sostratos made a mental note to do something about that, at the same time wondering if he would remember it when the *Aphrodite* sailed away from Kallipolis. The Kallipolitan sipped the wine. Try as he would, he couldn't keep his face straight. "This was worth waiting for, I must admit," he said. "How much for the jar?"

"Sixty drakhmai," Menedemos answered, as he had up in Pompaia.

This Hellene howled louder at that than any of the Pompaians had. He and Menedemos were throwing arguments back and forth when somebody yelled, "You whoresons! You wide-arsed, turd-eating bastards!" a good deal louder than Menedemos had called out the virtues of his silk and wine and perfume—loud enough to drown out every other sound in the agora, in other words.

"Uh-oh," Sostratos said—quietly, but with great sincerity. He and Menedemos had idly wondered what had happened to Alexidamos the larcenous mercenary. Now they'd found out. Sostratos, for once, could have done without the enlightenment.

"Throw me off your stinking ship, will you?" Alexidamos shouted, even louder than before. "Leave me to be barbarians' meat, will you?" He carried no spear, but drew his sword and trotted toward the men from the *Aphrodite*.

Sostratos wore no sword. Neither did Menedemos. Neither did the other two sailors from the akatos. Few men did wear swords in a polis. If a man wasn't safe among his fellow Hellenes, where would he be? *Nowhere*, went through Sostratos' mind.

"Stop him!" someone exclaimed. But nobody seemed eager to stop Alexidamos. Who would want to try, unarmed, to stop a man with a sword in his hand and murder in his eyes. *And, for all these people know, he really does have some good reason to want revenge against us.* There were times when Sostratos wished he weren't so good at seeing the other fellow's point of view.

"Good day," said the Kallipolitan who'd been haggling with Menedemos. His departure showed a turn of speed that wouldn't have disgraced a sprint at Olympos or any of the other Panhellenic festivals. When Sostratos looked around to ask for help from Aristeidas and Teleutas, he didn't see the latter, either. He cursed under his breath. *He trips in the street and runs from trouble. Many goodbyes to him!*

"Whoresons!" Alexidamos shouted again. "Abandoned catamites!"

Aristeidas looked ready to take to his heels as the furious mercenary charged across the agora. So, for that matter, did Menedemos. Sostratos' cousin was a formidable sprinter in his own right. *I wish I were*, Sostratos thought. *But if I run, he'll catch me from behind. What man wants his death-wound in the back?*

Sostratos didn't want his death-wound at all. Since running would do him no good, he stooped, plucked a stone from the mud, and flung it at Alexidamos with all his strength. Had he missed, things would have gone hard for him—something he paused to think about only later. But, by then, Alexidamos was only three or four strides away; Sostratos had nearly waited too long to do anything at all. The stone struck the mercenary right in the nose.

The wet splat made Sostratos' stomach lurch. Blood splashed as Alexidamos' nose, already kinked by a scar, flattened and smashed. Alexidamos gave a great bellow of pain. He kept coming, but his hands—including the one with the sword—went to his face.

Menedemos jumped on him. Sostratos grabbed at his right arm and twisted the blade away from him. Aristeidas added his weight to the struggle. The three of them quickly subdued the mercenary.

As Sostratos helped hold Alexidamos down, he listened to the chatter of the Kallipolitans all around. "Should we seize them?" somebody asked.

"I don't see what for," someone else said. "They were only defending themselves. He attacked them for no reason I could see." The mutter of agreement that rose relieved Sostratos in no small measure.

A third local said, "If the soldier thinks they wronged him, better he should take them to law than slice them up." That produced more mutters of agreement. The fellow added, "He must think he's an Italian or a wild Kelt, to act the way he did."

Menedemos distracted Sostratos, saying, "I didn't know you could throw so straight."

"Neither did I," Sostratos answered, which made Menedemos laugh. Sostratos went on, "I did what I had to do. Out of necessity, throwing"—a paraphrase of Homer's *out of necessity, fleeing*.

"I understand." By his smile, Menedemos caught the allusion as well as the truth behind it. "Grab this lovely fellow's sword, Aristeidas. We don't want him getting his hands on it again."

"We sure don't," the lookout agreed. "But he'll never be lovely again, not with his nose looking like a beet you just stepped on."

"Too bad." Sostratos and Menedemos spoke together. Menedemos added, "Where did that cowardly wretch of a Teleutas disappear to? By the gods, I ought to pitch him off the ship."

Before Sostratos could answer that, there was a commotion in a nearby street. Teleutas reappeared in the agora, at the head of a dozen sailors carrying assorted implements of mayhem. When he paused to look around and find out what had happened, the expression on his face would have done credit to

a comic mask. "You didn't even need me," he said indignantly.

"Well, now that you mention it, no," Sostratos answered. "But thanks for bringing help anyway."

"I still think he just ran off," Menedemos muttered. But he did no more than mutter, for Teleutas *had* returned promptly, and the reinforcements he brought might have been useful.

"What do we do with Alexidamos here?" Aristeidas asked.

"One of the useful things you might do would be to pluck that dagger from the sheath on his belt," Sostratos told him. After Aristeidas had done that, Sostratos said, "Listen to me, Alexidamos."

"To the crows with you, you stinking son of a whore." Alexidamos' voice didn't sound right. He probably couldn't breathe very well through that ruined nose. "You've maimed me. May the gods curse you forever."

"This is what you get for being a thief," Sostratos replied. "I told you once, you'd better listen to me. If we let you go, will you leave us alone after this?"

A considerable silence followed, punctuated by wet snuffling noises as the mercenary struggled for air. At last, he said, "How can I say no?"

Menedemos spoke before Sostratos could: "You'd better mean it when you say yes. Otherwise, we might as well cut your throat and offer you up for fair winds, the way Agamemnon did with his daughter before he sailed off to Troy."

Considering the misfortunes that befell Agamemnon after he sacrificed Iphigeneia, that didn't strike Sostratos as the wisest threat to make. But Alexidamos was not inclined toward literary criticism. "You're more trouble than you're worth," he growled. "You've shown me that twice over now."

Menedemos looked a question at Sostratos. Sostratos was mildly surprised to find his opinion sought. He shrugged and said, "I don't think we'll get any better promise out of him. It's either let him go, kill him, or stay here and go to law against him."

"May that not come to pass!" Menedemos exclaimed. "We might be stuck forever, and we haven't got the time to waste." He relaxed his grip on the mercenary. Sostratos and Aristeidas followed his lead. Menedemos said, "All right, Alexidamos. Count yourself lucky."

Gingerly, Alexidamos felt of his nose. He hissed in pain at the slightest touch, and cursed at the blood on his fingertips. It was running down his face, too, but he couldn't see that. "Lucky?" he said. "I'm going to be ugly for the rest of my days on account of you—" Remembering he didn't have the advantage, he swallowed a couple of choice epithets.

"You *are* lucky," Sostratos said. "You still have the rest of your life." *Even though I did my best to knock your head right off your shoulders when I threw that stone.* "You were ready to rob us of ours, the same way you tried to rob us of our peafowl eggs."

Alexidamos didn't answer. He staggered away, still dripping blood. "May we never see him again," Menedemos said.

"I thought we were rid of him when we put him on the beach," Sostratos said, "and then especially when we didn't see him in Taras."

"So did I," his cousin said. "We'll be gone tomorrow. We can keep enough men here till then to make sure he doesn't try anything. If we hadn't spent two nights in a row at sea, and if this weren't the last chance before we sail back to Hellas to let the men get their share of wine and women, I'd leave port now."

"You say that?" Sostratos demanded. "You say that after risking everything on the trip to Syracuse?"

With a shrug, Menedemos replied, "We made a lot of money in Syracuse. I don't see much chance for profit here, to you?"

"Nobody could make much of a profit in Kallipolis, and that includes the Kallipolitans." Sostratos spoke with great conviction. He also spoke quietly, lest any of those Kallipolitans hear him and think he slandered their city. He intended to, but he didn't want them to know it.

A moment later, Menedemos donned a wide, artificial smile. "Hail, best one," he said to the local who'd been dickering for fine Khian when Alexidamos made his unexpected appearance. "Good to see you again."

"Have things, ah, settled down?" the Kallipolitan asked. Then he answered his own question: "Yes, I see they have. Well and good. Where were we?"

"We were right here," Menedemos replied. *And we stayed here, while you ran like a rabbit with a pack of Hipparinos' Kastorian hounds baying at your heels,* Sostratos thought. He exhaled noisily through his nose in lieu of sighing. Doing business with a man too often meant you couldn't tell him what you thought of him. Smoothly, Menedemos went on, "Here, why don't you have another taste of a wine Dionysos himself must have specially blessed? The genuine Ariousian of Khios doesn't come to Kallipolis every day, or every year, either."

The cup they'd borrowed had got broken in the scuffle with Alexidamos. They had to pay for it and get another from the potter. When the local tasted the sweet, golden wine for a second time, his eyes got big. Sostratos smiled to himself; he'd seen that before. The Kallipolitan had to work to keep eagerness from his voice as he said, "Now, you named some ridiculous price before the ruction started."

"Sixty drakhmai the amphora," Menedemos repeated calmly.

"Yes," the local said. "I mean, no. I thought that's what you said, and I won't pay it. I'll give you twenty, and not a drakhma more."

"Good day, sir." Menedemos politely inclined his head. "It's been pleasant talking with you."

"Are you mad?" the Kallipolitan said. "You had to open the jar to give me a sample. It won't keep—wine never does, not after you broach the amphora. How much will you get for vinegar? You'd better take what I offer, and be thankful you're getting that much."

His smug smile said he'd played this game with merchants before. He'd probably got away with it with a few of them, too. *Another small-town, small-time chiseler,* Sostratos thought. Aloud, he said, "Good day to you, sir, as my cousin said. And to the crows with you, too." He didn't have to waste politeness on a cheat.

The Kallipolitan's eyes widened again, this time with a different sort of astonishment. "But…But…" he floundered. "You have to sell the stuff, and—"

Sostratos had enjoyed bedding some girls less than he enjoyed laughing in the local's face. "We don't *have* to do a cursed thing, O marvelous one." Not for the first time, he stole Sokrates' sardonic salutation. "We just ran the Carthaginians' blockade to get grain into Syracuse. We have more silver than we know what to do with, friend. If you don't want the Ariousian—and if you don't want to pay our price for it—we'll give the jar to our sailors to drink."

"I've never had a merchant speak to me that way in all my life," the Kallipolitan said. Sostratos believed it. All he did was shrug. Menedemos matched him. The Kallipolitan spluttered wordlessly, then caught his stride: "Oh, very well. If you insist on being unreasonable, I suppose I can go to thirty drakhmai."

Normally, that would have been the start of a dicker. A dicker *had* started before Alexidamos interrupted things. Now, Sostratos just tossed his head. He said, "No," and not another word.

"Thirty-five, then." The local turned red. Anger or embarrassment?

Embarrassment, Sostratos judged. "My cousin told you sixty," he said. "Sixty it will be." He had, for once, the freedom of not caring whether or not he sold the wine. It felt exhilarating, as if he'd had a couple of quick nips from the amphora himself.

"You're not being reasonable," the Kallipolitan protested. "Here, now—I'll give you forty drakhmai. That's more than your precious Khian is worth."

"No," Sostratos said again. "Our price is sixty. If you want the wine, you'll pay it."

And the man from Kallipolis did pay it. He took a while to talk himself into it, and tried to get the two Rhodians to agree to forty-five, fifty, and fifty-five drakhmai first. Sostratos yawned in his face. Menedemos, who could be the most engaging of men when he wanted to, turned his back. The Kallipolitan stomped away. When he returned, a slave behind him, he threw a leather sack full of drakhmai at Sostratos almost as hard as Sostratos had thrown the stone at Alexidamos. Sostratos carefully counted the coins before dipping his head to his cousin.

As the local had the slave carry the amphora back toward his house, Sostratos sighed and said, "Thus we bid farewell to our brief layover in Kallipolis, a small polis where nothing interesting ever happens."

Menedemos stared at him, then started to laugh. "If only it were so," he said.

"Now we just have to hope Alexidamos doesn't go after any of our tavern-crawling sailors tonight," Sostratos said.

"No." His cousin tossed his head. "If that gods-detested mercenary is in any shape to go after our boys tonight after what you did to his beak, he's tougher than Talos, the man made all of bronze."

Sostratos considered that. "Well, maybe you're right."

✧

Diokles pounded his bronze square with his mallet hard enough to make a lot of the *Aphrodite*'s sailors wince as the merchant galley left the harbor of Kallipolis. Menedemos leaned forward toward his crapulent crew and favored them with the smile of a man who'd stayed sober. "Next stop, boys, is Hellas," he said.

He got a few answering smiles. He also got a few answering groans. Diokles said, "Some of 'em don't want to live long enough to get to Hellas."

"But they all will by this afternoon," Menedemos replied. "Hangovers don't kill you. You just wish they would."

Sostratos mounted to the poop deck. "And how shall we go back to Rhodes?" he asked. "Around Cape Tainaron again, or by the diolkos across the Isthmus of Corinth?"

"I don't know yet," Menedemos answered. "We have a good notion of the risks at Cape Tainaron. But who knows what's happened in and around Corinth while we've been out here in Great Hellas? How can we guess whether we should use the diolkos till we know who controls the polis?"

"Hmm," Sostratos said, and then, "You've got something there, no doubt about it."

"Nice of you to admit it," Menedemos said. His cousin made a face at him. Ignoring it, he went on, "We can put in at Korkyra and hear the news there before we decide what to do."

"You're not going to sail southeast toward Zakynthos and reverse the way we came?"

"No. It's getting late in the sailing season for me to want to chance so much time on the open sea," Menedemos answered. "The cranes will be flying south for the winter pretty soon, and not many people want to do much on the water after that. How did Aristophanes put it in the *Birds*?"

"I don't know. How *did* he put it?" Sostratos said. "If you remember it, it was probably foul."

"That's not fair," Menedemos said indignantly. "Aristophanes could write lovely verses about anything at all."

"Or sometimes about nothing at all," Sostratos said.

"Not here," Menedemos said. "It goes something like this:

'Time to sow when the croaking crane migrates
to Libya
Which tells the shipmaster to lie idle after hanging
up his steering oar.'"

"Well, all right. That isn't bad," Sostratos allowed.

"Do you think you can stand being so generous?" Menedemos said. He loved Aristophanes both for his poetry and for his bawdy wit. Sostratos, he knew, admired some of the verse but wanted nothing to do with the lewdness that went hand in hand with it.

To his surprise, his cousin answered seriously: "Being generous to Aristophanes isn't easy for me, you know. If it weren't for the way he pictured Sokrates in the *Clouds*, the Athenians might not have decided to make him drink hemlock."

"He's been dead for a hundred years—" Menedemos began.

"Not quite ninety," Sostratos broke in.

"Not quite ninety, then. Fine. Why are you getting so exercised about it?"

"Because he was a great and good man," Sostratos answered. "That's reason enough—more than reason enough. They aren't so common that we can afford to lose them."

"From everything *I've* heard, he was an interfering old busybody," Menedemos said. "Even if Aristophanes hadn't said a word about him, plenty of people still would've wanted to get rid of him."

For a moment, Sostratos looked as shocked as if he'd said Zeus did not exist—more shocked than that, even, for some bright young men these days did dare doubt the gods. But his cousin, as usual, thought before he spoke. At last, he said, "There may be some truth to that. He never did worry much about what other people thought before he opened his mouth. Platon makes that very plain."

"There you are, then," Menedemos said. "If it was his own fault, why are you blaming Aristophanes?"

"I didn't say it was *all* his own fault."

"Ha! Now you're backing oars. You can go one way or the other, O best one, but you can't try to go both ways at once," Menedemos said.

"I think you're trying to be as difficult as you can," Sostratos said.

"I'd sooner talk philosophy—or gossip about philosophers, which isn't quite the same thing—than

think about pirates," Menedemos said. "Since I don't usually care to do that, you'd best believe the pirates worry me."

"You could have decided to make for Zakynthos instead of taking the short way across the Ionian Sea," Sostratos said.

Menedemos tossed his head. "I told you, it's too close to crane-flying season. Too much chance of a storm's blowing up for me to make the long journey across the open sea. But the pirates will be out. They'll know what honest skippers are thinking, the gods-detested bastards."

For once, though, the usually cautious Sostratos was the bold of the two of them. "I still think you're worrying too much," he said. "If a pirate sees our hull, what will he think? He'll think the same thing half the fishermen in Great Hellas—and over in the Aegean, too—have already thought: that we're pirates ourselves. We don't look anything like a round ship, after all. And he'll leave us alone."

"Here's hoping you're right." Menedemos looked back over his shoulder toward the rocks of Cape Iapygia, the southeasternmost point of Italy. Soon it would disappear from view, and the *Aphrodite* would be out of sight of land till Korkyra or the mainland of Hellas or Macedonia crawled up over the eastern horizon. "But dogs eat dogs. Why shouldn't pirates eat pirates?"

"You've said it yourself: we've got enough men aboard to put up a good fight," Sostratos said.

Menedemos' laugh was less cheerful than he would have liked. "Well, maybe we'll find out if I'm as smart as I think I am."

They got their chance to find out sooner than he would have liked. It wasn't Aristeidas who sang out, "Sail ho!" but a sailor who was pissing from the *Aphrodite*'s stern. Menedemos turned to look back over his shoulder, as he had for Cape Iapygia. He had to follow the sailor's pointing finger to spot the sail, which wasn't much different in color from the sky or the sea. Whoever captained that ship didn't want it seen.

"Fast," Diokles remarked as the sail got bigger and the hull came into view. It too was painted greenish blue, so as not to stand out against waves and sky. "Almost bound to be a pirate, with that turn of speed and that paint job."

"I was thinking the same thing." Menedemos raised his voice: "Take your weapons, men. We may have a fight on our hands."

The skipper of that other ship was bound to be making calculations about the *Aphrodite*. Yes, she was a galley, but she didn't try to disguise and she was on the beamy side for a rowed vessel. That made her an akatos, not a pentekonter or hemiolia—probably not a pirate ship herself, but still a vessel with a formidable crew, one not to be taken lightly.

When Menedemos got a better look at the pirate ship, he saw she wasn't quite so long and low as he'd expected. She carried two banks of oars, though the rowers' benches of the upper deck aft of the mast could be taken out in a hurry to stow the mast and yard and sail. "Hemiolia," Sostratos remarked, coming up onto the poop deck: he'd noted the same thing.

"Which would mark her for a pirate even without her paint job," Menedemos said. "Not much use for hemioliai except to steal from slow ships and run away from fast ones."

"They might make naval auxiliaries," said Sostratos, who sometimes showed himself altogether too good at looking at all sides of a question to suit Menedemos.

But the hemiolia coming up behind the *Aphrodite* was without a doubt, without argument even from Sostratos, a pirate. Menedemos, who couldn't conveniently take down his own mast, could and did order the sail brailed up to the yard and put a full complement on the oars. As he'd done twice before, he swung his ship toward the pirate, showing he was ready for a fight if her skipper wanted one.

That skipper didn't run, as the other two had done. But he didn't attack the merchant galley, either. Instead, he shouted across a couple of plethra of seawater: "Ahoy! You coming from Italy? What news?" His Greek held a peculiar accent, perhaps Macedonian, more likely Epeirote.

"You have news of Hellas?" Menedemos shouted back. The pirate captain nodded, which proved him an Epeirote or something of the sort—Macedonians dipped their heads like proper Hellenes. Menedemos went on, "I'll trade what I know for what you do. I won't give it away."

"All right," the other captain called. "I tell you, Polyperkhon still has Corinth and the isthmus and

Sikyon to the west, and he's made friends with the Aitolians north of the Gulf of Corinth."

That was worth knowing. Menedemos spoke of Agathokles' dash to Africa, with the Carthaginian fleet on his heels. "I don't know how long he'll be fighting there, but the war between Carthage and Syracuse won't be the same any more."

"You're right about that, trader," the pirate agreed. "I tell you, too, Polyperkhon has from Pergamon the youngster called Herakles, the son of Alexander the Great and Barsine. He says he will make the youth king of Macedonia."

"He's not really Alexander's son," Sostratos said quietly. "He's just a pretender Antigonos raised up…I think."

"I know that—I've heard the same stories you have," Menedemos answered. "But whoever he really is, he's plenty to make Kassandros pitch a fit in Macedonia."

"Well, yes," Sostratos said. "When you think about what Kassandros did to Alexandros and Roxane, you know he doesn't want any heirs to the Macedonian throne running around loose. They hurt his own position."

"What's Polemaios doing?" Menedemos called to the pirate.

"He's still down in the south of the Peloponnesos," the fellow answered. "If that was me, I wouldn't go anyplace Antigonos could get his hands on me. If Old One-Eye caught his nephew now, I bet he'd keep him alive for *months*."

"You're probably right," Menedemos said. "Speaking of Antigonos, what do you know about the war between him and Ptolemaios?"

"Not a thing," the pirate said, shrugging. "Who gives a fart what happens way over in the east?" He seemed suddenly bored with talking instead of plundering, and shouted orders to his crew. The hemiolia glided south, looking for prey easier than the *Aphrodite*.

"Which way will you go?" Sostratos asked.

"Over in Corinth, Polyperkhon's got trouble with Kassandros and Polemaios both," Menedemos said. "That makes Cape Tainaron a better bet, I think." Sostratos clicked his tongue between his teeth, but didn't try to tell him he was wrong.

XII

"Telos behind us at last," Sostratos said. His cousin made a face at him, for the Aegean island's name sounded nearly the same as the word for *at last*. Grinning at Menedemos, he pointed eastward. "And there's Rhodes ahead."

"A good thing, too," Menedemos said. "No guessing how much longer decent sailing weather will hold."

"You've been grumbling about that ever since we left Syracuse," Sostratos said. "The weather couldn't have been much better."

"That's true, but it didn't *have* to stay good," Menedemos replied. "And when have you ever known a sailor who didn't worry about the weather?"

Sostratos didn't answer that. He eyed the birds overhead flying south for the winter. Sure enough, there was a long, straggling line of cranes, bigger than any of the other birds he could see. Aristophanes had had it right. *But he was still wrong about Sokrates*, Sostratos thought.

If he said that, he would start a real quarrel, and he didn't feel like one now, not with the *Aphrodite* so close to home. Instead, he chose something he reckoned harmless: "It'll be good to get back to our family."

But his cousin only grunted. "Good for you, maybe," he said at last. "You wait. My father will say he could have done better and made more money."

He's probably right, Sostratos thought. *Uncle Philodemos is never satisfied.* Aloud, he said, "Why don't you just smile and dip your head and tell him he's bound to know best?"

"Ha!" Menedemos rolled his eyes. "For one thing, he cursed well *doesn't* know best. And for another, if I told him he did, he'd fall over dead from the shock. I don't want his blood on my hands even by accident, the way Oidipous had Laios'."

And you're just as stubborn as your father, and you won't yield to him even by a barleycorn's breadth. One more thing Sostratos thought it better not to say. He did say, "Whether the two of you argue or not, he'll be glad to see you. We've come back safe, we only lost one man, and we made money. What more could he ask?"

"More money, of course," Menedemos replied.

"Oh, foof!" Sostratos said. "Once we get into port, the family will throw a celebration the polis will buzz about all through the winter. Your father wouldn't do that if he didn't care about you, and you know it. My mother and sister will be green with envy because they aren't men and won't be able to come."

"Maybe." Menedemos did his best not to sound convinced. "I wonder if my father's second wife will even care."

"Of course she will," Sostratos said. "Baukis is young—I remember that from the wedding, though I doubt I've seen her since, naturally. She'll want something she can gossip about with her friends."

"Maybe," Menedemos said again. He turned away from Sostratos, plainly not wanting to discuss it further. Sostratos wondered if he was angry at his father for remarrying after his mother died. If Uncle Philodemos had a son by his new wife, that would complicate the family inheritance.

As the *Aphrodite* neared Rhodes, the island stretched across more and more of the horizon. "The vines look good," Sostratos said, even though he was too far away to make any real guess about how they looked. It let him talk about something besides the family, which Menedemos plainly didn't want to do. Trying his best to come up with the light chat that his cousin managed as if by nature, he went on, "Not that we'd ever get sixty drakhmai the amphora if we shipped Rhodian to Great Hellas."

"No," Menedemos said, and made a production out of steering the akatos. *So much for light chatter*, Sostratos thought mournfully.

The fishing boats that bobbed in the blue, blue Aegean didn't flee when their skippers spotted the *Aphrodite*—most of them didn't, anyhow. The fishermen knew few pirates dared venture into the well-patrolled waters near their island. "We can certainly be proud of our fleet," Sostratos offered.

"Yes. Certainly." Again, Menedemos spoke as if he were being charged for every word he uttered. Sostratos gave up until the merchant galley rounded Rhodes' northernmost promontory, passed the fleet's harbor, and sailed into the sheltered waters of the great harbor, from which it had set out that spring.

"It *is* good to be back," he said then.

"Well, so it is," Menedemos admitted—something of a relief to Sostratos, who'd begun to wonder if his cousin ever intended to speak more than a couple of words to him. Menedemos wasn't shy about talking to the rowers, of whom he had ten on a side at the oars: "Come on, boys—make it pretty. The whole polis will be watching you, and there's not a Rhodian man breathing who doesn't know what to do with an oar in his hands."

Thus encouraged, the rowers showed what a well beaten-in crew could manage, following the stroke Diokles set with perfect precision as Menedemos guided the *Aphrodite* to an open berth. "Back oars!" the keleustes called, and the men did that as smoothly as everything else. As soon as they'd killed the merchant galley's momentum, he called, "*Oöp!*" and they rested at their oars.

Sailors heaved lines to men on the wharf, who made the akatos fast. Sostratos tossed an obolos to each roustabout, and another little silver coin to a fellow to whom he said, "Hail, Letodoros. Run to the houses of Lysistratos and Philodemos and let them know the *Aphrodite*'s home and safe. They'll have something more for you there, I expect."

"Thanks, best one. I'll do that." Letodoros popped the obolos into his mouth and went off at a ground-eating trot.

"Won't be long now," Sostratos said to Menedemos.

"So it won't." His cousin still stood between the steering oars, as he had throughout the voyage. Menedemos drummed the fingers of his right hand on the starboard tiller. "It won't be *so* bad," he said, as if trying to make himself believe it. "We *did* make a profit, after all, and a good one. Nobody can deny that."

"Nobody will even try to deny it," Sostratos said. "You'll see. And you're the one who claims I worry too much."

Menedemos fidgeted while they waited for their fathers to come down to the harbor. Sostratos paid the sailors what he owed them since he'd last given each of them silver, and wrote down the payments so no one could say he hadn't got his due. Watching Menedemos, he thought, *I wouldn't twitch like a man with fleas even if I didn't have anything to do. I might feel like it, but I wouldn't do it.*

After he paid off Diokles, he clasped the keleustes' hand and told him, "I hope you'll sail with us again next spring."

"I hope so, too, young sir," the oarmaster answered. "Never a dull moment, was there?"

"Too few of them, anyway," Sostratos said, which made Diokles laugh.

"Oh, by the gods," Menedemos said softly. "Here comes Father." He'd attacked a Roman trireme with no visible trace of fear, but quivered to see a middle-aged man approach the *Aphrodite*.

Sostratos waved. "Hail, Uncle Philodemos," he called. "We've come back with every man we started out with but one, and with a tidy profit."

"What happened to the one man?" Philodemos rapped out. He aimed the question not at Sostratos but at his own son.

"Hail, Father," Menedemos said. "He died of an arrow wound he took in a sea fight."

"Pirates?" Philodemos asked. "The Italian waters are lousy with 'em. Polluted bastards all ought to go up on crosses." His right hand folded into an angry fist.

"Yes, sir," Menedemos agreed. "But this wasn't a fight with pirates. The Romans sent a fleet of triremes to raid a Samnite town called Pompaia just as we were sailing away from it, and one of the triremes took after us."

Philodemos raised an eyebrow. "And you got away from it? That must have taken some fine sailing. I wasn't sure you had it in you."

Menedemos grappled with that, trying to decide whether it came out a compliment. Sostratos spoke up before his cousin could: "We didn't get away from it, Uncle. We wrecked it—used our hull to break its starboard oars. After we crippled it, then we got away."

"Really?" Philodemos said. Not only Sostratos and Menedemos but also a good many sailors amplified the story. Menedemos' father stroked his chin. "That does sound like a smart piece of work," he allowed.

"There," Sostratos hissed. "You see?" But Menedemos ignored him.

He was miffed, but only for a moment, for he saw his own father coming down the wharf toward the *Aphrodite*. He waved again. Lysistratos waved back. "Hail, son," he said. "Good to see you again. How did everything go?"

Uncle Philodemos didn't say it was good to see Menedemos, went through Sostratos' mind. *He may have thought it, but he didn't say it.* "Hail," he answered. "We're here. We made money. And we got rid of all the peafowl and all of their chicks." Relentless honesty made him add, "Well, almost all the peafowl. One peahen jumped into the sea. That was my fault."

"Many goodbyes to them," Menedemos said. "They're gods-detested birds, no matter how pretty the peacock was. The Italiotes and barbarians who bought them are welcome to them, believe you me they are."

"They did make nuisances of themselves in our courtyards, didn't they?" Lysistratos said. "But I'm sure the two of you will be glad to come home and sleep in your own beds again. That was always one of the things I liked best about getting back from a trading run, anyhow."

"I don't know, Father," Sostratos said. "I've spent so much time on the planks of the poop deck, the mattress will probably feel strange the first few days. And then there was the night on the sacks of wheat when we were going down to Syracuse."

"Syracuse?" Lysistratos and Philodemos said together. Menedemos' father went on, "What's the news from Syracuse?" and Sostratos realized the *Aphrodite* was the first ship coming into Rhodes with word of everything that had happened in the west.

He and his cousin told the story together. Menedemos told more of it. Of the two of them, he'd always had the quicker tongue as well as the quicker feet. Sostratos got his chances to talk after Philodemos' frequent questions, for each one would throw Menedemos off his stride for a little while. Questions from Lysistratos didn't faze Menedemos at all, Sostratos noted.

When the two young men finished, Philodemos clicked his tongue between his teeth. "You took some long chances there, son," he said, his tone suggesting he might have other remarks when not so many people could hear them.

"I know, sir, but we got by with them, and they ended up paying off well," Menedemos replied, with something less than the cheeky brashness he'd shown through most of the journey.

"Just how much money did you make?" Philodemos asked. Menedemos looked toward Sostratos. Sostratos had told his cousin the answer, but Menedemos had no confidence in it. Here in his home port, Sostratos saw no point in keeping it a secret. He told his uncle, and had the satisfaction of watching the older man's jaw drop. "You're joking," Philodemos said.

"And five oboloi," Sostratos added. "No, I'm not joking at all."

"*Euge!*" his father said, and clapped his hands together to show just how well he thought it was done. "That's…splendid is the only word I can find." Lysistratos clapped again. "I'm proud of both of you."

"We also still have a little silk and a little Ariousian and some perfume on board," Sostratos said. "They won't bring so much here as they would have in Great Hellas, but they'll bring something."

Lysistratos beamed. Even Philodemos didn't look too unhappy. Sostratos waved to Himilkon the Phoenician, who was heading over to find out the news. *We did it*, he thought. *We really did it, and now, at last, we're back. It feels even better than I thought it would.*

☼

Menedemos sat in the andron in his house, sipping from a cup of wine and wishing he were somewhere, anywhere, else. Even the men's chamber itself left him disappointed. Here in Rhodes, it was pretty fine. Set it next to Gylippos' in Taras, though, and it wasn't so much of a much.

But he wouldn't have minded the andron so much if his father hadn't been sitting a couple of cubits away glaring at him. "You idiot," Philodemos said. "What on earth or under it were you thinking of?"

"Profit," Menedemos answered in a low voice. His father always managed to put him in the wrong. With a flash of defiance, he added, "We got it, too. We got a lot of it."

Philodemos waved that away, as of no account. "You came much too close to getting exactly—exactly, I tell you—what you deserved for such a piece of foolishness. What did your cousin think of it? Was he as mad to put on wax-glued wings and imitate Ikaros flying up toward the sun as you were?"

Menedemos thought about lying, but reckoned he was too likely to get caught. Reluctantly, he tossed his head. "Well, no. Not quite."

"Not quite?" Philodemos put a world of expression into his echo. "What does that mean? No, don't tell me. I can figure it out for myself. Sostratos has some sense, at least—more than I can say for my own flesh and blood."

To cover his feelings, Menedemos took a long pull at the wine. He wished he could get drunk right now, so he wouldn't have to pay his father any attention at all. But Philodemos wouldn't let him forget that, either, and they'd be living in the same house till spring. However much he wanted to, however insulted he felt, he couldn't storm away, either, not unless he wanted to create bad blood that might last till he could sail away again.

What can I do? he wondered. Changing the subject was the only thing that came to him. He said, "We heard on the way back here that the war between Ptolemaios and Antigonos got going for all it was worth. Nobody really expected the peace to last, but even so...."

"It's going, all right," his father agreed with a certain gloomy satisfaction. Philodemos was willing to criticize the follies of others besides Menedemos. "Ptolemaios sent his general Leonides up to Kilikia to seize the cities on the coast from Antigonos."

"And he did it?" Menedemos asked.

His father dipped his head. "He did it, all right—till Antigonos heard what had happened. Then old One-Eye sent out his son Demetrios, and Demetrios ran Leonides out of Kilikia and all the way back to Egypt. Ptolemaios sent messages to Lysimakhos and Kassandros, too, they say, asking them for help to keep Antigonos from getting too strong, but he sure didn't get much."

"But Antigonos' nephew Polemaios turned on him," Menedemos said. "That has to be a heavy blow to Antigonos, losing the fellow who was his right-hand man."

"'Was' is right," his father said. "That's Demetrios' place now, Demetrios' and his younger brother Philippos'. Antigonos sent Philippos up to the Hellespont to take on Polemaios' lieutenant Phoinix, and Philippos whipped him almost as hard as Demetrios whipped Leonides."

Menedemos whistled softly. "I hadn't heard that before. You have to admire Antigonos. He's never at a loss, no matter what happens to him."

"If you're a fat partridge in a bush, do you admire the wolf who wants to eat you?" Philodemos said. "That's how Rhodes looks to the marshals. And the thing about Antigonos is, he frightens all the others enough to make 'em band together to try to pull him down. You mark my words, son: those Macedonians

will still be knocking heads together when you're as old as I am."

"Thirty years from now?" Menedemos tried not to sound scornful. He also tried to imagine what he would be like if he reached his father's years—tried and felt himself failing. "That's a long way off."

"You mark my words," Philodemos repeated. "The generals have been going at each other ever since Alexander died. Why should they stop? What would make them stop?"

"One man winning," Menedemos said at once.

His father looked thoughtful. "Yes, that might do it," he admitted. "But if one of them looks like winning, all the others gang up on him, the way everyone is against Antigonos now. That's how it's gone so far. Why should it change?"

"*Panta rhei,*" Menedemos replied.

"'Everything flows'?" Philodemos echoed. "Some philosopher or other, isn't it? I thought you left showing off how much you know to your cousin."

"I'm sorry. I usually do." Menedemos liked his father much better when he was slighting Sostratos than when he was praising him.

Philodemos grunted. "Well, that's not much of an apology, but I suppose it's better than nothing."

You always find fault, Menedemos thought. *If I cut my liver out for you, you'd complain that the priest didn't read good omens from it.*

But then his father said, "You beat a trireme? And you came home with that much silver? I suppose, all things considered, you could have done worse. Here, let me pour you some more wine." Menedemos was almost too startled to hold out his cup—almost, but not quite. But as Philodemos poured, he asked, "And how many husbands did you outrage in Great Hellas?" Even when he tried to praise, he couldn't do it unmixed with spite.

And Menedemos answered with quick truth when, again, he might have done better lying: "Only one."

His father muttered something under his breath, then sighed and asked, "Where was it this time? Will you ever be able to do business there again, or is it as bad as Halikarnassos?"

"Taras, Father," Menedemos said, and Philodemos grunted as if he'd been hit in the belly. Menedemos went on, "I don't think it's quite so bad as at Halikarnassos." He didn't think Gylippos' toughs had intended to kill him, but only to beat him up. The fellow in Halikarnassos had definitely wanted him dead.

"Not *quite* so bad." Philodemos looked as if he were sipping vinegar, not wine. "And Taras is an important polis, too, the first one you're like to come to on the way west from Hellas. What *are* we going to do with you, son?" Menedemos found it expedient to stay mute. His father grunted again, then said, "Well, at least you don't do things like that here in Rhodes, the gods be praised."

Menedemos didn't answer that, either. His father, fortunately, took silence for agreement.

"I was hoping I might hear my sister had been betrothed when I came home," Sostratos remarked to his father as they sat in the andron.

"And I was hoping I might be able to tell you Erinna was," Lysistratos replied. "I did have some discussions about it with—oh, never mind what his name was: what point to going into the details when these things don't work out?"

"What was wrong with him?" Sostratos asked.

"Not a thing," Lysistratos said. "But he made a match with another family for their daughter who's never been married. They aren't so well off as we are, but the girl's fourteen, not eighteen. He's more likely to breed sons on her than he is on Erinna. You can't blame him for having that uppermost in his thoughts. What are wives for but sons?"

"It's not Erinna's fault—" Sostratos began before checking himself.

"It's not anyone's fault that I can see," his father said. "It's just one of those things that make life difficult for mortals."

Gyges, the Lydian majordomo, stuck his head into the men's chamber. "Master, Xanthos is at the door. He wants to congratulate the young master on the *Aphrodite*'s safe return."

Sostratos rolled his eyes. "Speaking of the things that make life difficult for mortals…"

His father laughed, but told Gyges, "Bring him in. He can drink some wine with us. Sooner or later, he'll go away."

"Later," Sostratos predicted, but in a voice low enough to keep his father from giving him a reproving

look. A moment later, when the majordomo brought Xanthos into the andron, Sostratos got to his feet and bowed to the older man. "Hail, O marvelous one. How are you today?"

"Hail, Sostratos," Xanthos said. "It's good of you to ask. To tell you the truth, I do marvel that I failed to go down to the house of Hades while you were off in the west. My piles have been torture—and all the worse because I've been so constipated. And my shoulder joints ache whenever the weather gets damp. I dread this winter season, I truly do. I haven't been sleeping well, either. Old age truly is a misery; never let anyone tell you otherwise."

"Here you are, Xanthos." Lysistratos gave the other merchant a cup of wine, no doubt hoping to slow the tide of words. "Drink with us. We have reason to be glad, with the boys home safe and with a tidy profit, too."

"That's good news, very good news, very good news indeed," Xanthos said, flicking a few drops out of the cup for a libation. "Pity your son here couldn't have heard me at the Assembly earlier in the month. I'm immodest enough to say I surpassed even my usual eloquence."

"What did you speak on?" Sostratos asked.

"On how we should conduct ourselves if the fighting between Antigonos and Ptolemaios gets worse," Xanthos replied.

"That *is* important," Sostratos agreed.

He didn't ask the plump merchant to summarize the speech. He knew better. And Xanthos didn't summarize it. He said, "I believe I can remember how it went," and launched into it, complete with gestures that looked as if they would have been more at home on the comic stage than in the Assembly. His main point was that, since Rhodes did so much business with Egypt, she should stay on Ptolemaios' side provided she could do so without making Antigonos attack her. That made good sense to Sostratos, but he mightily wished Xanthos hadn't taken half an hour to get where he was going.

"Stirring," Lysistratos said when Xanthos finally finished. He poured himself more wine, which showed just how much he'd been stirred. Sostratos held out his cup for a refill, too. His father didn't offer the oinokhoe to Xanthos.

"Tell me the news from Italy," Xanthos urged Sostratos.

"Up north of Great Hellas, the Samnites and the Romans are still fighting," Sostratos said. He started to tell the other Rhodian how the *Aphrodite* had wound up in the middle of that war, but decided not to. It would only have brought more questions, and maybe, the gods forbid, another speech. Instead, he went on, "And from Sicily, Agathokles has invaded Africa to pay the Carthaginians back for besieging Syracuse." He didn't say anything about how the *Aphrodite* had been involved there, either.

"Well, well, isn't that interesting?" Xanthos said. He sensed he was being thwarted, and cast about for an opening: "You sold all your peafowl?"

"All but one, that, uh, died before we got to Great Hellas." Again, he said not a word about peafowl eggs or peafowl chicks.

"Ah, too bad," Xanthos said. "That cost you some money, it did, it did." Sostratos gravely dipped his head. He didn't say anything. Much later than Xanthos should have, he began to suspect he'd outstayed his welcome. "Well, I guess I'll wander over and pay my respects to Menedemos and his father."

"Good to see you," Sostratos said. *Good to see you go*, he glossed silently. He was glad enough to clasp Xanthos' hand as the other merchant took his leave. So was Lysistratos. Son and father looked at each other. When they heard Gyges close the door behind Xanthos, they sighed in unison. "Is there any more wine left in the oinokhoe?" Sostratos asked. "He's windy without eating beans and cabbage."

When his father shook the jar, it sloshed. He poured some into Sostratos' cup, the rest into his own. "He means well," he said.

After hearing every word of Xanthos' speech before the Assembly, Sostratos was not inclined to be charitable. "So does a puppy that piddles on my feet," he said, and drank the wine his father had given him.

"I know what you're thinking," Lysistratos said. "I'll have you know, though, that I suffered worse than you. I've heard his speech twice now."

"Oh, poor Father!" Sostratos exclaimed, and put an arm around Lysistratos' shoulder. They both started laughing. Once they started, they had a hard time stopping. *It's not the wine*, Sostratos thought. *We didn't drink* that *much. It had to be Xanthos' speech.*

That would have paralyzed a man who'd drunk nothing but water his whole life long.

"We shall have to have a feast to welcome you back," Lysistratos said. "A couple of feasts, in fact: one for your sister and your mother, and the other a proper symposion where you and your cousin can speak at length of your adventures in Great Hellas. Did you truly beat a trireme in the *Aphrodite*?"

"We wrecked its starboard bank of oars, and that let us get away," Sostratos replied. "Menedemos was telling Uncle Philodemos about it just before you got down to the harbor. I'm sure, at the symposion, he'll make a much more exciting story of it than I ever could."

"Exciting stories are all very well after the wine's gone round a few times," his father said. "I'd also like to have some notion of what really happened, though." Lysistratos' smile was lopsided, the smile of a man who'd learned not to expect too much from the world. "It might even make the stories more exciting."

"I'll tell you everything, as best I remember it," Sostratos promised. "But you should also listen to Menedemos' version, and Diokles' as well. Then you can put them together for yourself and decide where the real truth lies." He laughed at himself. "Anyone would think I wanted to write a history one day. That's how Thoukydides says he went about figuring out just what happened in the Peloponnesian War."

"Seems a sensible way to try to learn things," Lysistratos said.

Sostratos snapped his fingers. "Diokles!" he exclaimed. "I do want to put in a good word for him. We couldn't have had a better oarmaster. Honest, sensible, brave when he needs to be—I'd love to sail with him as keleustes again next spring, but he'd make a good captain, too."

"I've always thought well of him, ever since the days when he first started pulling an oar," Lysistratos said. "I'll tell you what I do. When we have our symposion here, I'll invite him. I'm sure he can tell some stories of his own, and that will also let him talk with some other men who might want to offer him command of a ship."

"That would be very good, Father." Sostratos enthusiastically dipped his head. "It might be our loss, but Diokles deserves the chance."

"I should say so," Lysistratos agreed. "Considering how much silver you brought home, anyone who helped you earn it deserves a hand up from us. A man should lift up his friends and put down his enemies as he can, eh?"

"So Hellenes have said since the days of Akhilleus and Agamemnon," Sostratos answered. *And so Hellas has seen endless factions and feuds, too*, he thought, and then, *I wonder if that would make sense to any of Alexander's marshals. Probably not, worse luck, or they wouldn't be at one another's throats.*

Lysistratos pointed. "There's your sister, watering the garden. She'll be glad to see you."

Sostratos had heard water splashing from a hydria, too, but sat with his back to the courtyard. He'd guessed the slave girl, Threissa, was doing the work. "I'm always glad to see her," he said, getting to his feet. He walked out of the andron and called, "Hail, Erinna."

His sister squeaked, put down the water jar, ran to him, and threw herself into his arms. "Hail, Sostratos!" she said, and kissed him on the cheek. "When that wharf rat came yelling with news the *Aphrodite* was back, I almost veiled myself up and ran down to the harbor myself to come get a look at you as soon as I could." She grinned wickedly. "Wouldn't that have been a scandal?"

"It's not something girls of a good family do very often," Sostratos said diplomatically.

"I'm not exactly a girl of good family any more," Erinna answered. "The rules are a little looser for a widow."

"I suppose so," Sostratos said. "Father tells me you almost had a match this summer."

"Almost," Erinna agreed bitterly. "But then they decided to wed their son to a maiden instead. Look at me, Sostratos!" His sister seized his hands and held them. "Is my back bent? Is my hair gray? Are my teeth turning black and falling out?"

"Of course not." Sostratos answer was automatic. "By Zeus, you're still my little sister, and I'm a long way from an old man."

"Well, that other family treated me like an old woman," Erinna said. "When the other match came along, they dropped me as if they thought I'd be a shade in the house of Hades day after tomorrow. How am I supposed to have a family if no one wants to marry me any more?"

"You're always part of our family," Sostratos said.

His sister impatiently tossed her head. "I know that, but it's not what I meant, and you know it isn't. I meant a family of my own."

"Don't worry," Sostratos said. "You'll have one." *If we have to make your dowry bigger, then we do, that's all. We can afford it better than we could have before this voyage. The silver we made in Syracuse* will *come in handy, no matter how much I wish Menedemos hadn't taken such a chance to get it.*

"I hope so," Erinna said. "Childlessness is a terrible thing." Her smile seemed to Sostratos a deliberate effort of will, one that sprang from purposely turning her back on her troubles. She made her voice bright and cheerful, too: "Tell me about the voyage. Even if I am a widow, I'm a respectable woman, so I hardly get out of the house except to festivals and such, but you—you get to go across the sea. You know I'm jealous."

"You have less to be jealous of than you think," Sostratos said. "If you feel crowded and closed in here, imagine spending a night at sea aboard an akatos, where most of the men don't even have room to lie down to sleep."

"But you see something new every day, every hour!" Erinna sighed. "I know every bump and scratch on the walls of the women's rooms upstairs, every knot in the planks of the roof beams. Even coming out here to the courtyard feels like a journey to me."

He wanted to laugh, but he didn't. Men and women lived different lives, and that was all there was to it. So he spoke of meeting Ptolemaios' five in the Aegean, of the little earthquake while they were at Cape Tainaron, of Herennius Egnatius' toga in Taras, of seeing Mount Aitne and Mount Ouesouion, of his muleback excursion from Pompaia toward Ouesouion, and of the eclipse of the sun at Syracuse. He couldn't have had a more attentive audience; his sister hung on his every word.

Erinna sighed again when he finished. "When you tell me about these things, I can almost see them in my mind. How marvelous it must be to see them in truth."

"I'm just glad I saw the volcanoes when they were quiet," Sostratos said.

"Well, yes," Erinna admitted. "But even so." Her gaze sharpened. "When the man came running up here from the harbor, he was shouting about sea fights. You didn't talk about any sea fights."

"We really had only one," he said, and told her the story of the clash with the Roman trireme.

This time, his sister clapped her hands when he was done. "That was exciting," she said. "Why didn't you tell me about it before?"

Sostratos chuckled sheepishly. "Because it wasn't exciting while it was going on, I suppose," he answered. "It was terrifying. And seeing the Carthaginian fleet coming at us outside of Syracuse was worse. If that had turned into a sea fight, we couldn't possibly have won."

"Why did you let Menedemos go on, then?" Erinna asked.

Sostratos' mouth twisted into a wry, lopsided smile. His laugh was similarly sour. "My dear, it wasn't a question of my *letting* him do any such thing. I'm toikharkhos. He's the captain. The choice was his. I tried to talk him out of it." *I thought he was a fool. I thought he was a reckless idiot.* "When he said we were heading for Syracuse, what could I do? Leave the ship and swim home? It turned out well."

"Luck," Erinna said, and then, "Why are you laughing now?"

"Because you sound just like me," he told her. "But it wasn't all luck. Menedemos turned out to be right about that. Agathokles used the grain fleet to lure the Carthaginian ships away from the harbor and give his own navy the chance to get out and make for Africa."

"Can he take Carthage?" Erinna asked.

"I don't know," Sostratos answered. "Nobody knows—including the Carthaginians, I'm sure. But I do know they can't be anxious to find out. No one's ever tried to take the wars in Sicily to their country before."

"Alexander conquered the barbarians in the east," his sister said. "Why shouldn't Agathokles conquer the barbarians in the west?"

"I can think of two reasons," Sostratos replied. Erinna raised a questioning eyebrow. He explained: "First, the Carthaginians are still strong. And second, Agathokles isn't Alexander, no matter how much he wishes he were."

"All right." Erinna hugged him again. "It's so good to have you home. No one else takes me seriously when I ask questions."

"Well, if your brother won't, who will?" Sostratos kissed her on the forehead. "I'll be home till spring, so you'll have plenty of chances to ask them. But now I'm going upstairs." With obvious reluctance, she dipped her head and let him go. As he headed for the stairway, she picked up the hydria and went back to watering.

He was halfway up the stairs when Threissa started down them. "Hail, young master," the redheaded slave girl said in her oddly accented Greek. "Welcome home."

"Hail. Thank you," he said, and went up another couple of steps. The Thracian slave wasn't so pretty as Maibia had been. But Maibia was back in Taras while Threissa was here—and Sostratos had gone without a long time. "Come to my room with me," he told her.

She sighed. She couldn't say no, not when she was as much property as the bed on which he intended to have her. But she said, "All right," in a way that promised she would give him as little enjoyment as she could.

He considered ways and means. "I'll let you have a couple of oboloi afterwards."

He didn't have to do that, not with a family slave. "All right," Threissa said, but this time in a different tone of voice. "Maybe even three?"

Slaves are mercenary creatures, Sostratos thought. *But then, they have to be.* "Maybe," he answered. Threissa waited for him at the top of the stairs. They went down the hall together to his room. He closed the door behind them.

"Come on," Menedemos said as he and Sostratos made their way toward the gymnasion in the southwestern part of Rhodes, not far from the stadium and the temple dedicated to Apollo. "It'll do you good. We've been away too long."

His cousin accompanied him only reluctantly. "What you mean is, it'll do *you* good to show you can still outrun me and throw me when we wrestle. I don't know why you bother. We both know how that will come out."

"That's not the point," Menedemos said, which was at least partially true. "The point is, a proper Hellene doesn't let himself go to seed."

"I can think of quite a few things you do that a proper Hellene doesn't," Sostratos said tartly. "Why shouldn't I get to pick and choose, too?"

Since Menedemos knew he had no good comeback for that, he didn't bother trying to find one. Instead, he repeated, "Come on," adding, "No point in going back now. Look, you can already see the theater and the southern wall beyond it."

"And if I went back home, I could see Demeter's temple," Sostratos retorted. "Did you drag me out here to see the sights? I don't mind that so much. Going to the gymnasion is a different story."

"Quit complaining," Menedemos said, beginning to lose patience. "You can let yourself get all hunched-up and flabby, like a shoemaker stuck at his bench all the time or a barbarian who doesn't care what he looks like because he never takes off his clothes, or else you can try to be as much of a *kaloskagathos* as you can."

"I have much more control over whether I'm good than I do over whether I'm good-looking," Sostratos said. Despite his grumbles, he accompanied Menedemos into the gymnasion. They stripped off their chitons—being seamen, they didn't bother with sandals—and gave an attendant an obolos to keep an eye on the clothes while they went out and exercised.

Some of the men running on the track or grappling with one another in the sandy wrestling pits plainly didn't get to the gymnasion often enough. But others…Menedemos pointed. "There's a pretty boy, fourteen or fifteen, and handsome enough to have his name scrawled on the walls." His own name had gone up on more than a few walls when he was that age; Sostratos', he remembered rather too late, hadn't.

All his cousin said now, though, was, "Yes, and doesn't he know it? If he sticks his nose any higher in the air, he'll get a crick in the neck."

"When you look like that, you can get away with a few airs," Menedemos said. Sostratos only grunted.

They ran a few sprints to loosen up. Menedemos savored the feel of the breeze against his skin, the grass at the verge of the track flying by as he strained to get every bit of speed from himself he could. He also savored Sostratos in his wake, hearing his cousin's panting breath fade behind him time after time.

"You're a pentekonter, sure enough," Sostratos said. "Me, I'm just a round ship."

Menedemos' turn of speed drew the notice of a fellow a couple of years younger than he who also had the lean, muscular build of a runner. "Try yourself against me?" the younger man said. "I'm Amyntas son of Praxion."

"Pleased to meet you." Menedemos gave his own name, and introduced Sostratos, too. "I'd be pleased to run with you. My cousin will call the start."

"Good enough," Amyntas said. "Would you care to put a drakhma on the race, just to make it interesting?"

"Interesting, eh?" Menedemos raised an eyebrow. "All right, if it pleases you. Sostratos, turn us loose." He took his position on the track beside Amyntas.

"Ready?" Sostratos called. "Set." Both runners tensed. "Go!"

Amyntas went off like an arrow from a bow. Menedemos stayed shoulder to shoulder with him till they were within twenty-five or thirty cubits of the end of the stadion course, but Amyntas pulled away and won by five cubits or so. "I can do better than that," Menedemos said. "Try it again, double the stake to the winner?"

"Why not?" Amyntas said, not quite hiding a predatory smile as they walked back to the beginning of the course. Several men gathered to watch them now. Menedemos wondered if Sostratos would give him a fishy stare for gambling on his legs. But his cousin only shrugged and called the start again. *He's probably glad not to be running himself*, Menedemos thought, leaning forward to get the best start he could.

"Go!" Sostratos said, and Menedemos and Amyntas shot away once more. Again, Menedemos stayed close to the younger man till the race was almost over. Again, he couldn't quite keep up at the end. Again, he kicked at the dirt in frustration.

"That's two drakhmai you owe me," Amyntas said, not bothering to hide his grin now that he'd won.

"Let's double it one more time." Menedemos sounded like a man determined to win his way back to prosperity no matter how long it took—and no matter if it broke him first.

"Just as you say, best one," Amyntas replied as they walked back toward the starting line.

"Give us a start one more time," Menedemos called to Sostratos. "I'm going to whip this fellow yet, and I've doubled the bet to prove it." Some of the men who stood at the side of the track watching murmured among themselves. Amyntas' grin got wider; he had witnesses, in case Menedemos didn't feel like paying up.

They took their marks. "Ready?" Sostratos said. "Set....Go!"

Amyntas and Menedemos flew down the track side by side. As before, Menedemos hung at the younger man's shoulder till they were about thirty cubits form the end of the course. Then Amyntas, leaning forward for his final sprint, let out a startled grunt. Menedemos went past him as if his feet were suddenly nailed to the dirt, and won by three or four cubits.

"That's four drakhmai *you* owe *me*," he said cheerfully. "Or would you like to double the bet again?"

"Oh, no." Amyntas tossed his head. "I know what I just saw. You held back the first two runs to draw me in, didn't you?"

"I don't know *what* you're talking about." Menedemos' voice was arch. "Besides, how can I be sure you weren't trying to fool me there?" But he knew. Amyntas had been running flat out, and he hadn't been good enough. Menedemos chuckled. If he'd been fast enough to go to Olympia a couple of years before, Amyntas would have remembered his name. Nobody recalled the also-rans, but a man nearly fast enough to represent his polis at the Olympic Games was plenty fast to beat a fellow who picked up a little extra silver betting on his legs now and then.

"Why haven't I seen you round the gymnasion more?" Amyntas asked sadly. "I would have known better than to take you on."

"I just got back from Great Hellas," Menedemos replied, and the other man rolled his eyes in sorrow and chagrin.

They walked back toward Sostratos by the start line. Amyntas peeled off toward the building where the men left their tunics. "I hope he's not going to get dressed and skip out without paying you," Sostratos said. To him, it was the principle of the thing more than the money.

"I doubt it," Menedemos said. "He couldn't show his face here again for shame if he did—too many people watching. Shall we throw javelins while we wait?"

"Something to that," his cousin allowed. "Javelins? Why not? I'm not hopeless with them, anyway." And he wasn't. With his long arms, he threw fairly well—as Alexidamos had painful cause to know—though he would never be graceful. He matched Menedemos for distance, and almost matched him in accuracy throwing at a bale of straw.

Amyntas did come back. He gave Menedemos a fat, massy tetradrakhm with Apollo on one side and the rose of Rhodes on the other. "That'll teach me," he said.

"You'll win it back." Menedemos was willing to let him down easy. "Who knows? You may even use the same trick yourself one of these days."

"Why, so I may." Amyntas sounded surprised, as if that hadn't crossed his mind. Maybe it hadn't. Menedemos sighed. Amyntas didn't notice, as he hadn't noticed Menedemos holding back. Sostratos did, and contrived to look amused without smiling.

Having paid what he owed, Amyntas hurried away, as if afraid Menedemos would inveigle him into some other contest he was bound to lose. Menedemos turned back to Sostratos. "Want to wrestle?"

"Not especially," Sostratos answered. Menedemos' face must have fallen, for his cousin went on, "But I will, at least for a little while."

They dusted their arms and torsos with sand, to aid in getting a grip. Then they stood face to face, waiting. "Ready?" Sostratos asked. Menedemos dipped his head. Sostratos sprang at him. They grappled, grunting and heaving, each straining to throw the other off his feet. Sostratos' height did him no good in wrestling. If anything, the compact Menedemos had the advantage there, being closer to the ground. He got Sostratos on his hip, twisted lithely, and threw him down.

"Oof!" Sostratos said; he'd landed pretty hard. He was rubbing his right buttock as he rose. "I'm going to be sore about sitting down for the next couple of days."

"You made me work for it," Menedemos said. He did mean it; he often won a fall from Sostratos much more easily than he had there. And he wanted to keep him wrestling, too.

Before he could ask for another fall, his cousin said, "Shall we try it again?"

"Yes, if you like." Menedemos tried to hide his surprise. He couldn't remember the last time Sostratos had proposed such a thing. They squared off and grabbed each other, as they had before. Indeed, the second bout went very much as the first one had, right up to Sostratos' mistake. As Menedemos slid in to take advantage of it, he wondered if his cousin would ever learn.

He got his answer sooner than he expected. Instead of going up on his hip and then down in the dirt, Sostratos kept one of his long legs on the ground. Before Menedemos quite realized what had happened, his cousin had got round behind him, slipped an ankle in front, and shoved hard. Next thing he knew, he sprawled in the dirt himself.

He spat some out of his mouth, then said, "Well, well," as he got to his feet. Sostratos' face wore a grin as wide as that of a child with a toy chariot or a hetaira with a new gold necklace. He didn't throw Menedemos very often. Menedemos bowed, giving him credit for it. "Very nice. I thought I had you again, but I was wrong."

"I was hoping you would make the same move twice," Sostratos said. "I tried to steer you into it, the way you held back with that fellow who thought he was fast."

"*Did* you?" Menedemos said, and Sostratos delightedly dipped his head. Menedemos clicked his tongue between his teeth. He tasted more dirt, and spat again. "I'm never going to be able to trust you any more, am I?"

"I hope not," Sostratos told him.

They wrestled twice more. Menedemos won both times, but neither win came easily. He felt himself slower than he should have been. Instead of just wrestling, he was thinking about his moves before he made them, wondering, *If I do this, what does Sostratos have waiting for me?* Against an opponent who was skilled as well as clever, he probably would have lost both falls.

Sostratos noticed. As they rubbed themselves down with olive oil and scraped it off with curved bronze strigils, he said, "I had you looking over your shoulder there, didn't I?"

"As a matter of fact, you did." Menedemos mimed sorrow verging on despair. "A terrible thing, when I can't trust my own cousin."

"Trust me to go down like a sacrifice after its throat is cut, you mean," Sostratos said. "Maybe I'll be able to give you a real contest now."

"Maybe," Menedemos said. "Or maybe I'll find more tricks of my own." To his relief, Sostratos didn't look so happy about that. They finished cleaning themselves off and went back to reclaim their chitons. Then they left the gymnasion and headed up toward their homes in the northern part of the city.

Sostratos said, "Remember, my father's symposion is evening after next."

"I'm not likely to forget." Menedemos rolled his eyes. "And even if I did, you don't suppose my father would?" He didn't bother trying to hide his annoyance.

"If you looked on your father a little more tolerantly, he might do the same for you, you know," Sostratos said.

"Ha! Not likely," Menedemos answered. "If he looked on me a little more tolerantly, *I* might do the same for him. I'm not saying I would, mind you, but I might." His cousin sighed and said no more about it. That suited Menedemos fine.

Garlanded for a symposion, Sostratos always felt like something of an impostor. Most men donned gaiety with the wreaths and ribbons, as if it naturally accompanied them. He'd never been able to do that. And yet, a man who wasn't jolly at a symposion was an object of suspicion. There were times when he had to pretend to what he didn't feel, which did make him feel like a hypocrite.

Still, he might have been more at ease than Diokles. The oarmaster didn't come from a circle where symposia came along very often, if at all. His chiton and himation were good enough, but, a seaman to the core, he'd arrived at Sostratos' house barefoot. And he kept fidgeting on his couch, trying to find a comfortable position in which to recline.

To Sostratos' relief, the sypmosiasts had chosen his father as symposiarch. "Let it be five parts of water to two of wine," Lysistratos declared. No one could possibly complain about that, and no one did: it was the perfect mixture, not too strong, not too weak.

On the couch next to Sostratos and Menedemos reclined an olive farmer named Damophon. Like any prosperous landowner, he took symposia for granted. He didn't grumble at the mixture, but did chuckle and say, "I'll bet you boys drank stronger than that in Great Hellas. When the Italiotes put on a revel, they don't do it by halves. That's what everybody says, so I expect it must be true."

"Shall we talk of what people say and what is so?" Sostratos asked. But, at the same time, Menedemos also spoke up: "I'll say we did. This one affair in Taras"—the only symposion they'd been to in Great Hellas, but he didn't mention that—"it was one of wine to one of water till nobody could see straight."

Damophon paid no attention to Sostratos, but whistled at Menedemos' words. "One to one will do that, all right, and do it fast." Slaves passed out cups of the mixed wine. The olive grower sipped. He whistled again. "That's mighty fine stuff, that is—mighty fine."

Several other symposiasts were saying the same thing. Lysistratos smiled. He coughed a couple of times to draw men's eyes to him, then said, "That's Ariousian brought from Khios by my son and my nephew. We should thank the Italiotes and the Italian barbarians for being too ignorant to buy quite all of it, and for leaving this amphora for us to enjoy tonight."

The cheers that rose from the couches in the andron were louder and more fervent than might have been expected for so early in the evening and so mild a mixture. "*Euge*, Sostratos! *Euge*, Menedemos!" Xanthos called. "As I was saying in the Assembly the other day—"

Sostratos' father overrode the fat bore: "Since we've gathered together here to drink and to welcome Sostratos and Menedemos back to Rhodes after their safe and prosperous journey to the west"—more applause interrupted him—"my thought was that tonight we would speak of others who are on journeys or have returned from them, so that the long absent may be called to mind again."

Menedemos chuckled. "No dirty stories, not when your father's running things."

"If you need that sort of thing at *every* symposion, my dear, go off and live in Great Hellas," Sostratos answered. Neither spoke loud enough for Lysistratos to notice.

As was the custom, the guests began at the far end of the semicircle from the couches Sostratos and Menedemos and their fathers shared. Diokles, by

then, had drunk enough wine to blunt his shyness at drinking with men more prominent than he. He told a fine tale of shipwreck and rescue on the Lykian coast. Another man spoke of a brother who'd set off with Alexander and come back years later short an eye and three fingers on his right hand. Xanthos gave forth with an endless story that seemed to have no point whatsoever. Damophon told of ransoming his father, who'd been captured on a trading voyage by pirates from Krete.

And then it was Sostratos' turn. He rose. Dipping his head to Damophon, he said, "I don't think any man here would shed a tear if Krete sank into the sea, as the divine Platon says the island of Atlantis did in days gone by." No one contradicted him. Several men clapped their hands. He went on, "You meet Rhodians all over the Inner Sea. Menedemos and I ran into one on our journey to Great Hellas. Instead of making a long speech"—Xanthos wouldn't get the point of that, worse luck—"I was wondering if anyone here could tell me more about a soldier named Alexidamos son of Alexion."

Menedemos started to say something, then checked himself. Sostratos had only named Alexidamos; he hadn't told anyone what the mercenary had done, or even that he'd done anything. After stopping to think, Menedemos whispered, "Sly."

Sostratos bent down and whispered back: "You know me—I always want to find out."

"Alexidamos son of Alexion?" Damophon said. "A good-sized fellow a little older than you are, Sostratos, with a scar across his nose?"

"That's the man," Sostratos agreed, and didn't say anything about how he'd drastically revised Alexidamos' nose in Kallipolis.

"Alexion died five or six years ago," Damophon said. "I used to buy fish from him. Instead of taking his father's boat out, Alexidamos sold it and used the silver he got to buy his weapons. He said soldiering had to be an easier way to make a living than fishing. Where did you meet him?"

"Cape Tainaron," Sostratos answered. "We took him across to Italy. With all the wars in those parts, a soldier wouldn't have any trouble finding work."

From the couch Philodemos shared with Sostratos' father, he said, "With all the wars everywhere these days, a soldier has no trouble finding work."

"Wherever Alexidamos draws his drakhma a day and his rations, he'll likely lay his hands on more somehow or other," Damophon said. "His father was reliable, but I stopped buying from Alexidamos even before he sold the boat. He was the sort who'd drench yesterday's fish in seawater to make them look fresh. Any man can have that trick played on him once, but only a fool lets it happen twice." He glanced over to Sostratos. "Did he give you trouble?"

"Nothing we couldn't handle," Sostratos said, and Menedemos dipped his head.

When Sostratos reclined once more, Menedemos rose from the couch and said, "I'll give you the most famous return of all—Odysseus' return to Ithake, and to his own home town. Here's how Homer tells it:

' Then Odysseus of many wiles, answering him, said,
"I know. I understand. You order someone with
  discernment.
But let us go, and you lead all the way.
But give me, if you have one anywhere, a stick
On which to lean, since you said the road was rough."
He spoke, and flung his shabby pouch, full of holes,
Around his shoulder with a strap.
Then Eumaios gave him a staff that suited him.
The pair went off, but dogs and herdsmen stayed
  behind
To protect the farmhouse. He led the king to the city
In the guise of a wretched old beggarman
Leaning on his staff, and pitiful were the clothes
on his back.…'"

Menedemos recited from the *Odyssey* for some time. As always, the ancient tale drew in all who listened to it, no matter how well everyone knew it. Even Sostratos, sophisticate though he was, found himself falling under Homer's spell. *How does he do it?* Sostratos wondered. The same question occurred to him whenever he read Herodotos or Thoukydides. They were all writers he, like most Hellenes, despaired of matching.

When Menedemos took his place on the couch once more, his father rose from the adjoining one. Sostratos hoped Philodemos might say something graceful about the return of the *Aphrodite*, but he didn't. Instead, he spoke of how the Rhodians had ousted the Macedonian garrison in the city after news of Alexander's death arrived, and "how we had our freedom restored to us, and nothing for a polis is more important than its freedom. May we keep it in the future as we regained it in the past."

He reclined again. The symposiasts clapped their hands, Sostratos among them—and Menedemos, too, he noted. Philodemos *had* struck an important chord, all the more important because Ptolemaios and Antigonos were fighting again. When giants clashed, how could a dwarf like Rhodes stay safe? That comparison made Sostratos smile.

Host and symposiarch, Lysistratos got to his feet last of all. "I'll be brief, for we've got people waiting in the courtyard," Sostratos' father said. "A voyage to Great Hellas is always a risk. I thank the gods that my son and my nephew and almost all the crew came home safe. That's the most important thing. You always have another chance if it's true, even if the business end of things didn't go so well. But when they not only sailed west but came back with one of the biggest profits an akatos ever brought home—well, my friends, all I can tell you is that I'm proud to be kin to both of them. *Euge*, Sostratos! *Euge*, Menedemos!"

"*Euge!*" the symposiasts shouted, and clapped their hands and raised their cups in salute. "*Euge! Euge!*"

"Thank you all," Sostratos said. "A man who deserves special praise is our bold keleustes Diokles there. You couldn't hope to find a better sailor. *Euge*, Diokles!"

"*Euge!*" the symposiasts echoed. Diokles' lined features wore the bashful, proud grin of a boy praised for his beauty for the first time.

"Now everybody here will try to hire him away from us," Menedemos said.

"Tell me he hasn't earned the chance," Sostratos said, and Menedemos only shrugged. He couldn't do it, and they both knew as much.

Lysistratos beckoned to Gyges. He spoke in the majordomo's ear. The Lydian slave hurried out into the dark courtyard. As Sostratos' father had said, the entertainers were waiting there. A moment later, a couple of flutegirls in chitons of thin, filmy Koan silk pranced into the andron and began to play. The symposiasts whooped and cheered. A couple of them reached out to try to grab the girls, but they had no luck. Only a very raw slave would have let herself become a plaything so soon.

And then the men in the andron stopped reaching for the girls. There would be plenty of time for that later, and they'd done it plenty of times before. They whooped again, on a different note this time, and howled laughter, for into the room behind the flute girls bounded a naked dancing dwarf. His head and genitals were the size of a normal man's, his body and limbs sadly shrunken.

"Think I'm pretty funny, don't you?" he said in a light, true tenor as he spun in time to the music. "I'll tell you something, friends—if everybody looked like me, *you'd* be the monsters."

That made most of the symposiasts laugh harder than ever. Menedemos choked on his wine, and all but drowned. Sostratos had been laughing, too. He'd known his father had hired the dwarf; that was what had touched off his thought about the large realms Antigonos and Ptolemaios held, with little Rhodes doing her best not to get crushed between them.

But, though the dancing dwarf had made his gibe to amuse the symposiasts, it also made Sostratos think. Most people reckoned dwarfs less intelligent than normal men, but this fellow sounded bright enough. How did he feel, when he was able to make his living only by showing himself off for others to laugh at?

Sostratos thought about asking the little man. He thought about it, but not even his own sharp curiosity gave him the nerve to do it. After all, what was he but one more fellow who reminded the dwarf of his freakishness?

Instead, he got very drunk, even with his father's well-watered wine and shallow drinking cups. Maybe some of the symposiasts did end up rumpling the flutegirls. If they did, Sostratos didn't see it. They might have taken the girls out into the dark courtyard, or the symposion might just have stayed on the decorous side. After a while, he was dozing on his half of the couch.

What roused him was Menedemos' talent for quoting Homer. His cousin started to recite the section from the *Iliad* where lame Hephaistos bustled around serving wine to the other gods, who laughed at him despite his labor. "No," Sostratos said. "Find some other lines. Leave the little man here alone."

Menedemos gaped. "That's why he's here: to be the butt of our jokes. Look at the silly capers he's

cutting." Sure enough, the dwarf was waggling his backside like a coy courtesan, and he *was* funny.

But despite, or perhaps because of, the wine he'd drunk, Sostratos found the distinction he wanted to make: "Laugh at what he does, not at what he is."

"Why?" Menedemos said. "What he does isn't always worth laughing at. What he is, is."

Sostratos ran out of logical arguments. That *was* the wine. "If you can't find any other reason, don't mock him as a favor to me."

"All right, best one," Menedemos said, and kissed him on the cheek. "You're my cousin, and you're my host, and as a favor to you I will keep quiet. You see? I deny you nothing tonight."

"Thank you, my dear. You've made our homecoming perfect." Sostratos yawned. That was the last he remembered of the symposion, for he really did fall asleep then.

After the symposion at his uncle and cousin's house, several days of rain kept Menedemos close to home. What point to going to the gymnasion to try to run through mud or, worse, wrestle in it? What point to going to the agora when hardly anyone would be buying or selling or gossiping?

He wouldn't have minded so much being cooped up if he and his father could have walked past each other without growling. But they didn't get along, and being at close quarters only made things worse. Menedemos tried to stay out of Philodemos' way by taking one of the slave women into his bedroom and not coming out for most of a day, but that didn't work, either. When he and the slave did emerge, Philodemos grumbled, "She didn't do any work at all yesterday, thanks to you."

"Oh, I wouldn't say that, Father," Menedemos answered blandly. "She got very sweaty by the time we were through."

His father rolled his eyes. "I've got a cockhound for a son. Everything I've worked so hard to get will end up in some hetaira's hands when I'm dead."

"With what I brought home from Great Hellas, I could keep three of the greediest hetairai in the world happy for a long time, and the family would still be ahead," Menedemos said.

"That's what you think," Philodemos said. "You have no idea how greedy and grasping a woman can be."

"What I have no idea of right now is why I bothered coming home," Menedemos snapped. "It seems everything I've ever done is wrong."

"You said it. I didn't." Philodemos stalked out of the andron, his spine stiff with triumph. Menedemos made a face at him behind his back. Then he headed off to the kitchen; satisfying one appetite in his room had left him with another unslaked.

He took some olives and cheese. The cook warned him, "If you touch one scale—even one scale, mind you—on the mullet I've got there for supper, I'll snatch you baldheaded. I mean it. This is *my* domain, by the gods."

Laughing, Menedemos said, "All right, Sikon. Till you work your magic on that mullet, I don't want it anyway. Maybe a starving man would eat a raw fish, but I wouldn't."

He stood in the doorway, out of the rain, while he ate his snack. Sikon kept railing at him with the license a skilled and privileged slave enjoyed. Menedemos laughed. With Sikon yelling, he could afford to laugh. The cook's barbs didn't get under his skin and rankle, the way his father's did. He spat an olive pit out into the courtyard. It landed in a puddle with a splash. He ate another olive and spat again, seeing if he could make this pit go farther than the one before. When he spat a third pit, he wanted it to go father than either of the other two.

I wish Sostratos were here, he thought. *We could bet oboloi. I'd beat him, too, even if I had to make silly faces so he'd laugh and spit badly.* If he got into any kind of contest, he wanted to win it. Imagining how furious Sostratos would be if his antics ruined a spit made him smile. The next time they ate olives together...

His good mood quite restored, he looked across the courtyard. He could probably go back to his room without running into his father. Probably. He hung around in the kitchen, enduring Sikon's insults, for a while longer. He didn't want to risk that better mood, and it wouldn't survive another meeting with Philodemos.

What do I do when I get to my room? he wondered. *Play the lyre, maybe?* He shrugged. He was no marvelous musician. The lyre had hardly come off its pegs on the wall since his school days; the kitharistes

who'd taught him had been too free with the switch to give him any love for the instrument.

After a while, he squelched across the courtyard and started up the stairs. At the same time, someone else started down them. He cursed under his breath. If that was his father...But it wasn't; the voice that said, "Hail, Menedemos," was thin, light, and feminine.

"Oh," Menedemos said. "Good day, Baukis." He hoped his father's wife hadn't heard the curse; she might think it was aimed at her. He probably should have said, *Good day, stepmother*, but that seemed ridiculous when he was ten years older than she. He didn't have anything in particular against her. If she had children by his father, that might be a different story, for his own inheritance would shrink, but for now she was only a girl learning what being a wife was about.

Baukis came down the stairs towards him. She *was* young, her figure still almost boyish though she wore a woman's long chiton. She said, "It's not a *very* good day, is it?" Then she paused, as if waiting for him to contradict her. When he didn't, she went on in a rush: "I'm awfully tired of the rain."

"So am I," Menedemos answered. "I want to go out into the polis, to stroll in the agora, to exercise in the gymnasion, to see my friends and chat with them...."

"I just want the sun to shine again, to lighten up the women's quarters and dry out the courtyard, and to let me see farther than Lysistratos' house from my window." As a proper wife, especially one wed to an older, more conservative man like Philodemos, Baukis wouldn't get out of the house much. Being a man, Menedemos could go where he would. This little space was Baukis' world.

He hadn't thought about that before complaining of being shut up here. He changed the subject in a hurry: "Sikon has a fine mullet in the kitchen."

Her expression sharpened. She wasn't particularly pretty—she had buck teeth like a hare's, and pimples splashed her cheeks—but no one who spoke with her for even a moment would ever have thought her a fool. "A mullet? What did he pay for it?" she asked.

"I don't know," Menedemos said. "I didn't even think to find out."

"I'll have to," Baukis said fretfully. "Too much, unless I miss my guess. Sikon spends silver as if it grew on trees."

"What with the profit the *Aphrodite* made, we have plenty," Menedemos said.

"We do *now*," she said. "But how long will it last if we throw it to the winds?"

"You sound like Sostratos." Menedemos didn't mean it altogether as a compliment. With luck, Baukis wouldn't know that.

She just sniffed. "I don't think any man really knows, really cares, about money." Menedemos let out an indignant yelp, but Baukis went on, "Men don't have to manage a household, but wives do. Money and children. We'd better be good with those. We don't get much chance to deal with anything else."

"Well, of course," Menedemos said, and didn't stop to wonder if it felt like *of course* to Baukis. He'd heard similar things from the bored wives he'd seduced. That was probably why some of them had let him bed them, in fact—to get something out of the cramped and ordinary into their lives.

"I'd better go talk to him," Baukis said. "A mullet? That can't have been cheap. Excuse me, Menedemos." She slipped down the stairs past him and walked across the courtyard, raising a hand to her face to keep the rain out of her eyes.

Menedemos turned to watch her go. Her breasts weren't much more than a maiden might have had, but her hips and her walk were a woman's after all. *What does she think about such things, being married to my sour graybeard of a father?* Menedemos wondered. *Is she bored already? I wouldn't be surprised.*

He went up the stairs in a hurry, taking most of them two at a time. He trotted down the hall to his room, then went inside and closed the door behind him. For good measure, he barred it, too, and he couldn't remember the last time he'd done that. But what he ran from was in the room with him.

So was a good deal of darkness. The slave girl had wanted the shutters kept closed, and he'd humored her. He opened them, which turned things gray. He stared blindly out at the rain. Now he had another reason to wish it would stop. He wanted to flee the house as he'd fled up the stairs to this refuge that wasn't. He wondered if going out would do any good.

He doubted it. Wouldn't he take his troubles with him, as he'd brought them here?

And then he started to laugh. It wasn't really funny—not to him, though a comic poet might have disagreed—but he didn't know what else to do. *My father would kill me if he knew what went through my mind.* He laughed again, more bitterly than before. He'd had that thought many times, ever since he was a little boy, when things went wrong. His shiver had nothing to do with the chilly, nasty weather. This time, it might be literally true.

But oh, wouldn't that pay him back for everything?

"No," Menedemos said aloud. He kept talking, too, in a soft voice no one in the hall could have heard: "This once, my dear, you're going to have to be like your cousin and use your head. It's not always the best part of you, but it's the only one that will do right now."

Next spring, I'll sail away and not have to worry about it for half a year. Meanwhile, I've got plenty of silver. I can have as good a time as I please. Even my father won't complain too much more than he usually does. That should cure me. It has before, plenty of times.

He heard Baukis on the stairs. After she'd returned to the women's rooms, he went downstairs for some wine. Dionysos' gift brought ease from all cares.

Even so, Menedemos could hardly wait for spring

THE END.

HISTORICAL NOTE

Over the Wine-Dark Sea is set in 310 B.C. The Roman attack on Pompaia (the Greek spelling for Pompeii) is described in Book IX of Livy. The journey of the grain fleet from Rhegion to Syracuse, and Agathokles' use of the opportunity it gave him to escape from Syracuse and invade Africa, are told in Book XX of Diodorus Siculus. The solar eclipse described here took place on August 15, 310 B.C. Diodorus is also the main surviving source for the machinations of Alexander's marshals, which form much of the background for this novel.

Of the characters actually on stage, only Menedemos himself and Agathokles' brother, Antandros, are historical figures. Historical figures alluded to but not visible include Agathokles, Ptolemaios, Antigonos, his sons Demetrios and Philippos, his nephew Polemaios (also known as Ptolemaios, but given the former spelling here to distinguish him from Antigonos' rival), Kassandros, Lysimakhos, Polyperkhon, Seleukos, Alexander's son Alexandros, Alexandros' mother Roxane, Alexander's son (or suppositious son) Herakles, and Herakles' mother Barsine.

I have for the most part spelled names of places and people as a Greek would have: thus Rhegion, not Rhegium; Lysimakhos, not Lysimachus. Taras was known to the Romans as Tarentum, and is the modern Taranto. I have broken this rule for a few place names that have well-established English spellings: Rhodes, Athens, Syracuse, the Aegean Sea, and the like. I have also broken it for Alexander the Great, whose shadow dominates this period even though he had been dead for about thirteen years when the story opens.

All translations from the Greek are my own. I claim no particular literary merit for them, only that they convey what the original says.

✿

www.ingramcontent.com/pod-product-compliance
Lightning Source LLC
Chambersburg PA
CBHW082048220626

47052CB00007B/1252